SPOTTED HEMLOCK

She was not a nervous or fanciful girl. Moreover, she had been born and brought up in a country vicarage and was accustomed to the absence of lights in country places. Nevertheless, she realised that she would not be sorry to leave the rhododendron walk behind her and emerge on to the neat gravel drive which ran between the open lawns. She tried not to remember that the college was said to be haunted.

Just as she was within sight of her goal, however, her blood froze and her ears pounded. She found herself sick with fright. Blocking the exit to the rhododendron walk was a dim figure tall enough to block out the stars. It glimmered faintly white against the dark bushes. She stopped dead, gulping with terror.

"Don't let it come! Don't let it come!" she thought wildly. But come it did, and by the light of the single lamp which illuminated the entrance to the college grounds she saw that it was a horse-man all in white, a shapeless, apparently headless, figure riding a big-boned grey.

SPOTTED HEMLOCK

Gladys Mitchell

PaperJacks LTD.

TORONTO   NEW YORK

To Patricia and Joe Rowland
with love

PaperJacks

SPOTTED HEMLOCK

PaperJacks LTD.

330 Steelcase Rd. E., Markham, Ont. L3R 2M1
210 Fifth Ave., New York, N.Y. 10010

Published by arrangement with St. Martin's Press

St. Martin's edition published 1958

PaperJacks edition published October 1986

ISBN 0-7701-0483-5

CONTENTS

CHAPTER ONE

Rhubarb

'Nothing has ever moved me more than the sight of this splendid vegetation.'

The Swiss Family Robinson

'RHUBARB?' repeated Lord Robert. 'I hardly think so. I could enquire, of course.'

The occasion was the summer dance given by the students of Highpepper Hall, a place recognised by the Ministry of Agriculture and Fisheries as an approved institution for the training of gentlemen-farmers. Lord Robert, the younger son of a duke, whose inheritance consisted largely of piggeries and tillage, was in residence at the Hall for thirty weeks of the year, and spent most of this time as a gentleman and what he could spare of it as a farmer.

Noblesse oblige, plus a three-line whip from his Common Room chairman, had been instrumental in bringing him on to the dance-floor to do his part in entertaining a bevy of somewhat beefy beauty from Calladale, an agricultural institution for women, situated in a pastoral countryside some twenty-five miles from Highpepper. The no-man's-land between the two colleges had seemed sufficiently wide to discourage private and unnecessary fraternisation between the men and the girls. It proved, however, that the majority of the gentlemen-farmers possessed cars, and it was a sobering thought that the dances given alternately by the two colleges marked an unavailing attempt on the part of the authorities to sublimate conditions against which all disciplinary action had proved useless. The heavy weapon of rustication and the

7

heavier one of expulsion were used sparingly at Highpepper, and fines had proved but a challenge to the young men to break . those particular rules which appeared to have a monastic bias.

Lord Robert's partner, beneath some ill-advised make-up, was a fresh-faced, healthy girl of nineteen. She was at Calladale on a scholarship plus a very inadequate grant, and, although she was doing her best to disguise the fact, she was feeling both flattered and alarmed at finding herself in the arms of the aristocracy. She had introduced the abortive rhubarb-motif in a desperate attempt to provide common ground for discussion, for Lord Robert's interests, on the whole, hardly coincided with her own.

'You can grow it anywhere,' pursued the misguided girl.

'Oh, really?'

'Only, of course, it needs good rich manure.'

'Oh, quite.'

'Or you can force it. In a greenhouse, you know, or a cellar or shed. You put the roots in boxes and cover them loosely with soil and straw. Or you can put an old bucket with a hole in it over the top of the crowns and mulch well, all round, with plenty of stable dung. I suppose, as all of you at Highpepper go hunting in the season, you're very well off for dung, so, if you ever *did* think of growing rhubarb . . .'

'Oh, quite,' said Lord Robert. 'What about some coffee and a bite? There's a running buffet next door.'

The subject of conversation which had failed to strike an answering note in the breast of the noble lord had made some slight appeal to a commoner named Soames, who had also danced with the girl.

'It would be rather a rag,' he said meditatively to his friend Preddle when the dance was almost over.

'What would?' demanded Preddle. 'I'm much too exhausted to rag. Come on up to my room. I've got a bottle of Scotch. I really need a restorative after rockin' and rollin' those truly dreadful girls. Why do they seem to get heavier and uglier and clumsier every term?'

'Mother Nature would know,' said Soames, taking the stairs two at a time. 'Anyway, you're quite right about ragging them. It would be a waste of time and trouble. Are you going down tomorrow or leaving it until the weekend?'

'Oh, weekend, I think. My people are going to Cannes on Saturday, and I'll have more scope with them out of the way.'

The two young men gained Preddle's room and Soames sank luxuriously into an armchair while his host rummaged among sports gear for the whisky. Relaxed and comforted, the friends maintained silence. Preddle poured out the second drinks and Soames lighted a pipe. Then Preddle said :

'What was on your mind? What rag?'

'Rhubarb. Plant it all over Calladale on top of dead rats.'

'Crude, old boy.'

'All ragging's crude, if it comes to that.'

'Where would we get so many crowns?'

'Order them on the College notepaper, of which I achieved a few useful sheets while I was waiting for Sella-clough the other day. There was a whole rack stuffed with headed stationery on his desk, so I helped myself. Never know when it might come in useful. The nurserymen will think the rhubarb's an official order from College, and bung it along like nobody's business.'

'Bung it along? Yes, and where to? You'd need a lorry to do a job like that.'

'Old Brown goes down tomorrow. We could have the rhubarb crowns delivered at his house and unloaded there, just inside North Gate. We'd have to be on hand, of course, to reload it into the boots of people's cars and run it over to Calladale at dusk. We should need half-a-dozen extra chaps, not more, to help with the carting and planting. Don't want too many people in a rag.'

'What about the dead rats?'

'Old Benson.'

'Yes, of course. But we'll miss the cream of it, you know.'

'You mean we shan't be there when the girls dig it all up? No, but you can't have everything, and we'll hear about it all right.'

There came a tap at the door. It opened and disclosed the wistful countenance of their tutor, Mr Gardien.

'I heard you had whisky,' he said. Preddle rose to his feet. Soames took his off the mantelpiece.

'Come in, sir, do,' said Preddle. He rummaged among riding boots and tennis shoes and found another glass. 'I didn't see you at the dance, sir.'

'Too old for dancing. Spent the evening at the Tally-Ho in Garchester. Nice girls, those barmaids.'

'Preferable to the girls we've been supporting tonight,' said Soames. 'When do you go down, sir?'

'Tomorrow, with Mr Brown. Going rock-climbing in Cumberland. Thanks very much. Well, cheers. Do as much for you another time. Been drinking nothing but draught beer this evening. Offered no hospitality, with all you fellows at the dance. Beer always makes me thirsty. And what devilment were you planning when I came along?'

'Devilment? We're serious types, sir.'

'Don't forget I always listen at doors.' He drained his glass. 'Another spot? Thanks very much. I think I will. Remember the great coach-rag? No. Before your time. Well, mud in your eye.'

'How much d'you think he heard?' asked Preddle, when the tutor had gone. Soames looked nostalgically at his empty glass, pushed it forward to be refilled and then shook his head.

'He was fishing. He hadn't heard a thing. Even if he had, there was nothing that mattered. He'd probably join in if we asked him. All the staff suffer from retarded mentality.'

'What about us? Are we really going on with it?'

'Well, we've more or less committed ourselves, I feel. Put our hands to the plough, so to speak.'

'Put our hands to the spade, you mean. Don't you see that it will be the most frightful fag?'

'Never mind. Think of the girls digging up old Benson's rats. We'll be doing it for the good of their souls.'

'Girls don't have souls. They only have vital statistics.'

CHAPTER TWO

Phantom Horseman

'We had worked for some time, when we were disturbed
by the horrible noise made by our poultry.'

Ibid.

CALLADALE HOUSE was a late Georgian mansion to which
had been added, in mid-Victorian times, an excrescence of
a long left wing. Lecture-rooms were in the original building
and the wing had been converted into study-bedrooms for
twenty students. The rest of the girls and most of the staff
were accommodated in hostels erected, between 1920 and
1937, at various points on the estate. In addition, there were
cottages for the college electrician and the head gardener,
various sheds and greenhouses, piggeries, cattle sheds and
poultry runs. There were also garages for staff cars and
cart-sheds for the farm machinery, not to mention rubbish
dumps, compost heaps and a silo.

On the day before the autumn term began, the Principal,
Miss Katharine McKay, known to the students as Canny
Katie, was explaining the college ritual to a new lecturer.
Mr Carey Lestrange, the noted pig-fancier, had been called
upon at short notice to take on the duties of the senior pigman who wrote to say that he had broken his leg in a
climbing accident during the summer vacation, and was still
in hospital.

'It won't be for long,' Miss McKay had pleaded, 'and
you're just the person. I have to be rather careful in the
choice of my men.'

'Yes, of course,' said Carey gravely.

'Well, the way we work is this : first milking—won't affect you in any way, but you may as well learn the routine—is at six, breakfast at seven-thirty—try not to be late; sets a bad example—then work begins at half-past eight. Break is at a quarter to eleven—they get shockingly hungry, so we feed 'em cocoa and bread and jam for fifteen minutes— midday meal at one. Two-fifteen, beginning of the next work period. Two hours. Tea after that, and supper at six-thirty. Then the girls take a compulsory study-period from seven until nine while we mark the written work or prepare for next day. Lock-up is at eleven. All visitors must be off the premises on Saturday and Sundays by eight o'clock. All right? Oh, second milking at five-thirty, but, again, that won't be your pigeon. Here's your time-table. Stick to it closely, if you don't mind, otherwise there's chaos in a place like this, where everything works on a rota, and everybody alternates theory and practice.'

'Yes, I see. I'm accustomed to pretty accurate time-keeping at my own place, so I can promise not to let the side down.'

'Good. What about sleeping quarters?'

'I've got a fast car. I can sleep at home.'

'Means you won't need to be here for breakfast. All right, so long as you're ready to begin work at the right time. Don't let the girls slack. They're apt to try it on with new men. You're rather handsome. Don't let them get any crushes. Awful idiots, most of them. I suppose we were the same at their age.'

'Oh, I'm fast approaching my sere and yellow leaf. I should hardly cause twenty-year-olds to flutter.'

'Don't you believe it! Some of 'em would vamp their great-grandfathers if they could. It's no end of a nuisance having that Highpepper place so close. Twenty-five miles in twenty-five minutes is their average. Gentlemen-farmers, indeed!'

13

'Oh, yes, the fellows who raise nothing but their hats! I've been over there once or twice to talk pig. All the same, most of them are reasonably intelligent.'

'Rakes, every one. Oh, well, see you in the morning. And, I repeat, stay of one mind with Shelley. "I fear thy kisses, gentle maiden; thou needest not fear mine."'

'You terrify me,' said Carey. 'No wonder they say that the female of the species is deadlier than the male.'

'And a truer word was never spoken. Haven't you an aunt with three husbands?'

'Well, not all of them at the same time, you know.'

'Like to meet her.'

'I will invite her to the College Open Day.'

On the whole, he enjoyed his job, although his students' combination of intense concentration on work and equally intense concentration on the pursuit of young men amused, and, to some extent, repelled him. The girls, however, were easy to teach and Carey loved pigs. Then, the staff Common Room, although an extremely noisy place, proved to be a surprisingly comradely one. Its extroverted denizens he found sociable and amusing. There were three other men on the staff, and when the monstrous regiment of women became intolerable, as was inevitable at times, there was always the Tally-Ho in Garchester, where the feast of reason and the flow of soul could be enjoyed to the accompaniment of some of the best beer in England. This cathedral city and county town marked, indeed, the apex of a triangle whose twenty-five mile base was bounded on the west by High-pepper Hall and on the east by Calladale. It was almost equi-distant from both colleges.

Another inevitability was that, with half the time given over to practical work, there was a far more free and easy relationship between staff and students than would have been possible at a college offering a purely academic course. Carey became the recipient of girlish confidences, the repository of girlish secrets, the adviser in the nice conducting of love affairs. He heard of college squabbles and of difficulties at home; of plans and ambitions; of despairs and frustrations; of hopes and fears; of triumphs and disasters.

'In fact,' he confided to his wife, soon after he had taken up his duties, 'I might as well be their father-confessor and have done with it.'

It was also inevitable that, early in his new career, he should hear about his predecessor.

'The other Piggy wasn't a bit like you,' remarked a damsel named Gay, one afternoon, after Carey had demonstrated the steps to be taken to relieve constipation in a pregnant sow.

'In what sense?' asked Carey. 'Check the increased amount of bran you are using and go easy with that bland pig-oil. In fact, I should try the increased bran-content alone at first. It prevents clogging because it holds water in the lower bowel. Keep your gestation charts up to date, all of you. There will be a "snap" test tomorrow, in place of the lecture on types of bacon pig.'

'That's what I mean,' explained Miss Gay. 'The old Piggy never bothered like you do. As for snap tests—I can just see his groups standing for anything like that! Yet, for you, we just sit up and beg.'

'Naturally. I'm old enough to be your father. I *am* a father, at that. I'm accustomed to implicit obedience—or else!'

Miss Gay giggled.

'It isn't that,' she said. 'And it isn't the Romeo in you, because there isn't.'

'Isn't what? Look at that young boar we were so worried about last week. Putting him in with the little hog pig has bucked up his appetite no end. Nothing like rivalry to make a boar show what he's made of.'

'There you go again!' said the amused and exasperated

15

Miss Gay. 'I believe you'd take a lot more interest in us if *we* were pigs.'

'Well, of course I should. Pigs are infinitely more interesting than callow young women.'

'It's a good thing all men don't think alike, then. When are you taking us to that bacon-curing place? I hate to think of our pigs ending up as streaky and long back rashers.'

'I know. It *is* sad, but life's like that. I'm not sure that I myself wouldn't rather end up that way, though, appreciated to the last, and of some use, even in death.'

Miss Gay giggled.

'Even your jokes aren't a bit like his,' she said. 'But when I heard he'd broken his leg I was simply terribly upset. He was quite a heart-throb, you know. He came here from Highpepper.'

'Did he? I suppose he considered his talents were wasted among the Philistines.—Miss Morris, lift that piglet by one hind leg and the shoulders. No, you won't hurt him that way. Gentle but firm—that's it.'

'He couldn't manage the men, so I heard,' said Miss Gay, mucking out rapidly. 'Why is it that, when we let these animals out for exercise, they make straight for the nearest mud and then come back and rock and roll on my nice clean straw?'

'High body temperature, poor creatures.—Cod-liver oil for that sow, Miss Walters, and don't forget her mineral salts. How long have you had her in the paddock?'

'Best part of the day, Mr Lestrange.' Miss Walters was the rhubarb-fancier, but Carey did not know that.

'That's the idea. Keep her toned up with exercise. She'll have a rotten time if she gets too fat, poor old girl.'

'Piggy,' pursued the indefatigable Miss Gay, 'would have added a personal touch to that advice, if you see what I mean, Mr Lestrange.'

'Piggy by name but Wolf by nature, I presume?'

16

Miss Gay giggled.

'He isn't exactly U, like you,' she explained.

'He seems to have been good with pigs,' said Carey, leaning over and slapping a lop-eared Cumberland, 'and that's the whole point, is it not?—What about that youngster of yours with oedema, Miss Platt?'

'Like you said, Mr Lestrange—sloppy bran mash with an ounce and a half of Epsom salts, and small ordinary bran mashes three times a day.'

'That's the spirit.' He took an apple out of his breeches pocket and gave it to a young pig which was scratching itself against his gaiters. 'Well, knock off any time now, girls. I want to get home to my telly.'

'It's too bad you go home every evening,' said Miss Gay, 'and weekends, too. Think of the fun you could have.'

'I do—and shudder,' said Carey.

One morning, at his home in Oxfordshire, his wife Jenny had gone down to the piggeries with Ditch, Carey's pigman, to look at a new boar, when Mrs Ditch, who acted, in their small, square, stone-built house, as housekeeper, cook and general factotum, came to the Scandinavian-type pig-house with the tidings that the master was on the telephone.

Answering it, Jenny learned that her lord was staying the night in College.

'Sorry,' he said, when she took the call, 'but I shan't be home tonight. We've run into a spot of trouble.'

'What sort of trouble?'

'Only a gang of louts, but everything's in a mess. Fences broken, pigs let out, fowl-runs opened—all the works. Anyway, we're slaving like mad to get things shipshape, and I'm going to do a spot of sentry-duty tonight. Haven't told Miss McKay. She'd have a fit if she thought I wasn't getting my beauty sleep. But my pigman and I are rather cross about things. I have a lovely gilt in-pig, and I'm afraid this may have upset her. Pigs are terribly temperamental, as you

17

know. How's Ernest settling in? Yes, quite. The importance of being Ernest is that if he mates nicely with Barbara we ought to get a beautiful litter of Gloucester Old Spots, which is a pig I've always wanted to try.'

'If you've had a lot of destruction, why don't you call in the police?'

'Miss McKay thinks it may be a Highpepper rag. She's had their bloke on the phone and he's promised to brain-wash his lads, but, personally, I don't think it's ragging. It's nasty, which the boys, on the whole, are not. Anyway, don't worry. I'll see you tomorrow night, with any luck.'

Carey and his pigman stayed up until three in the morning and caught nobody. Carey had no lectures until after the mid-morning break, so he slept-in until half-past nine, made a leisurely breakfast in the Staff dining-room and then went for a short stroll in the grounds.

The pigs which had been released by the marauders had done a considerable amount of damage, most of which was still being tidied up by the students. Carey stopped beside a perspiring lass in breeches and leggings who was putting a flower-bed to rights, and pointed to a heap of rhubarb crowns and the extremely decayed carcass of a small mammal.

'How come?' he enquired. The girl straightened her back and leaned on the garden fork she was using.

'Isn't it horrible?' she said. 'We keep finding rhubarb and rats all over the place. This is the fifth lot that I know of. Those filthy louts! I'd like to get hold of one of them!'

'I doubt whether *this* is the work of louts,' said Carey, gazing at the remains of the dead rat. 'It looks more like ancient history to me. I should incinerate that carcass, if I were you. Let's hope the pigs didn't investigate the corpses too closely. It can't have done them much good if they did.'

By lunch-time seventeen more deposits of rats and rhubarb crowns had been discovered, and the Principal of Highpepper had been along to look at the damage. His view was that the gentlemen-farmers were innocent of the destructive raid on Calladale, but it turned out that, although Soames and Preddle had contrived to remain discreetly silent about the rats and the rhubarb, Old Benson, the local rat-catcher, had confessed to the sale of sundry corpses to 'some of the gentlemen' at the end of the previous term.

'*Not* a nice rag,' said Miss McKay, 'but if Mr Sellaclough declares that his men did no damage, I have no option but to agree. I do wish they would leave this College alone.'

That in some respects this was unlikely was demonstrated very shortly afterwards. In spite of Preddle's ungallant assertions, not all the Calladale students were uncouth in body and mind. Some, indeed, were both handsome and gifted, not the least pulchritudinous being one Rachel Good. From the point of view of Miss McKay, Rachel was inclined to belie her surname, but in the eyes of a certain Highpepper youth named Cleeves she was the rose of Sharon and the lily of the valley. In other words, at the end of the summer term they had plighted their troth, and, as Cleeves was a young man of substance, Rachel sported an engagement ring tricked out with rubies and was taken into Garchester to partake of ambrosia and the blushful Hippocrene far more often than some of her envious contemporaries thought was reasonable.

Miss McKay, canny though she might be, was no Mrs Grundy. She was prepared to grant her students a reasonable number of late passes each term without wishing to find out how they spent the hours between lunch and lock-out. She disapproved of engaged students because she believed that their entanglements interfered with their studies, but she was a just and reasonable woman and was prepared to admit that it took all kinds to make a world, and, that microcosm of it, a college.

On the morning of the second Thursday in October, Miss

19

Good applied for a late leave. The college secretary looked up the records.

'It's your third this term, Miss Good, but I'll ring Miss McKay.'

'How dreary of you, Louise! Come on! Be a sport! Give me a pass. Who's to know?'

'Miss McKay, of course.' The secretary connected herself with the Principal. 'Miss Good, asking for a late pass . . . she's had two . . . Very good, Miss McKay.' She put down the intercommunication receiver. 'She says you can go ahead, but you've got to be in by eleven.'

'The old sourpuss! Still, it's better than nothing, although Barry will create, I expect. She's always made it half-past before. Oh, well, if you'll just give me the card . . . Thanks a lot.'

Thursday was the Calladale half-holiday. It had been arranged between the two principals that Highpepper should take Wednesdays, but this pious attempt at sabotage was frustrated weekly by the Highpepper students, who, if they had any desire to escort Calladales to the pictures and take them out to tea or supper, cut the Gordian knot by cutting the Thursday afternoon lectures and chores. This inspired cutting was accomplished by Mr Cleeves on the Thursday of Miss Good's late pass, and an enjoyable time was had by both, Cleeves merely remarking, when his affianced referred to the cheese-paring dictum of Miss McKay, that, at any rate, eleven o'clock would be all right. There would be plenty of time for a four o'clock cinema followed by a dinner and drinks, and his Morris would get the girl back to Calladale before the expiration of her pass.

He was prepared to be as good as his word, but, as the car was within a mile of her college, Miss Good gave a sudden exclamation.

'My ring! I must have left it in that cloakroom place! I

took it off to wash my hands, and I must have forgotten to put it on again!'

'Oh, damn!' said Cleeves. 'I'd better go back, I suppose. Good thing the place is an hotel and not just a pub. I'll be able to get in all right. I'll ask at the office. Look, I'll put you down at your gates, if you don't mind. That will save me a bit of time.'

'Oh, yes. After all, you've still got another twenty-five miles to do. Oh, dear! I'm terribly sorry.'

'Yes, you *are* a little chump. I'll hang on to the ring when I get it, and let you have it back when I see you on Saturday.'

'I only hope it's still where I left it! Surely nobody would steal it, would they?—not in a nice hotel like that!'

Mr Cleeves was not prepared to bet on this, but he did not say so. He merely told his beloved not to fret, put her down at the gates of Calladale, turned the car and drove back at top speed to Garchester. Miss Good watched his rear lights until they disappeared round a bend, and then turned her steps towards the hostel, for she was not an in-college student.

The Calladale grounds, even apart from the acreage devoted to crops, pasture, hen-houses and piggeries, were extensive, forming, as they had done before the college took them over, the park and gardens of a very large mansion. There was no moon, and Miss Good, walking between tall rhododendrons on the half-mile trek to bed and board, began to realise that there was a vast difference between being driven in a smart, new Morris up to the students' entrance and being compelled to walk the distance between the college gates and the hostel in eerie autumn darkness.

She was not a nervous or a fanciful girl. Moreover, she had been born and brought up in a country vicarage and was accustomed to the absence of lights in country places. Nevertheless, she realised that she would not be sorry to leave the rhododendron walk behind her and emerge on to

21

the neat gravel drive which ran between the open lawns that fronted the hostel. She tried not to remember that the college was said to be haunted.

Just as she was within sight of her goal, however, her blood froze and her ears pounded. She found herself sick with fright. Blocking the exit to the rhododendron walk was a dim figure tall enough to blot out the stars. It glimmered faintly white against the dark bushes. She stopped dead, gulping with terror. Then, with a sob, she turned in her tracks and tore for the gate. She did not look round until she was out in the road. Gasping and winded, she flung herself down in a ditch and lay there, shivering and terrified.

'Don't let it come! Don't let it come!' she thought wildly. But come it did, and by the light of the single lamp which illumined the entrance to the college grounds she saw that it was a horseman all in white, a shapeless, apparently headless, figure riding a big-boned grey. The horse was going at a walking pace, but when it was out on the road it began to trot.

The girl in the ditch got up and tore along the rhododendron avenue to the hostel. This time no sinister, ghostly horseman barred the way. Neither was the front door barred, but an apologetic maidservant informed her that the head of the hostel wished to speak to her in the morning.

In her study-bedroom a reproachful friend awaited her.

'You *are* a fool! Why on earth didn't you get back to time? Considine is rabid. You've probably ditched all our late passes until half-term.'

'I've got an answer for her, but, of course, she won't believe it.'

'She might. She isn't bad. Did you run out of juice on the way home? If so, I wouldn't hand her that one. She won't believe that, even if it's true.'

'She won't be asked to believe it. I suppose you haven't got an aspirin or something. I've had the most awful shock.'

'Not . . .? I shouldn't have thought . . .'

'Of course not! He's a lamb. No. The fact is—I think I've seen the college ghost.'

'How many drinks did you have?'

'No, really, I'm not joking. Get off my bed. I'll tell you all about it in the morning. Oh, dear! I wish, just for once, we had dormitories instead of these little rooms. I'm scared to death. I know I shan't sleep.'

She did sleep, however, youth and a certain amount of that which biteth like an adder assisting—indeed, insisting upon—kind nature's sweet restorer. She awoke to a thin, late October sunshine and the consciousness that she was called upon to report to Miss Considine. In the clear light of day the ghost-story would sound palpably absurd. Better to make the lost engagement ring the excuse for overstaying her late leave, Miss Good decided. She advanced this plea. Miss Considine, a weather-beaten lady of fifty who taught the science and practice of vegetable gardening, looked concerned.

'That very expensive ring?' she asked. 'Have you got it back?'

'Well, no.'

'You've lost it entirely?'

'I—I hope not.'

'Look here, Miss Good, come clean. What was your reason for overstaying your pass?'

Miss Good looked unhappy.

'It *was* really about the ring,' she said.

'Yes?'

'My—my fiancé went back for it. We'd got nearly back to college when I remembered I'd left it at the place where we had dinner. He brought me back to the gates and, *honestly*, Miss Considine, I'd have had heaps of time to get in before lock-up if I—if I—this is going to sound silly . . .'

'If you mean that you saw someone on horseback in the

college grounds, it may interest you to know that he trampled down my brussels sprouts. So—now?'

'Yes, I did see someone on a horse. It was at the end of the rhododendron avenue. I ran back to the gate and hid in the ditch, and that's what made me late.'

'Hid in the ditch? Why on earth didn't you challenge him? It must be one of the people who broke down the fences and let out the pigs. We might have found a scapegoat and got hold of the names of the others.'

'But, Miss Considine, he was perfectly enormous and all in white and he didn't have a head! It was awful!'

'You little goose!'

'No, really! I—I thought it was a ghost!'

'Now, really, Miss, Good! What did you have to drink last night, you foolish child? Sit down, and tell me all about it. I can't go to Miss McKay with a tale like that!'

'But it's true! Really, really it is. I could have made you any sort of excuse, but this is the truth. I was petrified! I didn't think what I was doing! I just ran for my life and hid in the ditch until it went!'

'How do you know that it went?'

'It came out of the college gate. It passed quite close.'

'What did it look like? Could you see through it? What had you had to drink?'

The student looked reproachful and then said sullenly, staring down at the carpet the while:

'I'd had a Bronx and then we shared a bottle of Burgundy, but Barry drank more of it than I did, and we had coffee to finish up.'

'That shouldn't have been enough to make you tumble into the ditch. Now, look here, you saw this horseman twice, the second time closely. Forget this ghost nonsense and think hard. Couldn't you possibly identify him? Horses sound like Highpepper Hall, now I come to think of it, and, in spite of what Mr Sellaclough had to say, I'm not at all convinced that the previous damage and mischief was not the work of the Highpeppers. For the sake of the college, Miss Good, you've got to think hard. Cast your mind back to the last Highpepper ball. Does nothing seem to ring a bell?'

'No, it certainly doesn't. As I told you, he didn't seem to have a head.'

'That only means that he must have been wearing a hood. Look here, my dear, we must get to the bottom of this. We can't have people coming here and working destruction. And just remember that the quality of *mercy* may not be strained, but my *patience* will be if you overstay your late leave again, whatever excuse you may offer.'

She went to the Principal, who was not particularly impressed by her report.

'Girls?' said Miss McKay sceptically. 'Well, of course, they *can* tell the truth. Some of them even *do*. Ring up her young man and let's get the first part straight. His name's Cleeves. That much I know. Get his story. Simply ask him where he left her last night. If he says he drove her up to the hostel door, she's had it, and that's her last late pass this term.'

Cleeves, with no clue to guide him, decided that the truth would be more likely to prevail than would a lie.

'I decanted Miss Good at the college gates at a quarter to eleven,' he said. 'She had plenty of time to get in. I didn't drive her up to the door of her hostel because she'd left a ring behind at the hotel where we dined. Oh, yes, thanks, I've got the ring. Somebody had turned it in to the office and I was able to describe it, so they handed it over. I say, I hope everything's all right!'

'If you are asking whether Miss Good is all right, the answer is in the affirmative. Next time you take her out you had better not give her quite so much to drink. She thought she saw a ghost in the college grounds.'

'Oh, I say! It couldn't have been the drinks. She didn't have more than a thimbleful all the evening.'

'Then it was one of the Highpepper students fooling about. As he frightened Miss Good almost into hysteria, you might care to find out who it was. His horse trampled down my brussels sprouts. I set a very high value on those sprouts, and I'm out for blood.'

CHAPTER THREE

Posted as Missing

'. . . and if I may judge by the absence of beard, it is a female.'

Ibid.

OVER one thing, Miss McKay was in full agreement with Miss Considine.

'Unless the girl was suffering from hallucinations or a hangover, a ghostly rider on a grey horse spells Highpepper Hall. That being so, I do not feel inclined to make trouble. I've made a nuisance of myself there already, and not for the first time, either. We must keep watch and apprehend the gentleman if he appears again. Then, when we get his name, we can take appropriate action,' she declared.

The appropriate action had to be taken sooner than she expected and for a more serious reason than the trampling of brussels sprouts by a ghostly horseman. The head of another of the hostels came to her immediately she had concluded her discussion with Miss Considine to inform her that one of the students was missing.

'Missing?' Miss McKay drew a jotter towards her. 'Since when, Miss Paterson?'

'Well,' replied Miss Paterson, 'that's just the difficulty. You know that I spent this last week at the Autumn Show of root vegetables on Monday and Tuesday, and went on to that exhibition of new farming machinery?'

'Yes, of course. Oh, dear! You don't mean she's been missing for several days? What does your head student say?'

'She's still in quarantine, poor girl—suspected mumps. She

27

knows nothing about it, and I can't get much sense out of the rest of them. It seems that the missing student went to her room to put in an extra study period on Saturday night as (so she seems to have told the others) she wasn't satisfied with the marks she got for her last essay and practical test, and on Sunday, of course, what with my preparations for my journey and the fact that Sunday is a free day, so that the students don't even come in to meals unless they like—they even take turns to give each other breakfast in bed—it didn't dawn on me that anybody *could* be missing. I mean, I wasn't told.'

'No, I quite see that.'

'Then, you see, I had a very early breakfast on Monday, to give myself time to get to the first day of the Autumn Show in good time, so that I still didn't realise . . .'

'Quite so. No blame attaches to you in the matter at all. I think one of your students should have had sufficient common sense to report to *me*, though.'

'They said they didn't like to run the girl into trouble. They do not seem to have taken a serious view of her absence. Thought it was a case of Cat's Away, Mice Will Play, apparently. She is very well-off, of course, compared with some of my students, keeps sherry and biscuits in her room—that sort of thing. They just thought she'd decided to be A.W.O.L., that's all.'

'A man,' said Miss McKay briskly. 'That's the answer. Well, she'll have to be traced and found. Our ghostly friend, of course. I suppose, when Miss Good saw him, he was reconnoitring,' she added, to Miss Considine.

Miss Considine said that she doubted it.

'Why dress up in such a noticeable way if he wanted to elope with the girl?' she asked. 'Besides, why a horse? Surely a car would have been much more sensible.'

'Not as romantic. *Young Lochinvar* stuff, without a doubt.'

'It doesn't seem practical, all the same,' said Miss Paterson, who thereupon took herself off.

'Romanticism never *is* practical. That's the beauty of it, from *their* point of view. And you do realise, don't you, Miss Considine, that if it hadn't been for your little Miss Good and her absurd engagement ring, nobody would have known that this horseman had ever existed? To that extent, I'm grateful to her,' declared Miss McKay.

Miss Considine respected and liked her Principal, but she was not prepared to allow this remark to pass unchallenged.

'Oh?' she said. 'What about my brussels sprouts? *I* should have known, all right, that he existed.'

'Well, yes,' agreed the fair-minded Miss McKay. 'I'd better telephone Highpepper and ask which of their students is missing. Oh, dear! How tiresome these children can be! And just when we've got these wretched thefts on our hands! I suppose there's no connection?'

'Miss Paterson would not care to hear you suggest it.'

'Well, more of her students have missed money and valuables than people in other hostels.'

'But she says this missing girl is rich. Are you suggesting we are harbouring a kleptomaniac?'

'No. Everything that gets lost is an article of intrinsic worth—watches, a ring, a bracelet, jewelled earrings, money. I wish to goodness the little idiots would leave their boyfriends' presents at home instead of flaunting them here.'

'But where would be the fun in that? Rivalry is the spice of life when you're young. Oh, here's Miss Paterson back again.'

It was not the custom at Calladale for lecturers to knock formally on the door when they wished to consult their Principal, Miss McKay regarding this as an unnecessary waste of time. Miss Paterson, therefore, came striding in, and announced, with an air of triumph:

'There's no need to telephone Highpepper, unless you wish.'

'Not Highpepper? Why, where else would one of our students find a man romantic and foolish enough to run off with her?' demanded Miss McKay.

'I didn't mean that. I meant that if a Highpepper youth is involved, the students in my hostel will be certain to know who he is. You could then attack from that angle.'

'Something in that.' But Miss McKay was not wholly convinced. She decided to telephone Highpepper, only to learn that none of the student body was unaccounted for.

'Staff?' demanded Miss McKay, resolved to leave no stone unturned.

'Come, come,' said Mr Sellaclough, soothingly. 'All the same, if you'll hold on, I'll send round. Well, it will take some time. Suppose I ring you back?'

Miss McKay agreed to this, thanked him and added that, naturally, she was rather worried. This was not the attitude she took at the high table that evening at supper, to which Carey had been invited.

'It isn't a Highpepper thing,' she announced to the table at large. 'There is nobody there unaccounted for. It means, in my experience, that the girl is in a pet, or is feeling worried about her work, and has slipped off home. I haven't telephoned her people because it is up to them to let me know she is there. Of course, if they haven't telephoned by noon tomorrow I shall have to contact them. If nothing is known of her there, I shall get in touch with the police, but that should hardly be necessary. It would be such a boring thing for the college if anything got into the papers. You remember the case of that Miss Diggins we had?'

Murmurs from the senior members of the staff could be taken as agreement that they did remember the case of Miss Diggins.

'The little silly who ran off to her married sister because

she couldn't face her preliminary "Perennials" *viva*,' translated Miss Considine helpfully.

'That's the girl.'

'Yes, that was scarcely very sinister,' said Miss Paterson. 'So you think she has just run home? Yet I shouldn't have thought it, you know. She certainly wasn't the type to worry about her work, although I will admit that, so far this term, it hasn't come up to standard. Still, I believe it to be quite good. Oh, it will all turn out to have a perfectly ordinary explanation, I'm sure. It's quite a mistake to panic.'

'I wouldn't care to state that it turn out to have an ordinary explanation,' said Carey. 'I don't know much about the psychology of girls, but, taking into consideration all the facts, I should call this whole business rather odd. Of course, there may be no connection between the three things, but— what have we experienced already this term? First, there was that outbreak of hooliganism, about which we still know nothing. Then we have the headless ghost seen by Miss Good. Now—a missing student who isn't being run off with by one of the lads at Highpepper, and who has been gone longer than seems reasonable. If you don't want to call in the police, why don't you call in my aunt? She's the soul of discretion, and will sort it all out in no time.'

'But Dame Beatrice could not possibly be interested,' protested Miss McKay.

'Why not? Look here, you call her in. I'll guarantee she'll come like a shot unless she's tied up with some conference or lecture programme or something.'

'I could hardly hope . . .'

'Would you like *me* to call her?'

'Well . . .'

'She'll do a lot for a favourite nephew.' He liked and respected Miss McKay. 'I can understand that you don't want the police butting in until we know there's real cause. After all, the girl's of age. There's nothing to stop her going off with a man, which is what I, personally, would rather bet she's done. What kind of girl is she?'

Miss McKay repeated what she had been told by the various lecturers and then added :

'You've only had her in your pig-keeping classes for a week or two, I know, but I should be interested to hear what *you* made of her.'

Carey wrinkled his brow.

'She seemed rather a self-contained sort of girl, I thought, and rather more mature in her outlook than some of them. She was quiet and worked well—seemed to take her training very seriously indeed. I got the impression that she was trying to learn all she could as quickly as she could. In fact, I used to wonder whether she hadn't a stronger motive than some of them for taking the course at all.'

'I don't think her people were very keen. She was acting partly in opposition to them, I believe. I'm glad to hear on all sides that she was such a keen student, except that it makes her absence from the college all the more unaccountable. If you *really* think Dame Beatrice would come . . .'

'I'll telephone her at once. No, come to think of it, I've a free afternoon tomorrow because of that film show you're putting on in the lecture hall. I'll go over and see her, and bring her back with me, unless, as I say, she's dated up.'

His aunt, as usual, was delighted to see him, invited him to dinner and to stay the night, and promised to go back with him to Calladale in the morning. Carey telephoned Jenny to let her know where he was, and settled down to enjoy his evening.

After dinner he gave the elderly, quick-eyed and beaky-mouthed Dame Beatrice, psychiatrist and consulting psychologist to the Home Office, an account of the several happenings at Calladale since he had joined the staff there. She listened without interruption until he had finished.

'Well?' he said, after a lengthy silence had succeeded his remarks. Dame Beatrice shook her head.

'I think we may discount the original work of destruction,' she said. 'It was almost certainly carried out by a gang of louts. In putting matters to rights, the students, you say, came across alien matter in the form of rhubarb crowns and the decomposed carcasses of rats. These, you believe, may have represented a long-term (so to speak) bit of ragging on the part of some men-students from Highpepper. There follows the appearance of this ghostly figure on horseback seen only by Miss Good . . .'

'But testified to by the dumb mouths of Miss Considine's brussels sprouts, don't forget . . .'

'. . . coupled with the disappearance of Miss Palliser.'

'We don't *know* that it was coupled with it, you know. There's a considerable time-lag between Saturday and Thursday. Besides, if anybody wanted to spirit the girl away, it was surely a damn' silly way to do it?'

'I don't see that. A motor-car or motor-cycle would have been noisy.'

'Do you suppose the girl was a consenting party to being carried away?'

'It seems that she must have been. Consider the facts : here are these students in study-bedrooms in a comparatively modern building, twenty or so, at least, of them, I suppose. It is not likely that one of the girls could have been carried off at just before midnight against her will.'

'No, but there was only one horseman, according to Miss Good.'

'You mean there was only one horse.'

She drove with Carey to the College early next morning and was introduced to Miss McKay, who professed that she was very glad to see her.

'Mr Lestrange has told you of our problem, of course,' she said.

'He has told me all he knows, but that really amounts to very little. I had better speak to the other lecturers. Have you any *reason* to think that this girl has run away with a young man? I gather that that is your opinion.'

'It seems that I may need to revise it. It *was* my opinion, but I have telephoned Highpepper Hall, and, so far as they know, none of their students is missing. It was the first thing I thought of, naturally. Some of our girls take themselves very seriously and are apt to do foolish things in consequence. If you get nothing helpful from the lecturers, I must ring up the mother. I can't take the responsibility of keeping her in the dark if the stupid child really is missing. It will all turn out to be some sort of an emotional upset, no doubt. You know what these adolescents are!'

Dame Beatrice ascertained from Miss Paterson, a weather-beaten, grey-eyed Scot, that the girl, so far as she knew, was in no trouble. She hesitated and then mentioned the thefts.

'But you could talk to the students,' she said. 'Naturally, they get to know things about one another that never come to our ears. The girl was well-off, I am sure. There couldn't have been any temptation to steal.'

Dame Beatrice did talk to the students and at first it seemed as though she was going to draw blank. Then she met a girl who knew the missing student from schooldays.

'Norah got married in the holidays. I'm not supposed to tell anybody, but . . . well, *I* think she may have gone to her husband. She told me the other week that she'd had a letter from him. The only thing is, I should have thought she'd have asked for an Absence. After all, she didn't need to say it was her husband. A white lie wouldn't be out of place under the circumstances.'

'Do her parents know about the marriage?'

'No. She's turned twenty-one and didn't need their consent. She wouldn't tell them in case they refused to go on

34

paying her fees here, I suppose, although I think perhaps she pays her own.'

'Her husband could not afford the fees?'

'No, he isn't earning. He's an art student.'

'I see. Thank you very much for being so helpful. I will find out privately whether she is with him. At which art school does he study, and what is his name?'

'His name is Coles and he's at Belmont College of Art in London. I say, you won't tell Miss McKay, unless it's impossible not to, will you?'

'No, I will not, and Miss McKay is not, unless I mistake her, the person to press for information which I may appear to be reluctant to give.'

'Thanks ever so much, Dame Beatrice. I wouldn't want Norah to know I'd ratted on her.'

Dame Beatrice went back to the Principal and told her that she had what might prove to be a clue to the where-abouts of the missing student and that the search must be carried on in London.

'I suppose the little idiot isn't going to have a baby?' said Miss McKay. Dame Beatrice replied that this, no doubt, was a possibility, and was so obviously unprepared to say more that Miss McKay, wise in her generation, forbore to ask any more questions, merely adding that all she wanted was to make sure that the girl was safe.

George, Dame Beatrice's respectable and reliable chauffeur, drove her the ninety-odd miles to London immediately after lunch. She reached her Kensington house in time for tea and sent her secretary, Laura Gavin, to look up the address of the Belmont College of Art. It turned out to be in the neighbourhood of New Cross, and, as it was likely to have concluded its daily session by five o'clock, a visit to it had to be postponed until the following morning. Dame Beatrice had left her telephone number with Miss McKay in case the missing student should turn up again at Calladale, but by ten o'clock next morning no call had come through from the college, so she sent for the car and drove out to New Cross, having previously arranged for an appointment with the head of the art school.

She explained her business and the young husband appeared on a summons from his principal. Dame Beatrice wasted no time on preliminaries. She said:

'Mr Coles, I represent the Principal of Calladale, where your wife is a student. She has absented herself from college without leaving a message, and you will understand that we are anxious to know that she is safe.'

Her quick black eyes had not left the boy's face whilst she had been speaking, and it was clear to her, before she had concluded her remarks, that the lad was not prepared to give her much information.

'I've no idea where Norah is,' he said. 'I—I should think she must have gone home.'

'Did you write her a letter to say that you were not in your usual health, or convey any other information which might have caused her anxiety?'

'No, I didn't. I'm perfectly fit. Always am. I don't understand this at all. Who said I had sent her a letter?'

'Her friend, Miss Elspeth Bellman.'

Coles shook his head.

'Something wrong somewhere. I should think Norah had a letter from home about somebody there, and Elsie Bellman got it all mixed up. If you'll excuse me, I'll telephone. That's where Norah must be, at her home.'

He went out. Dame Beatrice looked up as the head of the Art School, who had left them alone for the interview, came back to the room.

'Any satisfaction?' he asked. 'I saw Coles come out. He doesn't look particularly worried.'

'I do not think he is. He is under the impression that the

girl has gone to her own home. Perhaps a member of the family is ill. He has gone to telephone the household.'

'You speak as though your own is a different opinion.'

'Do I? I do not hold an opinion. If the girl *has* gone home it must have been on a matter of some urgency, or surely she would have left a message or sent a telegram. I am extremely sorry to take up your time like this, but you will appreciate that the Principal of Calladale is anxious.'

'Quite.' He glanced at the clock on the wall. 'I'm teaching next period, but, until then, my time is my own. I've cleared up my correspondence and there's nothing else outstanding. Yes, I can imagine that the Principal would be feeling rather worried. Thank heaven, I'm only responsible for day students.'

Coles returned after about twelve minutes, during which Dame Beatrice and her companion had discussed the difficulties and responsibilities of being *in loco parentis* to boarders. Coles' expression had changed. He looked anxious and uncertain.

'She isn't at home. I don't know what to think now. Could she have lost her memory and wandered off somewhere? I can't imagine it. She wasn't worried about anything, so far as I know. It's worry that brings about amnesia, isn't it?'

'Not necessarily. If she'd received a bad knock on the head it could lead to amnesia. But are you *sure* there was nothing about which she might have worried?'

'She didn't like keeping our marriage from her mother, but, until I can earn, there's nothing else for it, and she knows that. She's dead keen on this agricultural college. We're going to begin a smallholding as soon as we've saved enough money. Norah has a job waiting for her at the end of her course—next June, that will be—and I'm hoping to do more pottery, and perhaps sell a picture or two and do some private work—interior decorating, you know. We're prepared to live very economically to get the money together, and I think my uncle will help with a loan. My people don't know I'm married, but they like Norah. She can come and stay during the vacations. Her mother thinks we're engaged. If we can keep the marriage quiet until June, everything should be all right, so I don't see any real reason for Norah to worry. What do you suggest I should do? I'm afraid I feel rather at a loss.'

'I shall return to college and consult Miss McKay. It seems to me that our only course will be to call in the police.'

'Oh, surely that shouldn't be necessary. There can't really be anything wrong. If I hear anything of her, I'll ring up Calladale at once, of course.'

'And if all is well when I get back, I will let you know.'

But when she got back to the college there was still no news of the missing girl. Miss McKay called in the police. A lean, alert, fatherly, middle-aged officer asked questions and became reassuring. His reasoning was that Miss Palliser (as she was still known to the college authorities) had probably upset herself about something and had gone off in what he described as 'a state.' There would be little difficulty, he anticipated, in locating her.

CHAPTER FOUR

Echoes of Highpepper

"Little tell-tale!" said my wife, "why have you betrayed me? I meant to have surprised your father." '

Ibid.

THAT the police would have little difficulty in tracing Mrs Coles (as she had turned out to be) or that, alternately, she would return home or to college when she had recovered from her emotional crisis, turned out to be wishful thinking. During the ensuing days, the police obtained no clue to her whereabouts and Dame Beatrice, with no more to go on and without their facilities for search, gave up the quest and went home. Her theory remained unaltered. The girl had left college voluntarily and did not intend to be found. She would reappear in her own good time, thought Dame Beatrice.

'I suppose there's a baby on the way, and, as she's still got her college course to finish and her finals to come, and as she isn't supposed to be married, it's all a bit difficult,' suggested Laura, Dame Beatrice's secretary and the wife of Chief Detective-Inspector Robert Gavin of the C.I.D.

'It is the most likely explanation,' Dame Beatrice agreed. 'Miss McKay has volunteered to keep me informed of the march of events, but I don't see what I can do to help. Why on earth couldn't the little silly wait to be married until she was clear of the college?'

This rhetorical question went unanswered, and the days passed. Miss McKay wrote at the end of a week to say that the police still had no clue and that she was in correspondence with the missing girl's relatives, but that (thank goodness!) they showed no signs of wanting to haunt the college. She added that, so far, the business had been kept out of the papers, but she felt that, sooner or later, publication of the fact that Calladale had lost or mislaid a student would have to be resorted to if the girl was to be traced and found.

'I can't think why the parents aren't making more fuss,' Miss McKay concluded. 'One would almost suppose that they know where she is and are not concerned. If that is so, I do think they might tell us and set our minds at rest. Meanwhile, college has to go on as usual. I suppose you couldn't spare time to come back and have another look round?'

Carey Lestrange had his own problems. One of these was the necessity of getting back, as soon as possible, to his own pig-farm. He put the point to Miss McKay, who received it with a plea that he would stay until his predecessor was able to resume duty.

'Yes, but when is that likely to be?' Carey asked. Miss McKay could not say, but promised to write and enquire. His second problem was to keep a correct relationship between himself and the more forthcoming of his students.

'The shameless baggages make unmistakable passes at me, although I'm old enough to be their father,' he complained to Dame Beatrice, when, in response to Miss McKay's pleading, she came back to the college. 'I think I'd better bring Jenny along and show them that I'm admirably suited.'

Jenny, his wife, came, and brought the two children. During the visit it dawned on those students who were showing the children round the estate that, all over the flowerbeds, tender clumps of rhubarb were beginning to thrust up their infant heads. As it happened, the early autumn had been free from frosts and therefore the crowns of rhubarb had not suffered much from the lack of protective straw. It was obvious that, in tidying up after the raid by the destructive band which had let the pigs out near the beginning of

40

term, the students had not discovered a tenth of the rhubarb and dead rats buried by the myrmidons of Preddle and Soames.

When the visitors had gone, driven back to Stanton St John by Carey, a Common Room meeting was called by the head student and volunteers were called for to clear the flower-beds of the alien vegetation. There was no rush to enlist. As one shrinking student, heavily backed by others, put it, the case rested not upon the rhubarb but upon the dead rats.

'They were dreadful before; they'll be worse now,' said the student. 'I think the college ought to hire a couple of men.'

'Make Highpepper do it,' said someone else. 'They put them there; make them dig them up again.'

There was so much feeling that, in the end, a deputation went to Miss McKay. She was sympathetic, but pointed out that she had no power to demand the presence of Highpepper men on the Calladale estates. She advised the students to put a good face on it and do the necessary work themselves.

This turned the horrid task into what was known at Calladale as a Hostel Pot-Luck. In effect, the various hostels drew lots, the unlucky one to undertake the work. It chanced that Miss Paterson's hostel drew the short straw, and, true to tradition, tossed up between the senior and junior section of the house, to decide which should be responsible for doing the chore during the Thursday half-holiday.

'This is the limit!' groaned one Anne Hopkins to the unlucky group of which she was a member, and which happened to be the seniors of Paterson's. 'Tell you what! I vote, when we've dug everything up, we let Highpepper have the lot back. We'll stick it all up against their luxurious garages, the rich, awful pigs! I know where we can leave it during the daytime, close enough to deal with it later. You know

41

where their back gates come down to the old Canborough road? Well, do you remember the stage coach, about fifty yards from the front of the Cloak and Dagger hotel?'

It was generally agreed, afterwards, that if the juniors (i.e. the first year contingent) of Paterson's had been unlucky enough to lose the toss on this particular occasion, matters might have turned out very differently. It was unlikely that they would have conceived the idea of trying to hoist High-pepper with its own petard and even more unlikely that they would have thought of the stage coach at the Cloak and Dagger as a possible receptacle for the rhubarb crowns. (The carcasses of the rats, it may be stated, were, for reasons of hygiene, incinerated as and when they were found.)

The Cloak and Dagger was patronised by the gentlemen farmers only when there was no time to go into Garchester, but it throve, nevertheless, on such custom as the young men and the local farm-labourers brought to it, and was a pleasant Georgian house with a long, flat front and a pull-in for cars. At either end of this long front there was a considerable piece of grassland, and on that to the left, as one faced the house, there was drawn up the ancient stage-coach to which reference had been made by the tutor of Preddle and Soames.

It had figured in one of the more picturesque Highpepper rags. It had been commandeered, harnessed up, filled with students in late eighteenth-century costume, provided with outriders dressed as highwaymen, and driven into Garchester to collect for the local hospital, an object so worthy that the landlord of the Cloak and Dagger had not had the heart to complain about the unceremonious filching of his property, particularly as the college had almost drunk his cellars dry in celebration of the exploit.

Apart from a regular cleaning up and re-painting once in every five years, the coach was completely neglected in the ordinary way, so that Miss Hopkins' idea of using it as a cache for the rhubarb crowns until they could be dumped by moonlight in the Highpepper policies was, so far as it went, a sound one.

The knowledge that a rag against the men's college was impending and that it could be carried into effect as soon as the ground was cleared of rats and rhubarb, lent such goodwill to the work that by three o'clock on the half-holiday, while all the rest of the college was at games or off the premises bent on relaxation or the pursuit of outside interests, the rhubarb was all gathered and stacked and willing hands were putting it into sacks.

A telephone message to the firm in Garchester who supplied motor-coaches for college outings brought a driver to the Calladale gates by four o'clock, and, with his assistance, the bulging sacks were loaded into the boot. Rhubarb and students were then driven to the back gates of Highpepper Hall, where the cargo was unloaded, under the direction of Miss Hopkins and Miss Casey, her second in command, and there was no lack of volunteers to reload it into the derelict stage-coach.

The stage-coach was on the blind side of the inn, so that there was little fear, at that time of day—it was a quarter to five—of the proceedings being overlooked, and the old road was always very quiet except when the gentlemen-farmers were about. The rhubarb sacks having been stacked by the roadside, the driver was bidden to drive on and to return for the students in half an hour.

As soon as he had gone, the students humped the sacks of sprouting rhubarb crowns from the parking-place of the motor-coach to the strip of grass which bore the stage-coach. Willing and careful hands unlatched the inside door. The creaking hinges gave a note between a moan and a scream which ought to have served as a warning had any of the girls possessed second sight.

On the floor was a heap of rags which gave forth an unusual and suspect odour, but a bold hand plucked the rags forth to make room for the rhubarb. Somebody screamed. There was a general sortie from the vicinity of the stage-coach. One student, less impressionable and possibly more realistic than the others, craned her neck—she had been at the back of the queue—gave a long, incredulous look at the contents of the coach, and exclaimed in shocked, Midlands accents :

'Good Lord ! It's poor old Palliser !'

CHAPTER FIVE

The Corpse Speaks in Riddles

'Ernest remarked that the flamingo had feet formed for running like swans and for swimming like geese, and he was astonished that the two faculties were given to the same individual.'

Ibid.

ONE of the many phenomena of the Atomic Age is the curious process of osmosis which has taken place in the speech-forms of the sexes. In earlier but still comparatively modern times, the remark, 'Good Lord! It's poor old Palliser!' would have justified a student, given such an exclamation out of context, in stating, without hesitation, that the speaker must be male. The remark had been made, however, by an insensitive and inquisitive student named Diana Coots, as she stared incredulously at the huddled body.

'We'd better phone the college,' said a hesitant voice, 'and tell them to send a doctor, or something.'

'Miss McKay . . .' began the realist who had named the corpse; but she was cried down. The nearest telephone was the one at the inn, but, for obvious reasons, the students were not anxious to make a connection there.

'I'll go to that house just inside the Highpepper gates,' volunteered a student named Jones. (Later, when the numbing effect of shock had worn off, she wondered why she had felt so efficient and so calm.) 'It belongs to one of the lecturers, so he's sure to be on the phone.'

Unfortunately he was not in and the house was locked up, so, buoyed up by the knowledge that the occasion was one of crisis and great importance, she braved the portals of

Highpepper Hall and soon found herself opposite the pigeon-hole which communicated with the secretary's office. Breathlessly she explained her need and her mission. The secretary, a curiously, but perhaps necessarily, cold-blooded young woman of twenty-eight, put a call through to the nearest police station and then to the Calladale doctor, whose telephone number Miss Jones, her brain still ice-cold from shock, happened to know and to recollect.

'And now,' said Miss Jones, 'I'd better ring up the college.'

The college, in the persons of Miss McKay and Dame Beatrice, in the latter's powerful car, beat the police by ten minutes and the doctor, because he was out on his afternoon round, by more than an hour. Dame Beatrice, therefore, was enabled to obtain a short but uninterrupted first sight of the body. This, although interesting, was of no great help because it was not her province to move it.

She closed the door of the coach upon the poor, huddled remains and withdrew Miss McKay from their vicinity.

'There will have to be a post-mortem medical examination, of course,' she said. 'So far as I could *see* there is no external injury sufficient to cause death, but until the body can be moved we cannot be sure of that.'

'It couldn't be suicide, or she would never have been found in such a strange place,' said Miss McKay. 'I'm so thankful you could come back to us. You are a tower of strength. It looks like foul play to me. But who would wish to injure the girl? Our students are *utterly* harmless.'

'Let us speak to the group over there. They have had a severe shock, and so may make available to us some information which, in cooler moments, they might prefer to keep to themselves.'

Miss McKay, uncertain as to the ethics of this opportunist theory, nevertheless saw its usefulness.

'This is no time to withhold information,' she agreed. 'Will *you* bounce it out of them, or shall I?'

'Perhaps, if you would begin, I could put a question or two later on, as the spirit moves.'

'Yes, that would be best. I shall resign to you, then, as soon as you think you have a lead.' She marched up to the huddled little group. 'Now,' she said briskly, 'you must tell us all that you can. First of all, who found out where she was?'

'I did,' said a Miss Brander. 'I opened the door and lifted up the rags—those on the grass—and there it was.'

'There were several of us round the coach,' said Miss Jones, 'but Brander was the one who opened up.'

'I actually recognised who it was, I think,' said Miss Coots, 'as soon as Brander did.'

'Ah,' said Dame Beatrice. 'How was that, Student?'

Miss McKay, recognising her cue, nodded.

'Well, the college blazer. You couldn't mistake it,' Miss Coots explained.

'Of course not. So, seeing the badge on the blazer pocket . . .'

'I just called out that it was Miss Palliser.'

'Ah, yes. On the strength of the badge.'

'Well,' said Miss Jones, 'it would stand to reason, Dame Beatrice.' She seemed about to go on when a surreptitious kick from Miss Coots silenced her.

'True, child. And now—since all sins'—Dame Beatrice, who had seen the warning kick administered, glanced at Miss McKay, who nodded—'must of necessity be swallowed up by death, exactly what were you all up to that you opened the coach door at all?'

Miss McKay tactfully moved out of earshot and Miss Hopkins, as the organiser of the expedition, stepped forward. She pointed to the sacks of rhubarb crowns which were lying near the wheels of the coach.

'We'd planned a rhubarb rag on Highpepper,' she confessed. 'The crowns are in those sacks. We're certain *they*

47

ragged *us*—with dead rats, too, as well as rhubarb !—and we thought we'd get our own back, that's all.'

'What was the plan of campaign? You could scarce hope to garden in mid-afternoon on the Highpepper estates.'

'No. That was the point of the coach. We thought we'd stack the crowns inside until—until——'

'Until opportunity offered,' concluded Dame Beatrice, with graceful tact. 'All is explained, I see.'

'I hope—I mean, it was all my idea in the first place,' blurted out Miss Hopkins. 'Nobody else is to blame.'

'Here come the police,' said Dame Beatrice.

The Superintendent excused the delay by stating that the local sergeant had referred the finding of the body to headquarters, as was only right and proper. He added that he might as well take a look, but that nothing could be done until his photographer and the police doctor came along. He glanced at the group of students.

'I understand that one of the young ladies found the body,' he observed. 'I might as well be taking her statement.' He opened the door of the coach and looked inside. 'Very decayed,' he said, with disapproval. 'It won't be a nice job, that post-mortem won't. Rats have been at her, what's more. Identification won't be very easy.'

'Unfortunately, it will be all *too* easy,' said Miss McKay. 'One of my students has been missing for the past three weeks or more, as I thought you knew. The police, I *thought*, had been trying to trace her.'

'Oh, ah, of course, madam. Then that will be your college blazer she's got on?'

'Exactly.'

'Well, perhaps if I could get a statement from the young lady who found her . . .'

'More or less, they all found her, Superintendent. I may add that I fancy they did so because of a misguided attempt at ragging, but, of course, I don't know.'

48

'Well, the young gentlemen here at Highpepper borrowed the coach on one occasion,' said the Superintendent, 'so why not your young ladies? The equality of the sexes—isn't that what they're brought up to believe in nowadays? But this is a bad business—a very bad business.' He shook his head lugubriously. 'Perhaps you'd better get the ladies back to college. I'll take their statements there.'

The body bore no signs of violence and the autopsy revealed no disease in any of the vital organs.

'Poison,' said Dame Beatrice, whose formidable medical degrees and whose official connection with the Home Office had obtained readily for her a permission to be present at the whole of the post-mortem examination, 'and by one of the alkaloids, I should say.'

'My opinion exactly,' said a man named Clotford, in charge of the college laboratory. 'Coniine, my bet.' He also had obtained permission to be present. Both were now back in college.

'Coniine?' Dame Beatrice nodded.

'More than likely. Anyhow, the organs will have to be Stas-Otto-ed if they're to isolate the alkaloid. But coniine is a pretty good bet. Easy to get hold of, round here.'

'The spotted hemlock, no doubt.'

'Yes. Got it mixed up with some vegetable or other. Or, rather, somebody got it mixed up *for* her. On the face of it, I'd be inclined to say this was murder. Why else should she have been put into the coach?'

'She could have been taken ill along the road and crawled into it to sit or lie down. She could have died in some innocent person's car and been dumped when this person panicked. She could have taken the stuff, knowing it to be poison, and crept into the coach to die. Of these hypotheses, two are, of course, untenable, and another is highly unlikely.'

'Oh?'

'You did not see the inside of the coach after the body had been removed, but I did. There were no signs of vomiting and—there were no rats. I searched carefully, and so did the police, although I don't know that we were looking for the same things.'

'But the theory that she might have died in someone's car and been dumped would still hold water. Why is it so unlikely?' asked Miss McKay, later on when she and Dame Beatrice were discussing the tragedy and Mr Clotford had returned to duty.

'Because, if she *was* dumped in the coach, she was dumped somewhere else first. There's not much doubt but that the rats got at the body before it was put into the coach. Somebody has guilty knowledge of how that girl died.'

Carey, brought into consultation later, pointed out that the root of the spotted hemlock could be mistaken for parsnip, its growth of leaves for parsley.

'You must remember that she was a student at an agricultural college,' said his aunt. 'She wouldn't be likely to confuse things of that sort, would she?'

'True enough. What, then, do you suspect?'

'Foul play, of course. What else?'

'Are you sure it couldn't be suicide?' Carey persisted.

'There are easier ways of killing oneself. Death by most forms of poisoning is not a painless one, and death by spotted hemlock, though not to be compared with the agonies of taking the roots of the water hemlock, is very, very unpleasant. The symptoms of taking water hemlock are burning in mouth and throat, abdominal pains, nausea, palpitations, vertigo and brief fainting fits, followed by the most terrible convulsions at intervals of about fifteen minutes. Unless counter-measures are taken before the second of these convulsions, during which the patient screams, vomits and grinds his teeth, death follows as a matter of course:

50

Poisoning by spotted hemlock is a paralytic illness, and quite often asphyxiation is caused by respiratory paralysis, although circulation remains comparatively normal. Of course, most of the cases one gets are those of children who have experimentally chewed the stuff, which looks and tastes rather like parsley, as you say.'

'Children will chew anything,' remarked Miss McKay, 'in spite of all they are told in schools. We have water hemlock in one of the college ponds, and the spotted hemlock is of fairly wide distribution round here, but it has done flowering by now. It flowers in June and July. One relates it to Ancient Greece. Did not Socrates die from drinking an infusion of spotted hemlock?'

'Yes, so we are told. Unfortunately for this poor girl, spotted hemlock is at its most deadly at this time of year, and we may suppose that her murderer knew it. But are you not rather rash to allow the water hemlock to grow on land where cattle are kept? The common name for water hemlock is the cowbane.'

'To tell you the truth, I noticed it only the other day, when I was taking a short cut back to college. I think I will have it uprooted and burnt. Not that cattle are ever put into that particular field. You don't mean that, after all, poor Miss Palliser took water hemlock and not spotted hemlock, do you?'

'No, no. But have you an expert on poisonous plants, either a member of staff or a student? If so, I should be glad to make use of her specialised knowledge.'

'Nobody, so far as I know. Ah, wait a moment! I believe the dead student herself had made some experiments. I must ask Mr Clotford. He will know. Well, now, Dame Beatrice, you've told us the symptoms and course of death by taking the water hemlock. How about the symptoms of poisoning by spotted hemlock? You did say it was a paralytic illness . . .'

'Before I answer that, I think I ought to inform you, Miss

51

McKay, that Miss Palliser was no longer Miss Palliser; she was a Mrs Coles. Moreover, I should have taken the body to be that of a woman of at least thirty. It is very odd.'

'Oh, I guessed she had married,' said the Principal, calmly. 'Our students do, from time to time, before they have finished their course. When she disappeared, it occurred to me very soon that she might have gone to her husband. Do the police suspect him of the murder?'

'They know of his existence. I wrote to him, and, in his acknowledgment of my letter he said that he had put himself immediately in touch with them, informing them that he was married to the girl.'

'At least that doesn't sound like a guilty conscience,' said Carey. Dame Beatrice caught Miss McKay's sardonic eye.

'I wouldn't bet on it,' said the Principal. 'Two decades of working with students have taught me that a tender conscience is now the most striking anachronism in the world.'

Young Coles presented himself at the college that same evening. Miss McKay received him sympathetically.

'I've been called to attend the inquest,' he said awkwardly. 'Is there anything you'd like me to say—or, perhaps, not to say—about Norah?'

'The proceedings most likely will be adjourned after evidence of the cause of death and evidence of identification have been given,' said Dame Beatrice.

'Oh, yes, I see.' He turned, tongue-tied, and fidgeted with the strap of his wristwatch.

'And now,' said Miss McKay, with practical kindness, 'I am going to turn you on to Dame Beatrice. You may tell her everything you wish, including, I suppose, your reasons for marrying Miss Palliser before her college course was completed.'

'Yes, there is that. It couldn't have anything to do with what's happened, though.'

'Of course not. But it may help to ease your mind and something useful to the police enquiry may come of it.'

'I can't think—it doesn't make sense!' the boy blurted out. 'Nobody could have—nobody could——' He turned aside again and stared moodily out of the window. Dame Beatrice gave one glance at the Principal and nodded briskly. Miss McKay went out. Young Coles, master of himself once more, pulled forward an armchair.

'No. You have that. I'm going to look out of the window while I talk,' said the elderly lady. She turned her back on him and heard the slight creaking of the chair as he sat down. 'How did you manage to persuade Miss Palliser to marry you before the end of her college course?'

'Does it matter? Her death couldn't have—I mean, there couldn't be any connection.'

'No jealous suitor? No possessive stepfather?'

'Oh, you know about that old swine!' Trained in assessing such matters, she detected relief in his tone.

'Is he old?

'Actually, no, only in sin. He's a good deal younger than the mother, as a matter of fact.'

'What cause have you to dislike him?'

'He gets under my skin.'

'Nothing definite?'

'He kicked me out of the house once—literally. That's why we got married—just to show him.'

'No, you don't mean that. You mean you persuaded Miss Palliser to marry you to assuage your wounded feelings.'

'Perhaps so.' His voice had gone flat again. 'Will you tell me a bit more about things? I'm pretty well in the dark. I don't even know when and where she died.'

'I can tell you approximately *when*, but *where* remains a mystery. She died between three and four weeks ago— probably even before she was reported missing. I am not in a position to be more explicit at the moment.'

53

'Will you tell me where she was found?'

'Yes, but you must try not to jump to any unwarrantable conclusions.'

'That means you suspect those young devils at High-pepper!'

'That is the unwarrantable conclusion which you must try to avoid. Your wife was found on the floor of a coach which acts as an original sort of inn-sign at a house called the Cloak and Dagger, not a hundred yards from the back gates of Highpepper Hall. I cannot avoid the thought that a student from that college would have gone further afield to dispose of a body.'

'Probably couldn't.'

'There is that, of course. The inquest may make certain things clear which, at present, are extremely obscure. Now for one or two questions. Please answer me as accurately as you can. When did you last see your wife?'

'The week before the beginning of term. She had a lot of preparation to do—holiday work for the lecturers—which she'd put off doing so that we could have as much time to ourselves as possible, so we came back from the seaside on the Saturday and term began on the following Tuesday week.'

'How often have you communicated with her since you parted?'

'Oh, a couple of times. We've never, either of us, been terribly good correspondents.'

'Did anything happen during the holiday to cause you any uneasiness?' She turned swiftly as she put this question. The young man flushed and looked down at his watch.

'I—no, I don't remember anything special.'

'Please think hard.' There was a long silence before Coles shook his head.

'Everything was perfectly normal, as far as my recollection goes. We had a mild row on the first day, but that's the

54

usual thing when two people who are rather desperately keen on one another get together after a longish absence.'

Dame Beatrice nodded agreement.

'Quite,' she said. 'And it was fun to make up the quarrel afterwards. Apart from the incident to which you have already referred, what reason had you to dislike your wife's stepfather?'

'He just simply gets under my skin. I can't explain. Some people are like that.'

'How long ago did you marry?'

'Last March.'

'Mrs Coles had then barely completed two terms of her college course?'

'That's right.'

'I am not clear why you were in such a hurry.'

A slight smile changed the boy's anxious expression.

'There wasn't the usual reason, if that's what you mean,' he assured her. Dame Beatrice nodded.

'I could understand it if you had been able to live together,' she said, 'but as you were not able to do so, and as certain felicities of married life were barred to you until your wife's college course was over, I do not see any advantage in your having entered the holy estate of matrimony so early.' She looked him full in the eye. Coles shrugged.

'I suppose I wanted to make sure of her,' he said. Dame Beatrice accepted this explanation and pigeon-holed it for future reference. It suggested that the young husband might have had a rival, either real or imaginary, and, if real, some interesting possibilities might present themselves. The *crime passionel,* although rare, was not unknown in Britain, she reflected. There were, however, other possibilities.

'I am going beyond my brief with my next question,' she said, 'but it is one the police may put.'

'Go ahead.'

'Do you know whether your wife had insured her life?'

He looked startled.

'Insured her life? I'm sure she hadn't. I don't see how she could have afforded to pay the premiums. She had no money except what her own father had left her, and that wasn't much.'

'Did her stepfather help to keep her?'

'I don't really know about him. I know her own father left a little bit and that her college fees were paid out of it. And she had quite a fair amount of money to spend.'

'How do you mean?'

'Well, she always paid for her own holidays when we went away together, and often stood treat in restaurants. I used to do the actual paying, but she often handed me the money beforehand.'

'But she never referred to any life insurance policy?'

'Definitely not. Look here, can you think of anything else the police might ask me? I've had a pretty bad knock, and I'd like to be prepared. Are they—I know it sounds a bit odd, but, naturally, one's read about these cases—are they likely to suspect me? Had I better get my alibi quite clear?'

'You have an alibi, then?'

'Good Lord! I hope so!'

'Then you had better be prepared with it. The husband or wife is usually first on the list of suspects.'

He shrugged, laughed, then bit his lip, as though recollecting what had happened to cause her to make the statement. He got up, then.

'Well, thank you for your help,' he said. 'I'd better say good-bye to Miss McKay and get back to Garchester. We shall meet again at the inquest, perhaps?'

'I shall be there.'

'Well, what do you make of him?' asked Miss McKay, when Coles had taken his leave and gone. Dame Beatrice waved a yellow claw.

'I must have notice of that question,' she said. 'I want to look over Mrs Coles' wardrobe.'

Miss McKay asked no questions. She touched the buzzer for her secretary, who delivered Dame Beatrice into the charge of the head student. There was little wardrobe accommodation in the study bedrooms, and, beyond a suit obviously retained for best wear, a dance frock, a stuff frock for ordinary college wear, and some sweaters, blouses and changes of stockings and underclothes, there was nothing very much in the missing student's room and certainly nothing to excite remark. It was not what was there, but what was not there, which interested Dame Beatrice.

'Are there any clothes in a trunk in the boxroom or the basement?' she enquired.

'Yes. Most people keep clothes in their trunks, and then, of course, we are allotted lockers for such things as dungarees, Wellingtons and dairy dresses,' the head student replied.

'Yes, I see. I should like to look into her trunk.'

She was shown this and, for form's sake, she also inspected the dead girl's locker in the basement. She shook her head.

'Did the student not possess a dressing-gown?' she asked. 'And I have seen only one pair of pyjamas.'

'One pair would be in the wash, but there ought to be a third,' said the head student. 'And a dressing-gown—I don't know for certain. She may have used her overcoat.'

'But that also is missing, and she was not wearing it when she was found. Will you please keep this little expedition of ours strictly secret from the rest of the college?'

'Yes, of course, if you wish, but would you not like me to try to find out about the dressing-gown?'

'The overcoat seems far more important. Considering the time of year, one can deduce that it does exist somewhere. No doubt your reactions to that supposition are the same as my own.'

'I take it you mean that if it's not in college, it must be somewhere else. The question, I suppose, is—where?'

'Exactly.' She beamed upon the student and returned to acquaint Miss McKay with the negative result of her researches.

'We didn't fathom her,' said Miss McKay. 'But, of course, a girl who will contract a secret marriage in the middle of her training may be a darker horse than I had suspected. I wonder how far on the police are in their investigation? So far, they haven't troubled the college. I suppose that is because she was found twenty-five miles away. All the same, I shall be surprised if we are not overrun as soon as the inquest is over. What, if anything, will come out at the inquest, I wonder?'

'Probably nothing but the cause of death.'

'You actually named spotted hemlock as the vehicle. How was that?'

'That was simply guess-work. I had noticed the spotted hemlock about the neighbourhood. Of course, the murderer has had bad luck. It was by the merest chance in the world that your students took up the piece of material that hid the body from view. Who could have supposed that they would want to use the stage-coach?'

'Ah, yes. I have asked no questions in case I might hamper the police or your own enquiry, but I should be interested to know what caused them to explore the interior of the coach. I realised at the time, of course, that they were up to mischief.'

'They were seeking a hiding-place for some sacks of sprouting rhubarb.'

'Oh, I see. Preparatory to rendering unto Caesar the things they presumed to be Caesar's, I take it? Ah, well, since they did not succeed in their object, there is no reason for me to appear in the matter.'

'I made some enquiries at the inn, and it appears that the

presence of an unspecified heap on the floor of the coach would have brought no investigation from the owners, as they never went near it except to paint it every fifth year in order to preserve the bodywork.'

'Is there anything else I can do for you? Any way I can be of help?'

'Well, I wish I could find some way of meeting the girl's mother and stepfather. I should very much like to hear what they have to say.'

'I can arrange that, I think. I shall have to invite them to college after the inquest to collect the poor girl's things. Then you can meet them on neutral ground, as it were, and under non-suspicious circumstances. Will that do?'

'Most admirably. I wonder who was the last person to see her before she encountered her death? In the case of a murder by poisoning, the actual killer need not have been on the spot.'

'We don't seem able to find out. In other words, I don't think there was any one particular person. You know how it is in a hostel. The students are almost always in groups, and that is the way we like it. A gregarious student, on the whole, is a happy student. You still cling, I suppose, to the idea that Miss Palliser—I mean, Mrs Coles—was spirited away on that horse Miss Good saw?'

'I still think that, if she was not, coincidence has an even longer arm than I have ever suspected.'

'I still don't know why the parents have troubled the college so little. I wonder what made the mother marry again? It does not seem to have been for financial reasons, from what one can gather. I'll tell you one thing, though— not that it could have any bearing upon what has happened, but—I don't like the sound of that stepfather. I wonder whether he has children of his own? I also wonder whether Mrs Coles left a will. Not that I know whether she had anything very substantial to leave.'

'Are you arguing that the stepfather may have killed the girl to get possession of her inheritance, not knowing that she was married? It is possible.'

Miss McKay wagged her head.

'Wills cause more trouble and more bad feeling than wars,' she pronounced solemnly. 'But, of course, we have yet to discover whether a will was involved. If not, we may have a crime of jealousy, although one can hardly credit that one of our students would be mixed up in that sort of thing. They always seem such pedestrian, ordinary girls.'

'Yes, I know what you mean, but how can one tell? Of course, pedestrian, ordinary girls do get themselves murdered, I suppose.'

'Oh, dear!' exclaimed Miss McKay. 'There goes the refectory bell. I don't know about you, but at the first sign of trouble I eat like a horse. Come along.'

While the plates were being changed for the second course, the college secretary was called away. She came back with a message.

'Miss Palliser's parents are here, and would like to see you.'

'Tell them I won't keep them waiting for more than a few minutes. I shall indicate, without actually committing myself to a spoken lie, that you are a member of the staff, if you don't mind,' she added, in an aside, to Dame Beatrice. 'I met the mother once, but not the stepfather. I shall be interested to know what you make of them.' She finished her meal, drank a cup of black coffee and then, with an apology to the rest of the high table, rose and made her way, with Dame Beatrice, to the visitors' parlour.

CHAPTER SIX

Case History

'These are, I think, guinea-pigs, but of a particular kind.'

Ibid.

THE dead girl's stepfather wore a black armband and a black tie. He was a swarthy Italianate man, short and of stoutish build, with clear, amber, cat-like eyes, a broad nose and a slightly paunched belly. The mother bore no possible resemblance to the dead girl and did not appear to be old enough for the relationship between them. Her first words were in explanation of this.

'Of course, I was only twenty-three when Norah was born,' she stated, 'and I had Carrie at sixteen, although he did marry me later. I don't deserve this trouble should come upon me.'

'No, of course not,' said Miss McKay, in a sympathetic voice. 'Nobody deserves this sort of trouble. Is there any light you can possibly throw on the matter?'

'You're only thinking of the college,' said the woman, beginning to sniff. 'But it's worse for us than it is for you. People are beginning to say my daughter must have been a bad girl.'

'Was she?' Dame Beatrice gently enquired. The question was put in such a beautifully-modulated voice that the mother could scarcely take offence at its essential baldness.

'I don't know. That's the trouble. I just don't know. We've talked it over . . .' she glanced at her husband . . . 'Mr Biancini and I . . .'

'So he *is* an Italian,' thought Dame Beatrice. 'I wonder what light that might shed?'

'Yes?' said Miss McKay.

'But we can't come to any conclusion. We were relying on you to give us . . . well, a lead.'

'If I had had any reason to suppose that your daughter was an undesirable member of this place, she would have been sent down long ago.' Miss McKay's voice was extremely firm.

Mrs Biancini burst into tears. Her husband rose from the hard-seated chair he was occupying, went over to her, seated himself on the broad and comfortable arm of hers, and put an arm around her shoulders.

'O.K. Take it easy, Dee-an,' he said. 'So Norah was *à la* whatever it takes, with you?' he enquired of the Principal. Miss McKay replied curtly :

'I have already said so.'

'You called in the police at once?'

'Yes. We called the doctor, too, of course, in case there was anything to be done. Unfortunately, there was not.'

'Yes,' said Mrs Biancini, mollified, 'I'm sure you did everything you could. Shall I—I suppose I'll be allowed to see her before they nail her down?'

'Of course. In fact, I'm afraid that you will be called upon at the inquest for proof of identity. Haven't the police told you that? You must be prepared. It is not a pleasant task, and I'm sorry you have to be called upon to face it.'

'I've been so upset I haven't taken much notice of the police. They've come bothering round, of course, but there was nothing we could tell them about Norah that they didn't know already.'

'Did you tell them she was married?' The question was put by Dame Beatrice in the deceptively dulcet tones she had used before.

'Married?' Mr Biancini almost fell off the arm of his wife's chair. 'You're not serious?'

'Perfectly serious. You did not know, then?'

'Certainly not! Since when?'

'Since the beginning, or near to it, of the summer,' said Miss McKay. 'More probably during her first Easter holiday from college, or at the end of the Easter term.'

'Did *you* know, Dee-an?' Mr Biancini still appeared to be dumbfounded.

'Of course not.' Mrs Biancini was entirely mistress of herself again. 'How could I? She never used to tell me a thing. Neither of them tells me a thing.'

'In other words, she did not care for the idea of your second marriage,' said Dame Beatrice. 'Children are odd, in that respect. They never seem to think that their mothers have a point of view, too. My own son, Ferdinand Lestrange, although a broadminded man and one of some vision, never quite accustomed himself to my second marriage and its aftermath of a half-brother. Children, especially sons, are curiously self-centred, one finds.'

This speech had the effect that Dame Beatrice had anticipated.

'Sons!' snorted Mrs Biancini. 'I don't know about sons! Daughters are quite enough for me! Norah's father died when she was ten. I brought her up, working my fingers to the bone, until she was seventeen. Then I met Tony.'

Mr Biancini smirked.

'It was at a dance,' he explained. 'I was bored, frustrated —no, I'll be honest—just plain bored. Then Dee-an turned up, an older, more sophisticated woman. I fell for her and married her.'

He and his wife exchanged glances of mingled congratulation and caution. Then Mrs Biancini smiled.

'Just like that,' she said. 'Norah, of course, didn't like it. She adored her mum.'

63

'But not sufficiently so to prefer your happiness and sense of security to her own,' suggested Dame Beatrice.

'Oh, well, that's all over now, poor girl,' said the stepfather. 'Let's hope none of it was her own fault.'

'It couldn't be suicide,' said Mrs Biancini quickly. 'I've told you I don't know whether Norah was a good girl, but she wouldn't do a thing like that to us.'

'Do you wish the murderer to be found?' asked Dame Beatrice. 'I agree with you that it was not suicide.'

'Yes, that I do—and punished!'

'Then tell me all you know.'

The woman glanced at her husband.

'Perhaps, Mr Biancini . . . ?' suggested Miss McKay, beginning to rise. Mr Biancini got up.

'O.K.! O.K.!' he said, and followed her out. Dame Beatrice and the mother were left alone.

'Was it that artist boy?' asked Mrs Biancini. 'She was always bringing him to the house for free meals. I got quite sick of it.'

'A Mr Coles?'

'That's the one. What's he got to say for himself?'

'But little; he is armed and well prepared.'

'Oh? Prepared for what?'

'I was quoting from Shakespeare's *Merchant of Venice*. You are familiar with the passage?'

'I dare say we did it at school. Just let me get at that young beauty! He'll need a suit of armour to protect himself, I can tell you! Leading my girl astray! How dare he think of marrying her? I never heard of such a thing!'

'There are worse things than a legal union, surely?'

The woman's face darkened.

'I know I made a mistake myself,' she said, 'but that's as may be. I looked forward to a bit of Norah's company and . . . I won't deny it . . . a bit of her money when she'd finished her college course. I mean, when you've kept a girl until she's in her twenties, you can't be blamed for wanting some return.'

Dame Beatrice wagged her head. 'And when she was at home, what kind of person was she? Did she seem discontented, for example?' she enquired.

'Not as long as she got her own way. It was me marrying again that unsettled her. You're right about that. I did wait until after she'd sat for her General Certificate, too, before I told her what I was going to do. Of course, she wasn't with me very much, in a sense, between sixteen and seventeen. She had her school-friends and Saturday morning games—she was in all the school teams—a proper open-air type—and then, of course, I saw nothing of her, evenings, because I'd have the radio on in the dining-room and she'd be doing her homework on the kitchen table.'

'What about holidays?'

'I couldn't afford them,' said Mrs Biancini. 'She had her bike, and that was all I could manage. She only had *that* because it saved the fares going to school.'

'But you wouldn't call her an unhappy girl?'

'She seemed happy enough to me, but what I say is that children confide in anybody rather than their mothers, once they're turned fourteen.'

'Was she a quiet girl?'

'Very quiet. I used to wonder, sometimes, if still waters ran deep. And now I know they must have done. Whatever could have made her rush into marrying that boy? He hasn't got a penny to his name! What did she want to do it for? He didn't get her into trouble, I hope?'

'He says not.'

'Humph! I'm not at all sure I'd take his word for it! I don't trust those artistic types. It wouldn't surprise me if . . . oh, well, I'd better not say it, I suppose.'

'I understand you, but I agree that it should not be said.

Was she a girl who formed many friendships with young men?'

'Oh, she was normal, as to boys. I didn't pass any objection so long as I knew who she was out with, and she was willing to bring them home and introduce them properly. But, there! You never know what girls get up to, out of your sight! This marriage of hers—I'm not sure it hasn't upset me as much as the—as much as her passing away.'

She took out her handkerchief again. Dame Beatrice waited until she had recovered, and then asked gently:

'When did you last see your daughter?'

'During the summer holiday. She was at home for a few days and then said she had made plans to go away with this young art student. She'd been away with him before. I made no objection. Lots of young people go away together and have a good time and nothing wrong in it. And as for Tony, he was ever so good to her. Gave her the money, and quite a bit over, to spend there, and carried her bag to the station and saw she got a seat on the train, and everything. Not her own father could have done more to give her a send-off—I'm sure of that. Quite put himself out, he did, his own train going an hour later.'

'Was her husband with her?'

'No. He was to meet her down there the following day. He'd got something to do—a holiday job, I think—and couldn't get away until the Sunday, or so she said. It seemed a pity for both of them to miss the Saturday, as they had to pay all the same.'

'I see.' Dame Beatrice made a note on Miss McKay's blotter. A notebook, she thought, might frighten the witness into silence.

'Then she came home at the end of the fortnight and was with us a couple of days before she went off to stay with her aunt at Harrafield. She was there about ten days and then she came home for a week before going back to the

66

college. And to think that, all the time, she was married!'

'I suppose she really *did* go to her aunt?'

'Oh, she went, all right, because I got a postcard stamped at Harrafield, to say she'd arrived safely. Besides, her aunt would have let me know at once if she hadn't arrived.'

'Is the aunt your sister?'

'No, my late husband's.'

'The police may want her address.'

'They're welcome. It's the Hour-Glass Hotel, near the centre of the town. She's the manageress there. Norah and I used to visit there together until I married Tony. But Sarah took exception to that, and told me I needn't bring him there again. Nice, wasn't it? You'd have thought we weren't respectable! I told her if *that's* how she felt, we wouldn't trouble her any more for the rest of our lives. I *was* wild with her rudeness, I can tell you. Still, I wouldn't stop Norah going. She was very fond of her aunt. Well, you've been very understanding, I'm sure. See you at the inquest, I expect? And now I'd better have a natter with Miss McKay before I go.'

'Before you go, Mrs Biancini, there are just one or two points I should like cleared up. First of all, are you staying in the neighbourhood?'

'Yes, and have been ever since we heard the news. We're putting up with a Mrs Spear who lets lodgings down in the village. It's where we put up last year for the College Open Day and that. She's very nice, although I must say I'd like to show her how to make a batter pudding. Tony's so fond of them.'

'Yes. You do realise, don't you, Mrs Biancini, that, whatever Norah's reason for leaving college may have been, she went voluntarily?'

'I suppose so.'

'Can you suggest anybody, apart from her husband (whom, I may say, I have interviewed), who had sufficient interest in her, or influence over her, to wish to smuggle her away? You see, from the night she left college to the time the students found her body, she was, so to speak, lost without trace. Cannot you throw any light whatever upon her disappearance?'

'If I could, I would, and quick enough, too. Don't you think I've had enough of all this sort of thing from the police?'

'I'm sure you have. What made you let her come to college in the first place?'

'Well, the idea *had* been for her to get a nice job in a bank. Several of the girls from her school had gone into banks, and it seemed refined sort of work, and not above what she could do. But she and Mr Biancini didn't seem to hit it off, as I've tried to explain, and nothing would satisfy her but to get away from home.'

'Quite natural, under the circumstances, I should have thought.'

'As I said before, I didn't see it at all fair on me,' said Mrs Biancini. 'Still, if that's how she felt, there it was. She took her G.C.E. and passed in five subjects and then stayed on until she was eighteen so as to start here. They won't take them before eighteen if they can help it. I mean, they *do* take them at seventeen, going on eighteen, if it's exceptional or means family hardship, but she didn't come under either of that. There was the bit of money her father left her, you see. She came in for that at eighteen. Too young, I thought, so I used it to send her here and give her all the pocket-money she wanted.'

'Does that mean that she could have been in control of the whole sum, once she went to college?'

'Oh, yes, according to the law, I suppose, and I gave her just what she asked for. It was her own money, after all, just in the bank for her use and no strings tied to it except my

68

late husband's wishes, which, of course, I should always respect.'

'Quite so. Now please forgive me for asking such a question, but—what wishes had your husband expressed about the destination of the money supposing that your daughter died before you did?'

'No wishes at all. Norah was always a hale and healthy child, and she was only ten years old, as I've said, when her father died, so it wouldn't have occurred to him, I suppose, to think I might outlive her.'

'So the money has remained in your account, and would have done so until your daughter left college. How old . . .?'

'Just turned twenty-two.'

'But I thought you said she entered college when she was eighteen?'

'Well, no. She *was* to have done, but I was a bit doubtful about spending the money, so she went and helped her aunt for her keep and her pocket-money for a bit. Then she turned restless and said she didn't have a future and must be trained. She picked an agricultural college, and I gave in. Anything, so long as she was contented.'

'May I ask—or perhaps the police have already asked it—how large a sum is involved?'

Mrs Biancini shook her head.

'The police *have* asked,' she said. 'I told them and I can't see any harm in telling you. It isn't enough for anybody to be tempted into killing Norah for it.'

'One can never be sure of that sort of thing, Mrs Biancini.'

'All right, then. It amounted to round about three thousand pounds, that's all. I've paid her college fees outright for the two years, and put a matter of five hundred into my current account for her clothes and pocket-money and that, and there's something over two thousand left of it in my deposit account.'

'I am sure you have been most thoughtful.'

'I hope so, I'm sure. You can't always do for the best.'

'Would you have any objection to my going to visit her aunt as soon as the inquest is over?'

'Certainly not. Why should I? Not that she knows any more than we do, for I've asked her, thinking she might have been more in Norah's confidence, as she'd worked for her.'

'As your daughter stayed with her for some time before she went to college, I hope to be able to find out something which will help us to trace the murderer.'

'I doubt whether her aunt can cast any light on what's happened. Oh, dear! Oh, dear! And to think how nicely everything was going on! All of us reconciled at last, and such a lovely summer holiday, and now this has to come on us out of the blue, as it were! It makes you think we weren't born to be happy, don't it?'

'There is just one more point, Mrs Biancini. Did your daughter seem in any way—physically, in particular—old for her age, would you say?'

'I don't think so. I wasn't all that old when she was born, and neither was her father. Of course, she always had her head screwed on the right way, if that's what you mean.'

It was not at all what Dame Beatrice meant, but she did not press the point. She said:

'When you spoke of reconciliation just now, you were not, I take it, speaking of Norah?'

'No, I was speaking of my other girl, Carrie. Such a trouble she's always been, but she's promised us faithful to go straight. That's who we got reconciled with this summer, only it didn't work out.'

CHAPTER SEVEN

Machinations of a Paternal Aunt

'. . . we could not but admire the grace of form which
raises this kind of ass almost to the dignity of the horse.'

Ibid.

'So, whatever the motive of the murderer, it scarcely seems
as though money could have entered into it,' said Miss
McKay to the police. 'I refuse to believe that the mother
killed that poor girl for two thousand pounds, or the stepfather, either.'

'Stranger things have happened,' said the local Detective-
Inspector. 'We shall keep an eye on Mrs Biancini and on
him. Two thousand might come in very useful to a gentleman of *his* kidney. Not that he'd have got it, with a husband
in the offing.'

'And of what kidney, exactly, is he, Inspector?' Dame
Beatrice enquired.

'All foreigners can bear watching, madam.'

But with this insular comment Dame Beatrice was not
content.

'It appears,' she said to Miss McKay, 'that the aunt and
the niece had had quite a lot to do with one another. They
may have been in sympathy. The girl may have told the
aunt, her father's sister, things which she did not tell her
mother. I shall go north and see her.'

'Not until after the inquest, I presume,' said Miss McKay.
The inquest, adjourned at the request of the police, produced
nothing new and resulted in a verdict that the subject had
died from an administration of coniine, but whether she had

71

administered it herself, or had had it administered to her, the coroner's jury refused to decide.

Dame Beatrice, driven by George, her chauffeur, to the Hour-Glass at Harrafield, decided that the receptionist was also manageress. Dame Beatrice was shown to her room and had not been there for ten minutes before there was a knock at the door. The compliments of the manageress, and would Dame Beatrice care to take a private glass of sherry in the sitting-room?

The sitting-room, obviously the sanctum of the manageress, was a comfortable little den at the back of the reception office. It was well-furnished, showed a television set, a portable radio and a surprisingly well-filled bookcase containing, Dame Beatrice noted, works on spiritualism, theosophy, poltergeists, cookery and gardening.

The dead girl's aunt followed her gaze.

'I don't care for gardening myself,' she said. 'I bought them for Norah. Funny you should be down here from the college. I suppose you know all there is to know? I was terribly cut up when Dodo wrote. I was very fond of Norah. Too bad when Dodo, who always *was* very foolish, took up with that Tony Biancini. I feel bad about it, because it was here she met him. They used to go out and about together, but I thought nothing of it because of the difference in their ages, but there you are, you see. If a middle-aged woman is going to make a fool of herself, there's nothing you can say that will stop it. Still, it brought I and Norah together. I used to feel quite sorry for the girl, and, of course, she took it real bad when they married. No wonder, with my poor brother such a good husband and father. I thought Dodo owed something more to his memory than to go gallivanting into marriage with the son of an Italian waiter and a Maltese waitress from a little chop-shop off the Strand. That's what he is, that Tony. He told me so himself, before him and Dodo got so thick. Dee-an, he calls her. *I* never did, nor did my poor brother, either. Doris she was christened and Dodo she's been ever since, until this wedding came about. One thing, she didn't have it white—or so I was told. I got an invite, but, of course, I didn't go. Couldn't, I *said; wouldn't,* I meant. I should have thrown my hymn-book at the pair of them!'

Dame Beatrice nodded sympathetically.

'The college,' she began, with some diplomacy but less ingenuousness, 'wondered whether you could possibly throw any light on your niece's death.'

'So that's why you're here! I thought it was rather strange, you turning up and putting the address of the college on your letter. Well, I only wish I *could* tell you something that would help! But who would have done such a wicked thing? That's what I ask myself, morning to night I do. Who could have done it? There doesn't seem anybody, does there? I suppose'—she hesitated and then plunged—'I suppose it couldn't be a joke . . . what the students call a rag . . . that went wrong?'

'That is a point which will have to be considered,' said Dame Beatrice. She did not add that, in her opinion, it was nearly the most unlikely explanation that could be offered. 'But there's a lot of clearing-up to be done before we go as far as that. You see, these are all agriculturalists. They do *know* about plants and it was some preparation made from a wild plant which caused the death.'

She described the findings at the inquest.

'I *thought* they'd adjourn it,' said the aunt. 'So far as I've read'—she nodded towards the bookcase—'they always do. Do you know when the funeral is? Dodo didn't say in her letter, but I feel I must go, though we're that short-handed—still, we're not full, being October, so the maids will have to manage. Cook will keep an eye open, I dare say.'

'Were you surprised to hear of your niece's marriage?'

'Why, no. You see, I helped them over that. Dodo doesn't

73

know—not that I really care—but I let Norah get married from here. In the Easter holiday it was, the Wednesday after the Bank Holiday. I gave the reception for them, too. Being in the hotel business, it helped, you see. Everything was on the spot and I made the reception my wedding present, and, when the guests knew it was my niece, they clubbed together and gave her a cheque—not a large one, you know, but it was very nice of them, I thought—and a special cake-knife to cut the cake. Oh, we had a lovely time of it that day, and then . . . this!'

She blinked and swallowed, but she was a self-controlled woman and did not break down. Dame Beatrice sipped sherry and gave her time to recover. The aunt blew her nose and then smiled.

'I thought I'd got over giving way,' she said. 'Yes, they were married from here, and I'm glad to remember that. They were ever so much in love. You could see that from a mile off. They hadn't really known one another long, and I don't really know why they couldn't have waited until Norah had finished with college. Still, you can't dictate to Cupid can you, now?'

As Dame Beatrice was unable to imagine herself dictating, or attempting to dictate, to the son of Venus, she treated this as the rhetorical question that it was and did not reply.

'Your niece, then, had no idea of living at home for a time when her college course was concluded?' she enquired.

'Between you and I,' replied the aunt, 'it wouldn't have done. Dodo doesn't seem to have known anything about it, but, from what Norah told me once, that Tony is a wolf. Anything is grist that comes to *his* mill. She didn't like to be in the same house with him more than she could help. Why, she spent hardly any of her college holidays at home, you know. She came here before she was married, and this summer she went off with young Coles to one of those holi-

74

day camps—not that it would appeal to me, but I suppose they're all right for young people.'

'Which was the one at which they stayed?'

'Why, that big one at Bracklesea, the one that only opened a couple of years ago.'

'Wasn't that rather expensive?—I mean, for a young man without employment and a girl still at college?'

'I believe Tony Biancini subbed up. Norah did tell me once that she hated taking his money, but that it cost such a lot to pay for her husband's holidays as well as her own. I told her I thought it was foolish. "He'll get to thinking he's bought you, body and soul," I said, "and that's a situation you don't want to develop," I said. "These Italians may have their greasy ways," I said, "but they know the value of money better than anybody, without it might be the French, where I *did* hear tell, when I was a girl, they put a big pebble in the pot with the vegetables when they haven't got any meat to give a flavour.'

'I understood from Mrs Biancini that her first husband left some money for Mrs Coles to be spent on her education, the residue to go to her when she left college.'

'That's right. My brother was quite a warm man for our station of life. He was in the building trade, you know, and done well, I believe, out of war damage.'

'And Mr Biancini? You mentioned just now that he was in the habit of giving money to Mrs Coles. Do you know anything of his financial position?'

'Not a lot. Him and I don't have much to do with one another. I don't trust him. I believe he's been the saving kind, though. He's been connected with hotels and restaurants all his life and I expect he's saved up his tips, if not some of his wages. Of course, with accommodation and all food found, and drinks at cost price, there's nothing to buy in our business except your clothes, you see, unless you *want* to spend money. Dodo did hint, once, as he'd won a State lottery in some foreign country, so that would account for it, too.'

'You have never wondered whether your niece's death was self-inflicted, I suppose?'

Miss Palliser frowned in concentration for a moment and then shook her head.

'I've thought and I've thought,' she said, 'but I can't honestly see it. There wasn't a baby on the way, was there?'

'No, no baby.'

'That would be the only likely reason, although, even then, she'd only got to show her marriage lines at home and at the college to clear herself, hadn't she? I don't see that as an obstacle. Anyway, as you say, it wasn't so. No, we can wash out any idea of she did it herself. Besides, with her knowledge, she'd have chose an easier way out, that's what *I* think.'

'Her knowledge?'

'She'd have chose the gas oven,' said Miss Palliser, 'and not one of those nasty poisons. She'd know it would bring on pains and make her sick, and she always did hate to be sick. "I'd rather die than be sick," she's said to me more than once when she was a child. Her little stomach wasn't all that strong and she often *was* sick, poor mite. "I'd rather die than be sick," she used to say. So she'd hardly have chose a nasty poison as the way out. Besides, she wasn't the right temperament. She'd married the man she wanted, and she was doing well at college, and she had no money troubles. No, we needn't think about suicide, thank goodness. Been different, perhaps, if it had been her older sister. Always in trouble, that girl. Of course, my brother got Dodo into trouble, so I always think that might account for it, although my father made him marry her later.

'How did Mrs Coles come to meet her husband? Do you know that?'

'Oh, dear me, yes. It was quite simple and all quite above

76

board. They met at an agricultural camp, before she went to college. They picked peas and lifted new potatoes—the June-July before she started in the September, it was. She spent the last fortnight of August here with me, before going back home to get ready for college, and I knew then that there was something in the wind, although, naturally, I wouldn't force her confidence. I guessed it was a boy-friend, but she'd had 'em before and I never dreamt, not with her going off on this two-year course at college, that it was serious this time.'

'You don't know, of course, Miss Palliser, whether your niece left a will?'

'I'm sure she didn't. Girls of her age have no call to be thinking about such things.'

'Sometimes, I believe, their husbands are apt to think about such things.'

'*He* wouldn't,' said Miss Palliser decidedly. 'He may be an artist, and, to that extent, careless about his morals, but he was that fond of poor Norah! It was a pleasure to see them together.'

'I am very glad to hear it.' Dame Beatrice wrote her off as a meddling and romantically-minded spinster, took leave of her and decided to revisit the bereaved husband. Coles had been present at the inquest but, as no evidence had been called except evidence of identification and of the cause of death, he had not appeared in the witness box, and was now, as she knew from the police, back in his obscure London lodgings.

She wrote to him asking permission to call, and received an almost illegible postcard in reply to say that he would be at home on the following Sunday morning between eleven o'clock and noon. There seemed nothing that could be done during the ensuing days, and she had little hope that the interview would prove fruitful.

77

CHAPTER EIGHT

A Lamb to the Slaughter

' "Let us set out," said I, "and prepare for some fatigue,
for we shall take a longer road than that by which we
came." '

Ibid.

DAME BEATRICE found young Coles unshaven, unkempt and
in his dressing-gown. He seemed much more depressed than
on the previous occasion when she had seen him.

'Tell you more about Norah? I don't think I can,' he said.
'There's only one thing you might like to know, although
I don't see that it has any bearing upon what's happened.
I didn't want us to be married until I'd done with the art
school and she'd finished her college course.'

'And what caused you to change your mind, Mr Coles?'

'*Force majeure.* Norah talked me into it.'

'Really? How was that?'

'I don't know. She was a lot more forceful than I am.
Besides, she was afraid of old Biancini. She hated him. I'm
not sure she didn't hate him more than I do.'

'She objected to her mother's marrying again, no doubt.'

'I don't think it was only that. I think Biancini was a bit
of a wolf, and it scared her. She said she would feel safe if
we were married. Of course, she was at home as little as
possible. She used to stay with an aunt at Harrafield, a very
decent type. I stayed there once or twice myself and didn't
have to pay anything, although it was a hotel—well, a sort
of glorified pub with a few bedrooms, actually.'

'I have visited the place. So Mrs Coles talked you into
marrying her before you were quite prepared to do so?'

'She said—and kept on saying it—that until she was legally married she wasn't safe.'

'*Legally* married? What other kind of marriage could there be?'

'The marriage of true minds, I suppose,' said Coles, bitterly.

'And . . . she wasn't *safe*?'

'I knew he was a wolf.'

'But I am given to understand that she disliked him and spent as little time as possible at home.' The conversation appeared to be going round in circles.

'Well, yes, that's true enough. But she had to be at home sometimes, for her mother's sake. She was very fond of her mother,' Coles explained.

'The second marriage must have caused her some heart-burning, though.' Dame Beatrice was determined to pursue this point.

'She was very bitter about it at first, but she got over it. She was really a very well-balanced sort of person. I can't believe she's gone. Of course, it's not as bad as if we'd lived together, but I still can't realise we never shall.'

He took a packet of cigarettes from the pocket of his dressing-gown, lit one and tossed the packet on to the table as he glanced at the clock.

'You still cannot suggest any reason why anybody should wish her out of the way?'

'No, I can't. She hadn't an enemy in the world, as far as I know. I keep turning it all over in my mind, but it's just a blank. The police keep nosing around and asking questions, but I can't tell them any more than I'm telling you.'

'She could not possibly have come by some knowledge dangerous to another person, I suppose?'

'The police keep harping on that. All I can say is that I don't know, but I shouldn't think it's at all likely. I mean, there she was, just a student. You don't pick up dangerous information in a women's agricultural college, surely?'

'But she wasn't in college all the time, was she? There were the vacations.'

'Yes, but, except for when she was away with me, or staying with this aunt in the north of England, she was at home. The police, naturally enough, I suppose, are gunning for me and Biancini, as the only two men in her life, but, much as I dislike that greasy Eye-tye, I can't see him killing Norah and certainly not by poison. Poison's a woman's weapon.'

'Armstrong? Palmer? Crippen? Certain Italian noblemen of the fifteenth century?'

'Italian? Yes, I see. Then you think Biancini might have done it? I don't agree at all.'

'I can imagine both more and less likely murderers. Where did you take your wife for holidays when you went away together?'

'Oh, all sorts of places. She paid for both of us, of course. I've got all I can do to pay my fees at the Art School and buy my canvases and paints and sub. up for these foul digs. I couldn't manage the kind of holidays Norah seemed to like.'

'What kind would those have been?'

'Seaside hotels.'

'Yes?'

'We've stayed at Bournemouth, Torquay, St Leonards . . .' He checked them off on his fingers. 'Not the most expensive places, needless to say, but well out of my calculations if Norah hadn't been able to stand Sam. My mother's a widow, you see. She does what she can, but it doesn't run to holiday hotels.'

'Hotels? Yes, I see. No, a student's finances would scarcely run to those. Did you never try—say—Youth Hostels?'

'No. Norah was an open-air type, but she hated hiking or cycling. After all, as she used to point out, she had the money and so it had to be an hotel or nothing. Otherwise, as I say, she preferred to stay with her aunt, and, of course, that was an hotel, too, in its way.'

'I see. An hotel or—nothing.' She gave him every chance to repair what seemed to her a serious, and therefore a very important, omission, but he merely repeated, with another agonised glance at the clock :

'That's right. An hotel or nothing.'

'Well, I had better leave you to dress and get round in time for the beginning of the Sunday licensing hours,' said Dame Beatrice, with her crocodile grin. He laughed awkwardly, and got up as she rose from her chair.

'Sorry if I made myself obvious,' he said. 'But, as a matter of fact . . . promised to meet some chaps for a game of darts. If you don't get there when they open, you miss the chance of the board. Popular game, darts, you'd be surprised.'

'Not at all,' replied his reptilian visitor. 'I throw quite a pretty dart myself when called upon to play, although not, at my age, in a public house.'

'Really?' He went to the mantelpiece and picked up three beautiful darts. 'These are mine. Rather nice, I think.'

Dame Beatrice took one from his hand and balanced it in her palm. Then she went to the back wall of the room and studied a mark in the wallpaper. As she had suspected, it was a small hole made by a nail which, no doubt, had once supported a picture, but both picture and nail had disappeared. She retired to the hearthrug, flicked the dart, and said :

'What did I tell you?'

'Well, I'm damned!' He spoke with awe. The dart was firm in the nail-hole.

' "But, being in, see that the opposéd may beware of thee," ' quoted Dame Beatrice solemnly. 'Nothing but hotels? Really? Wouldn't you like to think again?'

Coles looked thoroughly bewildered.

'Think again? Why should I? I'm telling the simple truth.'

Dame Beatrice eyed him narrowly. He met her gaze defiantly and then strolled across the shabby room and pulled the dart out of the wall.

'The simple truth?' she repeated, on a warning and questioning note. Coles swung round on her, his eyes kindling and his face flushed with anger.

'Just exactly what are you getting at?' he demanded. 'If you're trying to catch me out, you'll be disappointed. I'm not hiding anything. I've told you I know nothing about Norah's death, and I've told the police the same thing. What is it you expect me to come clean about? You've shown me you can play darts. What about cards? What about putting yours on the table?'

'Very well. Did you not take your wife to a holiday camp at Bracklesea this summer?'

Coles stared.

'That I most certainly did not.'

'Well, her aunt thought you did.'

'What! Did she tell you so?'

'She most certainly did.'

'Well, I'm damned! I wonder where she got *that* idea from? You don't mean that Norah went to one without me? She'd never do such a thing. She had a strong dislike of hordes of people and of any sort of herd-holiday. She wouldn't even go on a motor-coach tour because she said the sight-seeing was all regimented and arranged and you couldn't even choose your own hotels. She—it was the one grouse she had against college—that you had to do things by rule and time-table and what-not, and could never get away from other people. A holiday camp is the *last* place you'd ever get Norah to go to, I do know that. So, if her aunt thought we went to one, she must be bats.'

'It is just on twelve o'clock,' said Dame Beatrice, glancing at her watch, 'so I must not keep you longer. No doubt your friends will be waiting for you.'

'Yes, they soon will be. I generally go along on Sunday mornings. A game of darts and a pint don't cost very much, thank goodness. You don't blame me, I hope, for not sitting in sackcloth and ashes because I've lost my wife?'

'Certainly not. Enjoy yourself while you can. Did Mrs Coles leave a will?'

'If she did, I know nothing of it.'

As there was no means of proving the truth of this assertion, Dame Beatrice accepted it at its face value and took her leave. She had food for thought, and, by this time, one very strong conviction.

CHAPTER NINE

Discrepancies

'. . . come and see, I have discovered the skeleton of a mammoth.'

Ibid.

THE holiday season was, to all intents and purposes, over, and the holiday camp, of which Coles had declared he had no knowledge, was closed. As Dame Beatrice had realised that this might be so, she was neither distressed nor disheartened, but, penetrating the main gates, made her way to the office, which was attached to the permanent living-quarters of the full-time staff.

She was received by a bearded man of youthful appearance who announced that the camp was closed until the following Easter.

'Used to be Whitsun,' he announced, 'so you're luckier than you used to be. I can take a reservation.'

'It is good of you to say so.'

'Think nothing of it. When would you wish us to book you in?'

'I cannot say, at the moment. I am in quest of information.'

'Sure. I'll get you a brochure. Next year's isn't ready until December, but last season's will give you all the gen you need.'

'Thank you. I should like all the information I can get. Would it be possible for me to be shown over the camp?'

'I don't see why not. You don't look the sort to plant a bomb. I'll take you round myself.'

'That is extremely good of you.'

'Think nothing of it. Service, not self, is our motto. Half a sec. while I get you the book of words.' He retired to an inner room and returned immediately with a shining, well-produced prospectus, copiously illustrated in black and white and in colour. 'There we are,' he said. 'We have accommodation, as you'll see by that, for singles, doubles or family parties. If you're on your own you'll soon make friends here, and we don't blow bugles or stampede you about in herds. That sort of thing's old-fashioned and we're nothing if not up to date.'

The camp was extremely extensive. The accommodation, to which reference had been made by her guide, consisted of dozens of châlets and a large, three-storey hostel on the ground floor of which was a bar. A restaurant opened out of it.

'Bedrooms upstairs,' said the bearded man. 'You'll see in the brochure they cost more than the châlets. That's because in the hostel you've got running hot and cold and proper bathrooms. The châlets only get a cold tap and a bathhouse with showers, one bathhouse to every twenty châlets. Mind you, there's the swimming-pool—we'll see it in a few minutes —with sea-water and the latest filter-system—so there's plenty of chance to freshen up.'

Another enormous, detached building, situated in a large garden, proved to provide a ballroom and concert hall. These had their own cocktail and snack bar. Yet a third structure proved to be a covered roller-skating rink complete with soda-fountain and coffee bar.

Dame Beatrice duly admired everything she was shown. Her alert black eyes took in every detail, but she asked no questions, content to allow the guide to act as showman without interruption.

'Well,' he said, when once again the office and the staff

quarters came in sight, 'that's the lot. Anything more you'd like to know?'

'Nothing, thank you. Do you have many foreign visitors?'

'Plenty. Not Americans, though. A camp doesn't seem to meet their requirements. A pity, really, because most of them are very good mixers. We did have a posse of American Service chaps apply last year, but we didn't take them. We got the impression they were only after girls. That kind of thing, if it's blatant, can soon give a place a bad name. Not that I don't sympathise with the fellows. They're a long way from home.'

'I should not wish to come alone,' said Dame Beatrice, reaching the true object of her visit. 'Some friends of mine stayed here last summer or early autumn, and spoke very well of the accommodation they were given. I should require the same kind of thing for myself and friend, or for two young friends if, in the end, I am not able to take up my option. I suppose it would not be possible for me to see the visitors' book, so that I may ascertain where they were housed?'

'I don't see why not. There's nothing private about it,' agreed the young man. 'If you'd care to take a seat, I'll go and dig it out.'

Dame Beatrice was highly gratified, and said so. She had not expected such complete co-operation, accustomed though she was to getting her own way; but she had made a marked impression on the young man, whose dealings with elderly ladies had acquainted him mostly with their capacity for producing pointless conversation and unreasonable demands and complaints. He left her to go and find the book, and, returning with it, asked when her friends had stayed at the camp.

'I do not remember the exact dates,' she said. He found the page which marked the beginning of August and put the open book on a small table.

'Help yourself,' he said genially. 'Knowing their names and possibly their writing, you may find them quicker than I shall.'

Dame Beatrice had three names in mind—Coles, Palliser and Biancini, although why she was alert for the last she could scarcely have said. Two names appeared under Palliser and were on one line, which ran : *Mr and Mrs N. Palliser of Calladale House, near Garchester.*

'Here they are,' she said, 'but the number of their room or châlet, or whatever they had, is not filled in.'

'Oh, now I've got the name, I'm bound to have a record of their accommodation,' said the young man. 'Shan't be a jiffy. Let's see the date again. August 18th they booked in? Right.' He came back in a remarkably short time with a large plan of the camp, and spread it out for her to see. 'We keep the accommodation charted,' he said. 'Look, they had châlet one nine six. Our system is quite simple. It has to be, with the number of campers we get every week of the season. Their number on the camp register'—he pointed to it—'was seventy-eight, which means they must have clocked in very early and certainly didn't come on the special train, and here is the seventy-eight marked on the plan against their châlet. See?'

Dame Beatrice congratulated him on the clearness of the arrangements.

'So, if I pay a deposit,' she said, 'you think I could have the same châlet?'

'Sure. How long would you want to stay?'

'Oh, only a week, I'm afraid.'

'Suits us. The second week's apt to be a repetition of the first, after all. Shall we say a couple of quid? Less if you like, of course, but a deposit does seem to clinch it.'

Dame Beatrice produced two pound notes, was given a receipt, gave, in return, a date for the following June and had the felicity of seeing Laura Gavin's name put down in a large ledger. It seemed as though there must be some truth in the story that Norah Coles had stayed at the Bracklesea camp, but why in the name of Palliser and why had Coles denied that he was with her? Dame Beatrice put through a call to her secretary, who was in Kensington, engaged in bringing the clinical records up to date.

'Leave everything as soon as you can, Laura. I want you at the Stone House for a conference.'

'That Calladale business? I wondered how soon you'd let me in properly on that. I've practically finished here, and Gavin has been called to Nottingham. I'll come at once, and bring Junior.'

'No, no. It is much too late to come tonight. You must leave it until the morning. Henri shall get us a special lunch. He has been worried about me since I began making these excursions to Calladale College. He thinks they starve me.'

Henri, it turned out, had been worried to the point of sleeplessness.

'Lunch is nothing today,' he announced. 'A cutlet, a soufflé, a cheese. Tonight, at dinner, mesdames, you shall eat! Think of it, Madame Gavin, ma chère Miss Laura! Those meals at the college for women! One says a camp for displaced persons, no?'

As it had proved impossible to reassure Henri upon this point, Dame Beatrice did not attempt to do so this time, and neither did she inform him of the reason for her visit to the college. She knew what his conclusions would be if she told him that one of the students had been poisoned. Laura referred to this as soon as she and her employer were alone.

'Henri will swear it was the college dinners,' she affirmed; and Dame Beatrice saw no reason to contradict her.

'Henri is a monomaniac,' she observed. 'Well, dear child, the plot thickens.'

'Good-o. How thick has it become?'

'Very, very thick indeed. Do you think you could im-personate a reporter?'

'Second nature. Whom do I interview?'

'A bereaved husband.'

'The villain of the piece?'

'Well, mistakes have been made, and there seem to be so many and such curious discrepancies at present that he may be.'

She gave Laura an account of all that had happened, including her visit to the holiday camp. Laura, her fine body beautifully relaxed in a deep and comfortable chair, offered an appreciative whistle.

'He didn't mention that they went to a holiday camp; just called it a seaside hotel,' she said, summing up the information. 'I saw a very short account of the inquest and I noticed it gave nothing away. But I can't see why he should lie about going to the camp. Did *you* get anything important out of the inquest?'

'There was one very interesting point which I was most anxious *not* to have anyone disclose,' said Dame Beatrice grimly. 'The dead girl was said to be in her very early twenties, but the pathologist pointed out to me privately that he would have thought that the body he dissected was that of a woman of thirty.'

'I suppose he could have been mistaken?'

'We were both impressed by the maturity of the body, so he made a special X-ray test of the bones. The subject was definitely not *under* twenty-five years old.'

'Who identified the body?'

'The mother.'

'Well, she ought to know.'

'I should point out that the body could not have been at all easy to identify.'

'Been in the water, you mean?'

'No; in a cellar, I rather fancy.'

'Oh, Lord! Not rats?'

'Undoubtedly rats.'

'How utterly beastly! I once dived for a body which had drowned and been got at by crabs. It's something I'd like to forget. Anyway, what do you make of the situation?'

'I may know better what I make of it when you have interviewed the husband, but that will not be just yet.'

'Dash it, I'm just rarin' to go.'

'I know, but we must give him time to get over my visit, and the police another chance to get to work on him first.'

'Does he gain anything by her death?'

'He says he knows of no will. I put the question to him point-blank. I cannot tell whether he is lying. I am inclined to think, however, that he's telling the truth. If there is no will, I take it that he will inherit the money. That is, if the dead girl is indeed Mrs Coles. But if the dead girl is *not* Mrs Coles, I think we need to find Mrs Coles.'

'Mrs Coles the murderess?'

'Most probably not, but she might be able to tell us who the dead woman is and, if she could, that in itself *might* lead to a solution of our problem. It might, on the other hand, lead us into deeper problems.'

'*If* we can find her—Mrs Coles, I mean.'

'Yes. It may be quite difficult to do so.'

'How do we set about it? Are the police in on this?'

'The police believe that the dead woman is verily and indeed the missing student.'

'In spite of the report about her age?'

'In spite of everything, dear child. One can hardly blame them. The body has been identified by Mrs Coles' mother. No one is going to question her evidence. Technically, the girl has always lived at home. Nobody is going to challenge her mother under such circumstances.'

'Except us. Well, supposing that we are right, I still don't see where we go from here. How soon can I put on the mask of Fleet Street and go to interview the husband?'

'The inquest is to be resumed in three weeks' time, if the police are ready by then. I think you might go to see him a fortnight from now. Unless something turns up to change my line of thought, your task will be to extort from him where he went for his summer holiday, and with whom.'

'Sounds to me more like a B.B.C. job. Can't I stop him with my roving microphone?'

'Tackle it in any way you choose. I have little faith in your discretion but much in your imagination.'

'Fair enough. Meanwhile?'

'Meanwhile we go to Calladale and interview a Miss Good.'

'The one who saw the white horseman?'

'Precisely.'

'But what can she tell us? From what you say, I gather she was gibbering with fright.'

'A more tranquil state of mind will have intervened. Subconsciously she may have noticed something that will prove of value.'

'Such as?'

'Whether the horseman was tall, short, thin or stout.'

'Good heavens! You mean it might have been Mrs Coles, and not a man at all!'

'I mean it may have been Mrs Coles *and* a man.'

'Talk about *my* imagination! But, if it *was* Mrs Coles and a man, why the elaborate get-up? Why the whiteness? Why go out of the way to make yourselves conspicuous on a dark night? And, another thing, it would prove it couldn't have been an abduction.'

'Nobody has mentioned such a word, child, and my own opinion is, and always has been, that the girl went willingly; but, even if that were not so, the lack of a struggle would not necessarily mean that the abducted party was a willing participator in the affair. "I was stiff with terror ... I could not utter a word to save my life ... I thought I might fall off if I struggled ... I was so taken by surprise that I didn't know what was happening". . . all psychologists and all police courts have heard such remarks, and, the point is, in many cases they are true, *so far as the plaintiff knows.*'

'Oh, yes; the old bromide about the subconscious mind. Her conscious mind may have been horrified, but her mad, bad, cave-woman subconscious was really making whoopee all the time. You'll never get me to believe it, you know.'

'The Scots are an inhibited race.'

'And a jolly good thing, too! At least we're respectable, hard-working, thrifty, courageous, patriotic, reliable, canny, proud, dour, invincible, kind-hearted, poetic, strong-minded, tough, well-educated, religious, zealous, generous—I could go on for hours. Anyway, nobody can call the kilt an inhibited garment. You forget the kilt. And what about the bagpipes?'

'The kilt, or philabeg, came into being because the Scots would not trouble to learn to sew. The bagpipes came to Scotland from Ireland, as did poetry, whisky and religion.'

'You can't prove a word you say!'

Dame Beatrice cackled.

'Touchée,' she said pacifically. 'Please ring up Miss McKay and find out when it will be convenient for us to talk to Miss Good.'

Miss McKay would have liked to name the Thursday free afternoon as the most appropriate time for the visit, but she was a just and fair-minded woman, and she knew how resentful Miss Good would be if her weekly date with the lecture-cutting Mr Cleeve were cancelled. She suggested the following Tuesday morning, and invited Dame Beatrice and Laura to lunch.

'I am truly sorry to come bothering round again,' said Dame Beatrice, when they arrived, 'but I have a fine new theory about Miss Palliser, as I suppose she will continue to be referred to by the college, and, although I do not expect my interview with Miss Good to do much, if anything, to support it, I must try to clear her out of the way first.'

'You'll be a change from the police, at any rate,' said Miss McKay. 'We've had them morning, noon and night. Did you know that they have decided to keep an open mind as to whether the dead girl really *was* Mrs Coles? It seems there's a doubt.'

'No, but I thought they might do so. Shall we see Miss Good before lunch?'

'Yes, I think that would be best. She is on practical work this morning, but has an essay this afternoon. Let me see, now . . . yes, she will be down at the piggeries with Mr Lestrange. I am sure he'll be pleased to see you.'

Miss Good was also pleased to see them. Carey had just concluded an exposition, with demonstration, of the way to introduce a newcomer into a pen which already held a settled group. He had caught and anointed three pigs, the newcomer and two others, with pig-oil powerfully scented with aniseed, and Miss Good and three other students were each to take a pig of the remaining four and copy his method.

'And, of course, the pigs are all right—quite sweet, actually—but the smell of aniseed makes me retch,' said Miss Good. 'But if it's about that ghost I saw . . . and there's nothing else you'd want to see me about . . . well, I did realise afterwards that it might be Highpepper being silly, but, as I didn't think of that at the time, I didn't take any notice except to scram.'

'As who would not?' said Laura, who had been briefed by Dame Beatrice on the way down. 'But I do wish you'd tell me a bit more. I'm interested in ghosts, and this may have been a real one, after all.'

'Mrs Gavin was born in the west of Scotland,' explained

Dame Beatrice, 'where there is a long history of extra-sensory phenomena.'

'Oh, yes? I wouldn't know. But, if Mrs Gavin is interested in ghosts, as such, she's come to the wrong shop, I'm afraid. You see, what I saw couldn't have been a ghost. I know that perfectly well now. The proof is that the ghost's horse trampled Miss Considine's brussels sprouts. Looking back, it was obviously Highpepper. I can't see the point, all the same. I should think something came unstuck and the boy had to make a getaway. I mean, no rag was carried out, so far as we know.'

'Just a moment,' said Laura. She was carrying a brief-case and from it she produced a stiff-covered, shiny notebook of rather impressive size and very impressive thickness. It was nearly half-full of notes and weird drawings which she had manufactured on the preceding day in preparation for the visit. She skimmed through the notebook—they were in the Principal's sitting-room—as fine and private a place as the grave once the telephone had been disconnected and the door locked—and found a lurid picture of a headless rider and a headless dog in the middle of what looked like the destruction of the Cities of the Plain. 'You see, the *horse* may have been a real one.'

'The horse?'

'Well,' said Laura, temporising, 'we all know about the Gytrash, don't we?'

'I—I don't see the connection.'

Neither did Laura, but she continued, sternly :

'So you may as well describe the ghost to me. It was tall, you say?'

'I don't know. Anyone on horseback looks tall.'

'Broad?'

'Well, I couldn't really say.'

'Did it look like a man or a woman?'

'I was so scared, I just turned and ran.'

94

'It followed you, didn't it?'

'I don't think it *followed* me. I mean, I don't think it saw me at all.'

'Look here,' said Laura, upon inspiration, 'where *are* those brussels sprouts? I mean, you spotted the horse and rider at the head of the drive, I gather. Where had they been before that?'

A look of intelligent interest replaced the former expression of slightly puzzled distaste on the student's face.

'You know, I never thought of it that way before,' she said. 'Miss Considine told me about the sprouts being trampled just to prove to me I hadn't seen a ghost. The sprouts are in the kitchen garden, and that's about the most unlikely place you can think of for anybody to go riding. It's right round by the butler's pantry that was, and all that sort of thing.'

'Ah, that's if the person knew the layout here. Try to imagine a person having an assignment with somebody here, but having no knowledge of the geography, so to speak.'

'I don't see what you're getting at.'

But Laura, inspired with a truly magnificent notion, was not prepared to explain. She said :

'I wish you could remember the *size* of the rider. Haven't you any idea?'

Thus prompted, Miss Good replied reluctantly :

'Well, you know Anne Boleyn?'

'The apparent headlessness of the apparition, you mean?'

'Yes, so why should I suddenly think of Henry the Eighth?'

'Her husband, and responsible for the headlessness aforesaid?—No, by thunder !' Laura got up, smote the astonished and slightly resentful student a congratulatory blow between the shoulder-blades, and said urgently, 'The kitchen garden, my girl, and quick about it, before my brain has time to cool. As the barrow-boy remarked when he looked at an alligator's teeth, you said a mouthful, cocky.'

Dame Beatrice, with an alligator's smile, watched them go. She had been visited by a wild idea, too. She waited. The kitchen garden, as Laura had anticipated, was unusually vast. A strip of lawn separated it from the back of the house, and then it stretched far and wide, beautiful and austere. At that time of year it was given almost wholly over to brussels sprouts and cabbages, and these spread, downhill slightly, to a couple of ponds, a disused cottage and, finally, a gate which opened on to a lane.

Laura, nosing about like a hound which has picked up the scent, made rapidly for this gate and opened it.

'Nobody except the dustmen ever come in that way,' volunteered Miss Good, obviously on the defensive.

'And are the dustcarts horse-drawn?'

'No, not nowadays.'

'But a horse has been here. Look at the hoof-prints.'

'It must have been somebody from Highpepper, as I said.'

'And it might be your ghost of Henry VIII. Well, I must away and write up my report. Many thanks for your invaluable assistance. Sorry to have taken up your time. Of course,' she added, as they walked back to the front door together, 'there is nothing to show that the ghost *didn't* come from Highpepper. That needs to be borne in mind. I do agree with you there, *and* that something caused him to sheer off before there was any ragging.'

'Well?' said Dame Beatrice, when they returned to Miss Considine's room. 'Did the brussels sprouts enlighten you, I wonder?'

'Yes and no,' Laura replied. 'You know you had an idea that the ghost may have been *two* people? Well, that's exactly what it was. It reminded Miss Good of Henry VIII.'

'You couldn't call that proof,' said Miss Good. But Laura wagged her head solemnly.

'*I* call it proof,' she said. 'Of course, if we could have seen the hoof-prints the morning after you saw this apparition, we might have been able to show that the horse was more heavily laden when it left by the front gate than when it appeared at the back, but that's past praying for now.'

They took their leave of Miss McKay, and, when they were in the car, Dame Beatrice, with a leer, congratulated Laura on her detective work.

'I think we may take two things for granted,' she said. 'The horse *was* carrying two persons, neither of whom had to be recognised, and the collaborator with, or abductor of, Mrs Coles did not come from Highpepper.'

'Did not?'

'Nobody who knew anything about the environs of Calla-dale would have trampled Miss Considine's brussels sprouts, and any Highpepper student who had planned to abduct Mrs Coles would certainly have taken pains to familiarise himself with the topography, if he did not know it already.'

'Yes, but, if secrecy was the main object, surely the ghostly get-up was a bit noticeable?'

'Yes and no. You must realise that the effect on most of the students would have been the same as the effect on Miss Good. There is a legend here of a haunting.'

'Sudden and unreasoning panic? Oh, I see. No hanging about to investigate the phenomenon, but the hasty *sauve qui peut*? Something in that, no doubt. So what do we get? Somebody carried off Mrs Coles . . .'

'And, most probably, with her own consent, although not, I venture to think, upon horseback.'

'With her own consent? I don't altogether see the point. If it wasn't with her own consent she would have kicked up devil's delight, unless the horseman had some mental or moral hold over her, and so could force the issue? You in-dicated the possibility, didn't you?'

'Did I really? Pray continue your exposition.'

'Somebody didn't intend (we think) to betray his presence, but he did so by trampling all over the kitchen garden, not

97

knowing the geography of the college. That rules out the Highpepper youths, who must know it remarkably well. I say, though, there's something else we ought to consider. In fact, we ought to do more than actually consider it.'

'Ah! I wondered whether that might occur to you. You refer, no doubt, to the difficulty of actually identifying the pillion rider, if, by any chance, it was *not* Mrs Coles. After all, she had disappeared some five to six days earlier, don't forget.'

'Not Mrs Coles after all? What a sell if it wasn't! Anyway, this is where I make a noise like Fleet Street and go and see this young husband. Incidentally'—Laura looked suspicious —'you seem very pleased about something.'

'I was very pleased to note Miss Good's remark about the position of the butler's pantry, child, that's all.'

CHAPTER TEN

Phantom Holiday

'Ernest discovered on the borders of a little marsh, a quantity of bamboos, half buried in the sand. We pulled them out. . . .'

LAURA had given considerable thought to an age-old problem. What, she wondered, would be the best things to wear for the interview with the bereaved husband. That it might turn out to be a meeting of extreme importance to the enquiry she was well aware, and she knew that both men and women, particularly young men and young women, were influenced, even if unconsciously, by the clothes worn by interlocutors.

Tweeds and brogues?—Reassuring? Maybe not. Mutton dressed as lamb?—Apt to arouse suspicion. Careless-artistic? —Always of doubtful value with either sex. Trousers?— Depended on the man. Some could put up with them on a large and handsome Amazon; some could not. Laura settled for a well-cut suit with matching accessories.

'You look very nice,' said Dame Beatrice. 'One visualises the card-case and detects the slight, unmistakable odour of Debrett.'

'Oh, Lord! All I aimed at was to appear neat but not gaudy.' Laura ostentatiously consulted a small and extremely elegant gold wristwatch, her husband's birthday gift. 'Well, see you soon, and with lots of gen, or so I anticipate. By the way, if I'm to impersonate a reporter, what's my pseudonym?'

'I leave that to you, child. Your imagination, resourcefulness, choice of language, personality, courage, and sense of responsibility, coupled with your total inability to write shorthand, far surpass my own. Be you who you will. Perhaps, for the proper recording of your feats of derring-do, I had better be told, though.'

'You know,' said Laura suddenly. 'I don't believe I think much of this reporter business, after all. He may shy away if he thinks I represent a newspaper, especially if he's got a guilty conscience. Couldn't I be an old friend of the deceased? Ah, I'll tell you what! Couldn't I have been her Sunday-school teacher? How old is she supposed to have been?'

'Mrs Coles was twenty-two, I believe, although the body was so strangely mature that it is difficult to see how it could be hers, although medical science is not infallible.'

'So I could easily have been her Sunday-school teacher! You can become one at about fourteen, I believe.'

'You don't look like a Sunday-school teacher.'

'Oh, they come in all sizes,' said Laura, easily. 'The hunt is up! Suspect, here I come!'

'Which of you is the suspect?' asked Carey, who was visiting his aunt. Laura looked through him. 'I mean, if you go attempting to pass yourself off as a doer of good works, looking like that, you've a nasty surprise coming to you, my girl.'

Laura glanced down at her suit.

'Nonsense,' she said firmly. 'You don't have to look like Frau Frump to teach in a Sunday School. Besides, I shan't pretend I *still* do.'

'How are you supposed to know that she was married? Don't forget it was a deep, dark secret.'

'Oh,' said Laura airily, 'she will have told her old Sunday-school teacher, if nobody else. What are old Sunday-school teachers for?'

'I've never enquired. Oh, well, go ahead and do it your way, but don't say I didn't warn you.'

'You go and feed the pigs,' retorted Laura. 'You're neglecting your duties.'

'My duty is to escort you to wherever it is you're bound for, and make sure you don't run into trouble.'

'Who says so?' demanded Laura, looking haughty.

'Aunt Adela, so don't fuss. This fellow may be the murderer, for all we know. You can't go and visit him alone. Gavin would have our blood, and quite right, too.'

'How do I explain you?'

'I've very kindly given you a lift up to Town. You thought you would do some shopping, then you remembered that poor dear what-was-her-name had told you her husband was at this art school in London, so you felt you must look him up. Then I shall suggest giving you lunch and include him in. All right?'

'All right, then, but I don't suppose I'll get much out of him with you hanging around.'

'Yes, you will, girl. Besides, didn't you notice I've shaved? What did you think that was for? I'm not going to waste it on the pigs?'

They drove in Carey's car to his home in Stanton St John as soon as his work was over for the day. Laura stayed the night there, and they set off early next morning for southeast London. The art school was separated from the road by a short gravel drive at the end of which it was possible to park the car. Carey remained seated at the wheel while Laura went exploring. She soon located the secretary's office, tapped on the glass panel and asked at what time it would be possible for her to speak to Mr Coles.

'He's in Life,' said the secretary. A little taken aback, Laura remarked that she hoped so.

'Life-drawing,' the secretary explained. 'You can go in, if you don't mind the nude. Oh, it's a male model this week, so he won't be. Room 24. There's a rude drawing on the door. You can't miss it. Up there.'

With a presentiment, unusual with her, that she was going to muff the coming interview, Laura traversed the corridor indicated by the secretary and discovered Room 24 without difficulty. She knocked, but there was no answer, so, after waiting a moment, she went in. There were eight or nine students in the room, also the professor of life-drawing and the model. The latter, astoundingly reminiscent of the Olmec *Wrestler* statue from Mexico, was in position on a small dais. The students did not look up as she entered, but the professor, who had been standing behind the shoulder of one of the girls, came forward.

'I wanted to find Mr Coles,' said Laura.

'Mr Coles?' The professor looked vaguely round the room. 'Not here. Oh, Mr *Coles*! No, he has not attended for—I don't know how many sessions. He left in—let me see . . .'

'He just went out of the room for a moment,' said one of the men. 'You're thinking of his father, I believe, sir.'

'Then he'll be along'—the professor waved his hand—'at any time now. Speak to him in the corridor, if you please. The model has just had his rest, and we are anxious to press on.' He returned to his work. As she opened the door to go out, Laura heard him say, 'Deltoid, Mr Soper. No good unless.'

The corridor was draughty, but Coles did not keep her waiting long. She did not know him by sight, but as he put his hand out to open the door of Room 24, she said:

'Mr Coles, I believe. Could you spare me a few minutes?'

'Not if you're a reporter.'

'No, I'm nothing of the sort.'

'And not if you're one of those damned snoopers who claim to have known my wife before I did.'

That put paid to the Sunday-school teacher, thought Laura. She said:

'A friend, a man, drove me down, and I don't want to waste his time. How soon can you join us for lunch?'

'What *is* all this?'

'You and your wife spent a week at a holiday camp this summer, did you not?'

Coles stared at her.

'What *is* all this?' he repeated. 'Are you touting for a holiday camp? If so, it's no good coming to me. I've never stayed at one in my life, and don't intend to, and now, if you don't mind, I'd like to get back to my work.'

Laura knew when she was beaten. She said urgently:

'Do you declare that you have *never* stayed at a holiday camp?'

'Yes, I do. It's not *my* idea of a holiday. It's not cheap, either, nowadays. Anyway, what *is* all this about holiday camps? Other people have bothered me about them!'

'But you used to stay at hotels?'

'Oh, I see! You're from the police! I stayed at hotels only because my wife paid. And now you can go back to whatever God-forsaken police barracks you're attached to, you narking female busy, and let me get on with my job.'

He opened the door violently and let himself in, crashing it shut behind him. A sympathetic Carey gave Laura lunch and drove her straight back to the Stone House at Wandles Parva, where Dame Beatrice, having again forsaken the college high-table for the weekend flesh-pots provided by her French cook, had arranged to meet them.

Laura told the inconclusive tale, and added that she would never make either a policewoman or a reporter. Dame Beatrice cackled.

'But you have made Mr Coles emphasise the very thing we regard as being of primary importance in the case,' she said. 'I had no hopes of the interview at all, therefore you have had great success.'

'You mean it *matters* whether he went to that holiday camp?'

'Of course it does, child. If his *wife* went there, she went with somebody else. If *she* did not go there either, it means that somebody had some reason to impersonate her, or else that it was her sister, Miss Carrie Palliser, with a lover.'

'And as it doesn't seem absolutely certain that the murdered woman *was* Mrs Coles . . . the apparent age of the body . . .'

'Exactly. Here we have a very pretty kettle of fish. I am now going to interview Mr Coles myself, but not, this time, at the art school. Neutral territory is indicated, but some territories are less neutral than others. Suppose we send for him to visit us here?'

'He won't come.'

'Do you care to risk a small sum in support of that theory?'

'It isn't a theory; it's a broad-based fact. As it is, I've scared him stiff. I told you how he answered me. He must have a guilt-complex. You had better let him mature in cask for a bit.'

'No, no. We'll get him while he's still in a state of ferment. Your question about the holiday camp, coming on top of mine, will have given him furiously to think, and, if we assist his thinking, I have an idea that he may be prepared to give us some information.'

'I suppose it occurs to you,' said Laura, after a pause, 'that he may not really give a hoot about the whole businesss? He may be glad to wash his hands of the girl. And, anyway, he doesn't know that we think the dead woman may not be his wife.'

'True, and he must not be allowed to know it yet. To-morrow is Saturday, and I ascertained from the time-table, which I saw in the principal's room when I was at the art school, that they are in session on Saturdays from ten in the morning until midday. We have only to telephone, informing Mr Coles that we expect him to dinner, and that a car will be placed at his disposal, to receive an enthusiastic acceptance of our invitation. He was accustomed to sponge on his wife. He shall sponge on me.'

'Bless your heart!' observed Laura, sardonically. 'I know he won't come. I've got him terrified, I tell you.' But her scorn was wasted. Dame Beatrice did the telephoning herself and returned to announce to her secretary that Coles was coming to dinner on the Saturday evening.

'And how!' said Laura, sceptical to the last. Dame Beatrice reassured her.

'I can repeat the telephone conversation verbatim,' she declared. 'I rang the art school and obtained speech with the secretary, a most intelligent, willing and helpful girl. She located Mr Coles with the greatest of ease and he was soon brought to the telephone. I reminded him that he had met me, and gave him the invitation to dinner. The conversation then ran as follows. I quote.'

Laura grinned. She had spent several years in Dame Beatrice's employment but was still prepared for surprises.

'Uh-huh?' she said, non-committally.

'The conversation,' said Dame Beatrice, 'ran thus :

'*Is that Mr Coles?*'

'*Speaking.*'

'*Splendid. Dame Beatrice Bradley here. I visited you a short time ago, if you remember.*'

'*Oh, yes. Well, well! And how do we find ourselves?*'

'*Short of one weekend guest, Mr Coles.*'

'*Too bad. Anything I can do?*'

'*Of course. That is why I am speaking to you at this present moment. Are you able to join us?—The Stone House, Wandles Parva, Hampshire. Nearest station Brockenhurst, but, if you prefer it, I can send my car to pick you up and transport you hither. Don't bother about a black tie, or anything of that sort. We shall be a very small family party. By*

105

the way, do not be alarmed if you meet my secretary who called at the art school yesterday.'

'Not Lady Vere de Vere?'

('You see?' said Laura, smugly.)

'The same.'

'I knew she couldn't be a copper's moll, although I called her one.'

'That says a great deal for your sense of character.'

'Did you say you could pick me up in a car? I'm not sold on paying my fare. Haven't got it, to be precise.'

'Very well, then, Mr Coles. My chauffeur will be at your door at two o'clock this afternoon. You will be ready by then?'

'Washed, shaved, shriven, and with a rose in my coat. Good-bye.'

'So he's coming,' said Laura. 'It's a sobering thought. What a forty-guinea suit and my womanly charm could not accomplish, the promise of rich food and a chauffeur-driven car have pulled off with the greatest of ease. You called him a sponger, I believe. How right you so often are!'

Mr Coles had smartened himself up. He was also on the defensive, particularly with Laura.

'I realise,' he said, finding her in the dining-room before his hostess had come down, 'that there's method in this madness of inviting me here for the weekend, and you may as well know, first as last, that I'm not committing myself. I know the police think I'm responsible for what happened to Norah, but they're wrong. And if *you* think the same, *you're* wrong, too, Mrs Private-Detective Gavin.'

'There, there. Have a cocktail,' said Laura. 'I mixed them myself, so I know they're good. Now I'll tell you the people you're going to meet, and we'll get the worst over first, and that's my husband, Detective Chief-Inspector Robert Gavin of the C.I.D. However, take heart. He is not here in his official capacity.'

'If I spill anything to my own disadvantage, he will be,' said Coles, with a cocky grin. 'Mud in your eye!'

'Then there are Dame Beatrice's nephew, Mr Carey Lestrange, his wife, his son and his daughter, and that's the lot. Not so bad, eh?'

Coles stared into his glass, then swallowed the rest of his drink. He shook his head, but before he could speak there was the sound of voices outside, his hostess and her relatives came in with Gavin, introductions were made and acknowledged and shortly afterwards dinner was announced and the company sat down, in informal fashion, to dine.

Coles found himself between Carey's wife and Laura Gavin and, once he had conquered a tendency to give nervous half-glances at Laura's husband, that disarmingly quiet and handsome officer of the law who happened to be seated opposite him, he told the company various anecdotes and appeared to enjoy the meal.

When it was over, and coffee had been served, Carey drove his wife and children home. The other four, at Dame Beatrice's suggestion, went into the smaller drawing-room to take chairs round the fire. When they were comfortably settled, Dame Beatrice opened the proceedings with a warning.

'We are going to ask questions, Mr Coles. Remember that you are under no compulsion whatever to answer them. Detective Chief-Inspector Gavin is here quite unofficially and only so that we may all benefit from his experience.'

'Yes, quite,' said Coles. He cleared his throat. 'You won't mind my saying that I feel about as happy as a rat in a trap, will you?'

'Can't expect you to believe it, but there's no trap,' said Gavin. 'I expect you've been badgered quite a bit, though, haven't you?'

'My instinct when I spot a police uniform is to run away, screaming. I dream of policemen. Do they really believe I made away with Norah and hid the body in that old coach? Because I didn't, you know.'

'Well, they've no line to go on at present. I expect you'll find they've been equally embarrassing to her stepfather and her mother. They've got to ferret, you know, until they can start something moving. It's all routine for them. Try thinking of it that way.'

'It comes hard on innocent parties, all this probing.'

'I know it does. The only thing is, the innocent parties have nothing whatever to fear.'

'Never?'

'Well, hardly ever,' Gavin was impelled to reply. 'Look here, listen to the questions, and answer them, but only if it suits you, as Dame Beatrice suggests. All right?'

'Not by a long chalk. Very well. Carry on. I suppose it may help, in the long run.'

'That's the spirit. Fire away, Dame B.'

'I visited a holiday camp the other day,' Dame Beatrice began. 'It was the big one at Bracklesea, the one I believed I mentioned to you when we met at your lodgings.'

'Oh?' Coles glanced at Laura. 'And you made some enquiries and decided that Norah and I had stayed there together last summer. Well, as I told you and Mrs Gavin, I have never stayed at one of those places in my life.'

'I know you said so. Do you agree that your wife's maiden name was Palliser?'

'I do. But she isn't the only Palliser in the phone book, *and* she's got a sister, don't forget.'

'If I told you the dates concerned, would you be prepared to tell me where you were and what you were doing that week?'

'I won't commit myself to that, but you may as well tell me the dates.'

'Saturday, August eighteenth to Saturday, August twenty-fifth.'

Coles' face cleared.

'I was in Paris. The art school has a scheme. You go cheap. Horrible *pensions* and lousy grub, but at least it's Paris. I can get you twenty witnesses.'

'Where was your wife?'

'Staying with that aunt in Harrafield, the aunt who keeps that glorified pub—*she* calls it an hotel—the Hour-Glass.'

'That corresponds with our information.'

'What does that mean? Have you contacted the aunt?'

'Yes, we have. Her information, as far as it goes, is interesting. Look here, Mr Coles, you will have to face the fact that it is to the last degree unlikely that your wife spent that particular week with her aunt.'

Coles looked bewildered, but as an actor might do.

'Not?'

'I am afraid not. The aunt seems to have thought that you and your wife went to this holiday camp. The aunt believed she was covering up for you by pretending to Mrs Biancini that Mrs Coles was still staying at the Hour-Glass. According to you, you did not go to any such place as the camp, but were in Paris. My investigation indicates that it is more than likely that your wife went for a week to this place at Bracklesea while you were in Paris. What do you say to all that?'

Coles looked troubled but not angry.

'I don't say anything. It may be so. By that I mean she may have gone away with somebody else. She might even have mentioned it, for all I know. She'd be certain I wouldn't mind. I don't believe in being a dog in a manger. I wonder whether she *did* tell me? I couldn't possibly say, after all these weeks.'

'The two people who booked at the camp in the name

of Palliser were a man and a woman,' said Dame Beatrice. Coles nodded.

'That's what I meant when I said I wouldn't have minded. We'd agreed to live and let live and not get jealous or anything idiotic like that. I mean, one *must* be civilised.'

'It's so terribly civilised to murder somebody,' said Laura. Coles jumped to his feet, but Gavin laughed. Dame Beatrice put another question :

'Are we really to understand that your marriage was one of convenience rather than of love?'

Coles sat down, deflated and perplexed.

'It's what I told you. She talked, or, rather, nagged me into it, but I didn't murder her,' he said. As a riposte to Laura's inexcusable observation it was more than inadequate. Dame Beatrice glanced at him sharply, caught Gavin's eye and grimaced.

'All right, Mr Coles,' said Gavin. 'We're quite prepared to accept that— at this stage. How far do you trust the aunt's word?'

'Which aunt? Oh, you mean Norah's aunt! Well, she was jolly good to us. Rather a romantic sort of woman, one might say.'

'Romantic?' It was Dame Beatrice who repeated the word. Coles, who had been crossing one knee over the other, now straightened his legs and stretched both feet towards the fire.

'She—well, all her geese were swans, I expect,' he said. 'She really thought we were in love, I suppose. We weren't, of course. I had no idea of marrying Norah when I did. It just became one of those things.'

'So you don't exactly grieve for her?' asked Gavin.

'No.' The embryo artist frowned. 'If I had to tell the truth,' he said, 'I'd say I was jolly well out of it. Her death, you know. I'm free again. It's all I want now. In most ways the whole thing was a ghastly mistake. In some ways your news that she went off with somebody else for a week doesn't really surprise me. She'd done it before.'

There was a long silence, then Gavin said :

'So that's that.'

'And that's the fellow who murdered her, I'll bet.'

Laura caught her husband's eye, nodded, rose to her feet and said her goodnights. Coles looked agonised.

'Don't go,' he said. 'Don't leave me! I don't know *what* I might be talked into saying!'

'You won't be talked into anything,' said Gavin. 'What's the name of this fellow?'

But Coles shook his head.

'I never asked and I haven't a clue,' he declared.

'You will say no more,' said Dame Beatrice. 'Personally, I think we might *all* go to bed.'

But her guest, it seemed, was not prepared for this.

'I do wish you'd listen,' he said. 'I didn't love Norah. You might as well know it first as last. I have no money. I thought she'd come in for something substantial from her father, and, heaven knows, I can do with every penny I can get. You see, I've got talent. Not a lot, of course, but, with a bit of money behind me—have you any conception of what it costs to hire even a small art gallery for a one-man show?—I could make good. I saw my chance, as I thought. But then I weakened. Norah wasn't really what I wanted. Then I thought it all over again and decided that it might work. I was prepared to be perfectly fair as long as all she wanted was an uncritical husband. But, naturally, she wanted a good deal more than that. She wanted complete devotion, and that shot wasn't on the board. You can't mortgage your soul.'

'So Doctor Faustus discovered,' said Dame Beatrice. 'And then?'

'Nothing. We got married. But when I got the chance of this cheap trip to Paris, she went to stay with her aunt. Only —she didn't, according to you. She went to this holiday camp at Bracklesea. Well, we know what's happened to her since then!'

'How much did her father leave her?' Gavin enquired. Coles shook his head.

'Her mother kept a tight fist on it while Norah stayed at college. I don't think Norah herself knew how much it was.'

'I really think she did.'

'Then,' said Coles, 'there's only one thing for you to do if you want to find the killer. You'd better lay off me and find out what that swine Biancini was doing between August eighteenth and August twenty-fifth this summer. There's your murderer for you, and you can tell him I said so! Mrs Biancini dotes on him, and anything Norah had to leave will come to him in the end. You see if it doesn't!'

CHAPTER ELEVEN

Identification of a Lady-Killer

‘ “What do you call that horrid beast?” asked James.

“It is,” replied I, “the cocoa crab. I doubt if you would have succeeded in overcoming your antagonist without that lucky thought, for the cocoa crab has as much courage as cunning, and he may be a dangerous adversary for a child.” ’

Ibid.

‘OUR guest,’ observed Laura, when Coles had been conveyed back to London, ‘spoke quite a piece when he suggested that there might have been naughtiness going on between the porcine Biancini and that girl.’

‘Don’t jump to conclusions,’ said her husband. ‘All the same, it won’t do any harm to check up on the Wop. I can drop a hint in the right quarter and make a slight unmeritorious police job of it, if you like.’

‘What sort of hint?’

‘To begin with, a hint to suggest that he may not be a naturalised British subject. If he hasn’t taken out naturalisation papers he is an alien, and if he’s an alien he may turn out to be an undesirable one. And so forth, until we’ve collected his dossier.’

‘While I am no critic of sexual indiscretions,’ said Dame Beatrice, ‘it does seem to me that if Biancini did stay at that holiday camp with Mrs Coles and not with Mrs Biancini, it would do no harm to investigate further. Your scheme, my dear Robert, although ethically undesirable, sounds neat and practical. How soon may we expect results, I wonder?’

‘We shan’t be long,’ said Gavin, grinning. ‘We may not

be as well documented in certain respects as the *Sûreté*, but we can soon get the tabs on people when it's necessary. On the face of it, this murder of Mrs Coles looks like one of those messy little "got the girl into trouble and had better shut her mouth" crimes, and, if it is, then this holiday at the camp could bear investigation, especially if the Mrs Palliser of the register was indeed Mrs Coles.'

'But that's the odd thing,' said Laura. 'Ask Dame B.'

'The autopsy revealed that the girl was a virgin,' said Dame Beatrice.

'*Un mariage blanc?* Good Lord! Then I don't see where Biancini fits in. If he did take the girl away, it could only have been for one reason. I'm all the more determined to probe into this camp holiday. Of course, there's strong presumptive evidence that the Mr and Mrs N. Palliser of the camp register were not verily and indeed the Mr and Mrs Coles of whom we know, if Coles did indeed spend that week in Paris, but that doesn't necessarily involve Biancini.'

'Of Calladale House, near Garchester, don't forget,' said Laura. Gavin wrinkled his nose.

'Curious, that,' he admitted. 'Must have been the girl's idea, I should think. Anyway, I don't suppose she dreamed that anybody except the camp staff would ever bother about what was written in the book. I should imagine that the "Calladale House" business was sheer stupid snobbery, put on for the benefit of the camp officials.'

'Well, what's our next move?' asked Laura.

'I shall visit Mrs Biancini to find out what, if anything, she knew about the marriage,' said Dame Beatrice. 'I find it difficult to believe that she had no inkling at all, although I do realise that family relationships are anything but what they used to be. What did you make of Mr Coles?' She was addressing Gavin, who nodded.

'He may be a cunning young fox, of course,' he said.

'Sometimes the truth has the effect of pepper in the eyes. It leads to temporary blindness.'

'I see that you understand me.'

'Dashed if *I* do,' said Laura.

'Well, if he wasn't foxing,' her husband explained, 'he more than ever laid himself open to being offered the position of Suspect Number One when he admitted that he married the girl for her money.'

'Oh, that! But, to me, he's always been the most likely person to have killed her.'

'The choice of that coach as a hiding-place for the body?'

'He would have heard from her about the Highpepper rag. It made quite an impression on the Calladale students, you know, and it's become a legend in Garchester.'

'Yes, I see. Oh, well, suspect him, by all means, but I think you're barking up the wrong tree. What says Dame B.?'

'She must speak for herself,' said Laura, 'but I am under the impression that she agrees with you. If only the body had been identified with more certainty! I expect the unfortunate mum took one quick, shuddering glance and felt sick. Rats! Ugh!'

'Quite,' said Dame Beatrice. 'That cellar, or warehouse, or whatever it is, is being diligently sought for by the police. I wonder how Carey's predecessor is getting along?' she added suddenly. 'I must find out from Miss McKay which hospital he is in, and send him a bunch of grapes. It is only fitting that one who has been the means of putting a fat salary, albeit a temporary one, into my nephew's pockets, should be the recipient of tangible benefits. Not that grapes are everybody's choice, of course.'

'That's one thing about broken limbs. You can still *eat* what you like,' said Laura. 'When do we visit Mrs Biancini? And how can we be sure that Biancini will be out of the way?'

'That, of course, is the problem. I think we must take our

chance. It seems unsporting to decoy him away, since some amount of suspicion appears to be attaching itself to him. I shall not attempt it. We must not lower our standards of fair play. It would be un-English. The English are now the keepers of the world's conscience, having, in some respects, lost their own.'

The visit to Mrs Biancini was paid by Dame Beatrice alone. Laura had been prepared for this decision and was in no mood to contest it. For several weeks her baby son had been with her own parents in Scotland, so, as Gavin had secured some leave, Dame Beatrice suggested that Laura should spend it with him and the baby boy. She saw them off at King's Cross and from there was driven to the Biancinis' unpretentious home. Knowing how unpopular Coles was likely to be with his mother-in-law, she was ready with a question which she felt would not be resented.

'From a remark you made when you visited the college,' she said, leaning forward from a comfortable armchair, 'I gathered that you had expected financial help from your daughter as soon as she had secured a post at the end of her college course.'

'Well, am I to blame for that?' demanded Mrs Biancini, who, rather to Dame Beatrice's surprise, appeared to be flattered by the visit. 'I mean to say, bringing her up without a proper man's money, as I'd done until she was seventeen, there was no harm in me thinking she'd do something to prove her gratitude, was there, do you think?'

Honesty, and a strong sense of the deep injustice of this all-too-common parental attitude, caused Dame Beatrice to remain silent for a moment. When she spoke, it was not in answer to the question.

'Mr Coles,' she said, very mildly, 'seemed to think that he had something to gain from marrying your daughter.'

'Oh, that! He was quite right. As I told you before, Norah stood to come in for about two thousand pounds when she

116

left college. That would be a lot of money for a penniless ne'er-do-well like him.'

'What happens now?'

The question was so appallingly crude that Mrs Biancini could scarcely think quickly enough to show that she resented it. She took no trouble to word her answer carefully.

'We've got to get the lawyers on to that, unless Tony and I can do something about it on our own. Not a fiddle, I don't mean. Tony will know. He's good at finding the best way to go about things, but, of course, he'd never touch anything shady.' Mrs Biancini sounded so much on the defensive that Dame Beatrice was immediately interested. 'People call him Wop and Dago and Eye-tie, but he's a nice fellow and a good husband. Of course, he's got his faults. I don't dispute that. But, there! Girls are such silly creatures nowadays that you really can't blame a man, can you? What I mean, Tony has an eye for a figure, I'm bound to say that. But he's harmless. He'd never think of misbehaving himself. He's like all the Italians—just lively.'

'I had the pleasure of meeting Mr Biancini at the college, if you remember,' said Dame Beatrice. 'He has quite forgotten his summer holiday, I imagine, with all this trouble and upset coming upon you both?'

'His summer holiday?' (The trouble and upset were obviously sublimated by this time.)

'Yes. The camp, you know.'

'The camp?'

'The holiday camp at Bracklesea. You were with him there, were you not? I've often wondered what these camps are like. Do tell me.'

Mrs Biancini was more than surprised.

'I've never been to a holiday camp in my life. They're run for teen-agers,' she declared. 'And, anyway, we couldn't have gone this summer because Mr Biancini and me were visiting relations in Italy. Not that I'd call it a holiday, not if you knew his relations, if we'd had to stop with them. I moved on to a posh hotel, I don't mind telling you.'

It was Dame Beatrice's turn to appear to be surprised, but she did not take advantage of the opportunity. What she *did* take, feloniously, secretly and actionably, was a portrait of Biancini which had stood on the mantelpiece half-hidden by a fairly large clock. It disappeared while her hostess was interviewing a tradesman who chose an inopportune moment to call, and so terminated what might have proved to be a fruitful conversation.

Armed, unobtrusively (since it had been slipped into the brief-case she carried) with this adjunct to the enquiry, Dame Beatrice took her leave. There seemed no point in staying until her hostess missed the portrait, and, apart from that, she doubted whether she could work the talk back to any point which might seem to be profitable.

A police report, inspired by Gavin, came in reasonably soon. Biancini had taken out naturalisation papers in 1937 and nothing was known against him. He had been employed as a waiter, rising to head waiter in a respectable West End restaurant, had gravitated from there to being demonstrator for a firm of processed-food manufacturers—this on a commission basis—and had saved money. At the time of the enquiry he was stated to be a man of independent means who added to these from time to time as a stand-in for the waiters at important hotels and restaurants.

'A blameless life, in fact,' commented the deeply-disappointed Laura, when she came back from Scotland accompanied by a contented husband and a lively son and heir. 'And now what? We spent last night at Carey's. That's why we're so beautifully early.'

'There's plenty to come in yet,' said Gavin soothingly, in a tone which never failed to annoy his wife. Laura snorted belligerently.

'It will all prove useless,' she declared. 'I picked this

118

Biancini as the villain of the piece as soon as Dame B. described him.'

'I thought you'd plumped for Coles,' said Gavin mildly.

'Biancini's summer holiday activities can bear a little further investigation,' said Dame Beatrice. She produced the purloined photograph. 'Not, I imagine, the portrait of a blinking idiot,' she added, 'but possibly that of a rather daring philanderer.'

'You think he's the holiday camp Lothario?'

'His wife would not admit it. She says that they were together in Italy.'

'I don't see how you're going to prove or disprove that. To find out whether one particular man, giving a false name, visited that Bracklesea place last August is a sheer impossibility, anyway. Who's going to remember him out of all the thousands who attend?'

'I am optimistic. I think someone on the staff of the holiday camp *will* remember him if, indeed, he went there and not to his relatives. Italians are sociable and lively. He would not have hidden his light under a bushel. Then, too, he looks what he is—a man from a foreign clime. Oh, yes, I have great hopes of finding someone who remembers him if he *did* go to the camp. There is one problem, however, to be solved.'

'It need not be a problem,' said Gavin. 'Put a private enquiry agent on the job. Give him the photograph and let him snoop around.'

'Why can't *I* go?' asked Laura.

'Not if you're going to represent yourself as Biancini's indignantly suspicious wife,' said Gavin, grinning.

'Nothing of the sort. I shall be—now, then, what shall I be? I wasn't very convincing in my last rôle. I must think of something really fool-proof, this time.'

'Do as I say, and leave the job to an expert.'

'No Percy Pilbeams for me, thank you. I'll hit on something. Don't you worry.'

'But the thought of you "hitting on something" *does* worry me. Don't forget that you're the mother of my child.'

'Well, Dame B. can't very well go there again, now that she's established her *bona fides* as a member of next year's intake. They'd be certain to think she was a tile loose, if nothing worse.'

'I see that. That is the problem. No, Laura. For once I'm going to put my foot down. You are not going to get yourself mixed up in Biancini's private stew-pond. In spite of the apparent cleanness of his copy-book, I suspect some well-disguised but very present blots. Back me up, Dame B.'

'With pleasure. Do you know of a man we might employ?'

'Yes, there's an ex-C.I.D. chap I can put you on to. He's a reliable type and retired from the police only last year. He'll turn the whole camp inside out for ten guineas. Here's his address.'

Their bloodhound sent his report to the Stone House in the following week. He employed the professional jargon of the "private eye," but his account made interesting reading.

Dame Beatrice had sent to Calladale for a copy of any college group in which Mrs Coles had appeared. The three which were sent by Miss McKay showed the girl variously costumed—in a suit, in sweater, breeches and gaiters, and in a dance frock. The 'private eye' took these as well as the portrait of Biancini. It transpired that Mrs Coles had certainly spent a week at the holiday camp that August. She was picked out in all three groups by independent witnesses. The reason for asking for group photographs rather than for a portrait was to secure this sort of independent judgment.) The portrait of Biancini—a very good likeness—drew a blank.

'Well, if she didn't go there with Biancini—and she'd

hardly have gone by herself—who on earth *did* she go with?' asked Laura.

'A fairly simple bit of deduction should supply the answer to that,' said Gavin, smiling in a superior and irritating fashion. Laura kicked him. 'No, really,' he said. 'Don't you see?' He moved out of range. 'If she didn't go with Biancini and didn't go by herself, she went with a pretty obvious somebody else. No, and I'm not being funny,' he added hastily, catching a dangerous glint in Laura's eye. 'There's definitely a nigger in the wood-pile and it shouldn't be so very difficult to spot him. Look again at the set-up. Here we have a situation in which a girl still at college gets married, without her parents' knowledge and consent, to a young fellow who, himself, is still training and can't possibly support her, perhaps for years to come. She has the sympathy of a friendly but probably misguided aunt who enters into a conspiracy (she thinks) to let the young people spend a holiday together when the girl's mother believed her daughter to be staying blamelessly with the said aunt, and——'

'Yes?' said Laura, drawling it out as far as the broad vowel would let her.

'The young man, we may infer from the available evidence, cared little about the conspiracy, but took himself blithely off to Paris with a party of fellow-students. The girl (his wife, remember) went to a holiday camp so vastly and variously populated that she felt it unlikely she would be singled out for notice. She did not want to be noticed because she had gone there with a man whom we shall call X.'

'How original of us!'

'I know it isn't, but who are we to dispute the mathematicians' conception of what constitutes an unknown quantity? Now, then, this is where we enter the realm of guesswork. We know the marriage of this young Coles was

121

not a love-match. We know that the young man expected it to advantage him financially. What we don't really know, although we may hazard a conjecture, is what the girl got out of it.'

'Conjecture away.'

'At least she obtained the status of a married woman.'

'So did I,' grunted Laura, still rebellious, 'but I don't yet notice any particular advanage. All I've got is a husband who thinks I'm a moron and a baby who apparently lives to eat, sleep and provide other people with laundry-work.'

'Besides being a considerable financial responsibility. I know. I sympathise with both his parents,' said Dame Beatrice. 'But, to return to the point at issue, I can imagine certain circumstances in which to be married is a distinct advantage. You, whose acquaintance with the English classics is wide, if not profound, should be able to furnish instances.'

'Oh, *that* sort of thing!' said Laura. 'But that's all outmoded and unnecessary nowadays. I mean, nobody expects that an unmarried girl will be chaperoned to a dance. Nobody even seems to care much if she has a baby or goes off with somebody else's husband.'

'It matters if the somebody else's husband is in the kind of employment which the least breath of scandal would take from him,' said Dame Beatrice, who had followed the last speech with critical attention. 'If I understand our dear Robert's train of thought, that is the line he is taking. To take a married woman to a holiday camp would not, perhaps, seem the same as taking her to an hotel.'

Laura looked puzzled.

'Do you mean a parson?' she asked. 'I shouldn't have thought it would make any difference at all. The scandal would ruin him in any case.'

'I was not thinking of a parson. Perhaps I am a little too close to this particular case to be able to take a broad enough view of it. I had better return Mr Biancini's photograph and then I have two telephone calls to make, so you two can count on a nice *tête-à-tête* if you wish. Lunch is at half-past two today because the butcher punctured a tyre. If you like, you can take over the other room and put on the electric fire, and then I shouldn't need to disturb you when I've finished making my calls.'

'What I should be doing at this hour,' said Gavin, glancing at the clock, 'is getting back to Town, I'm afraid. What about it, Laura? Like to drive up with me and come back tomorrow by train?'

'Having achieved the status of wife,' said Laura primly, 'my first thought should be for my husband's child. However, as the said child has no particular use for me—Célestine can dish him out his meals and see to his general needs—I will accompany you with pleasure, unless my services are required here.'

'No, no,' said Dame Beatrice. 'You run along. *I'll* see to Ian Alastair Hamish, bless his heart.'

'Oh, well, he likes you ever so much better than he does me, so *that's* all right. Where are you going to give me lunch?' said Laura, addressing the statement to Dame Beatrice and the question to her husband.

'Your favourite Helmsdale Arms, if we start at once. I need not phone them to keep a table. They're not likely to be full up at this time of year.'

Dame Beatrice packed up the purloined photograph and returned it by registered post but without a covering letter. It was better, she decided, that Mrs Biancini should have her curiosity left unsatisfied rather than she should think that her husband had been suspected of deceiving her with her own daughter. On the ethics of the means she had used to obtain possession of the photograph she was too realistic and far too honest to dwell. She had needed the picture and the end—that of proving Mr Biancini's innocence in respect

123

of the matter under immediate review—appeared to have justified the means. The Jesuits, after all, had a word for it.

She telephoned Miss McKay.

'I have some enquiries to make which cannot be made over the telephone. Where can I meet you, and when?'

Her second call was to the aunt who managed the small hotel at Harrafield.

'Can you possibly give me the address of Mr Biancini's relatives in Italy?—the people with whom he spent part of his summer holiday?' The aunt could and did. 'And do you know of the hotel to which, at Mrs Biancini's request, they transferred themselves?'

'I wouldn't know what it's like. It's a place just outside Naples, on the road south. My sister didn't care for the relations, so they went there. The Vittorio, it's called, but I don't at all know whether it would suit you. People have such different ideas.'

'If it's on the road to Pompeii, it will suit admirably, I'm sure.'

'Of course, if you like those old ruins. Well, mind, I can't recommend it. Of course, you get choosy when you're like me and keep a nice place of your own, but my sister thought very well of it, although she said it was gloomy. One of Tony's relations works there, I believe.'

Dame Beatrice rang up the travel agency and booked two seats on an aeroplane going to Rome. There was no need to rush to Naples. She had learned and disputatious friends in Rome who would expect her to visit them. She wondered whether Miss McKay could be suborned into taking the extra seat on the aeroplane, but that was but a secondary reason for her visit to the Principal of Calladale.

The first person she saw as the car turned in at the college gates was the girl who had informed her that the former Norah Palliser had become Norah Coles. Dame Beatrice stopped the car and got out.

124

'Oh, good afternoon, Dame Beatrice. Did you want Mr Lestrange?' asked the student.

'Not particularly. I have an appointment with Miss McKay.'

'He'd be very disappointed to miss you. He tells his students an awful lot about you. I wish *I* took Livestock. He must be a lovely change after Piggy Basil.'

'Piggy . . . ?'

'Well, we never really knew whether Basil was his first name or not. They don't put our lecturers' names on the college prospectus. Miss McKay's goes on, but not the others. Look, must you go and see her at once? Mr Lestrange is lecturing on castration, and they all loathe it, anyway, and say they'd always get the vet. It's the most dreaded thing in the syllabus, but, of course, it's part of it all, so Mr Lestrange has to show them how it's done.'

'I am not at all sure that I would not prefer to be a trifle early for my appointment with Miss McKay. I should hate to interrupt my nephew at such a moment. Incidentally, I must be interrupting you, too.'

'Oh, our lot are only supposed to be filling in the root holes of mulberries with compost. I've plenty of time. The others can carry on quite well without me. It's not a bad job, so they won't mind. The compost we're using is only a mixture of loam, leaf-mould and soil. It even smells quite nice.'

'Mulberries? Do you rear silkworms on the leaves?' Dame Beatrice asked, beginning to walk up the path.

'One or two cranks have permission. Personally, I couldn't be bothered.'

'Which species of mulberry do you cultivate?'

'Oh, the Black Mulberry. It's supposed to fruit the best. Well, here we are. I'd better not come any further.' She glanced down at boots heavy with the rich, damp soil of autumn. 'I'll tell Mr Lestrange you're here.'

125

'Tell *me* one thing. This Mr Basil was unpopular, did you indicate?'

'Oh, no, I wouldn't say that. He was pretty well liked, on the whole. Of course, his jokes were rather grubby and he was always asking people to go out to dinner with him, not in Garchester, where we're known, but in little road-houses and rather furtive sort of riverside pubs. Incidentally, he used to meet Norah Coles quite a lot. It can't matter telling you that.'

'X?' said Dame Beatrice, under her breath. 'I think I *would* like to see Mr Lestrange before I contact Miss McKay,' she added aloud. 'I can find my way to the piggeries, so please don't let me keep you from your mulberries.'

The girl laughed, and tramped away, gallant and somehow pathetic in her heavy boots, leggings and stout, unglamorous breeches. Dame Beatrice gazed after her for a moment, and then walked round the side of the main building. There were students at work in the kitchen garden who directed her.

Operation Eunuch was over by the time she arrived, and Carey was washing his hands beside a tap on the end wall of the pig-house. Dame Beatrice was reminded irresistibly of the *Jackdaw of Rheims,* in which, when the Cardinal washed his hands, various nice little boys held the various toilet requisites. Except that her nephew looked not at all like a cardinal, and that the nice little boys were sturdy girls and students of farm procedure, the analogy was exact. One obsequious student held the towel, another the soap-dish, another the bowl of very hot water in which the preliminary ablutions were being performed, and another a second bowl which she brought from under the tap at which still another student stood ready to turn the water off.

'Well, girls,' Dame Beatrice heard her nephew say, 'you may find yourselves raising hogs in the backwoods of one

126

of the outposts of the Commonwealth one of these days, and if you do, this little bit of exposition will come in very useful, because you mayn't be in touch with a vet. *at all* when it comes to the right time to turn Nature's boars into civilisation's bacon pigs, and that's a job that's got to be done when they're six weeks old. Oh, hallo, Aunt Adela! Scatter, you children, and let me have all your notebooks in by tomorrow at twelve, don't forget.'

The students groaned and laughed, and left him alone with Dame Beatrice.

'I won't keep you,' she said. 'I expect you're busy.'

'My next lot come along in a quarter of an hour. Come and have a cup of tea.'

'Thank you, but I am due to visit Miss McKay. There is, however, something I want to ask you. What have you been told about the man whose place you are taking?'

Carey looked surprised.

'The chap they call the Piggy? Not a lot.'

'Would you be surprised, from what little you *have* heard, that he would be capable of persuading one of these girls to go on holiday with him?'

'I've heard rumours about him, but, under the particular circumstances in which I find myself, I've felt rather bound to scotch any information of that sort. Why?'

'I think I've found X, and he appears to add up, as Laura would say, to your predecessor, Mr Basil.'

'Good Lord! You don't mean the murderer?'

'I don't know whether I mean that, but, of course, one can't be sure. What are you going to do when you've drunk your tea?'

'Explain what you do when your pigs contract scouring, swine fever and tuberculosis.'

'Surely not at one and the same time? That, I feel, would make medical history, even among pigs.'

'Too right it would. It's an either/or proposition.'

They strolled towards the main college building. At the foot of the steps they stopped.

'Well,' said Carey, 'bye-bye for now, as one of my students rather regrettably puts it.'

He sauntered off. His aunt leered affectionately at his retreating figure, and then went off in search of the student from whom she had heard that Norah Palliser was married. She found her, as she had hoped, among the mulberries.

'Tell me,' she said, 'when Mrs Coles told you that she was married, did she happen to mention why she had decided to embrace the holy estate without waiting to finish her college course?'

'Actually, yes. I couldn't help sympathising, either. I mean, you can't trust anybody nowadays, can you?'

'I may be old-fashioned, but I confess that that seems to me a remarkably pessimistic point of view.'

'Oh, I don't know. People are always letting other people down, particularly the sexes. You'd be surprised how many people here have more or less broken hearts through being let down by some man or other. The Highpeppers are especially prone to it. Sometimes I think they aren't serious types at all.'

'Have you yourself . . . ?'

'Me? Oh, no. I've got a steady back home. He works for my father, so I've got the tabs on him all right. No, I was just speaking generally. If you'd tried to mend as many broken hearts as *I* have . . .'

'Dear me! And Miss Palliser did not intend to have a broken heart, I take it.'

'Miss Palliser? Oh, of course, you mean Mrs Coles. Too right. She was pretty hard-boiled, was poor old Norah, and she told me she had got Coles hooked while he was still impressionable. "He's not going to be the one that got away," she told me. Of course, she swore me to secrecy, but, well, you know how it is! I expect she swore a good many other

128

people to secrecy as well. Do they—do they think he killed Palliser?'

'Up to the present, there is no evidence to speak of. And now I must go and see Miss McKay.'

'Are the police getting *anywhere*, do you think?'

'I am not much in their confidence, but I think we may expect developments shortly.'

'Of course, if he wasn't laid up with a broken leg, I wouldn't put much past Piggy Basil,' said the student thoughtfully. 'He was a proper wolf and, though harmless, may have got into a mess.'

Dame Beatrice did not comment. She waved a cheerful, valedictory claw, mounted the steps and was about to ring the front door bell when another thought came to her mind.

'Miss Bellman!' she called after the retreating student. Miss Bellman turned and came back. 'You mentioned the Highpepper students, and it is clear to me, of course, that there would be a considerable field of mutual interest, let us say, between the two colleges. But how did Mrs Coles, *née* Palliser, whose home is not far from Northampton, come to be acquainted with Mr Coles, who lives in lodgings in London?'

Miss Bellman shook her head sadly.

'It was one of those pick-ups,' she said.

'Yes?'

'She picked him up at a dog show—Crufts, I think it was— the spring before she came here in the September. He'd gone to draw dogs, and she'd gone to show a couple of Pekes. Then they met again lifting potatoes.'

Before she sought out Miss McKay, Dame Beatrice had a word with the college secretary.

'Yes,' said the secretary, in answer to a question, 'a letter *did* come for Mr Basil. Only one. I re-addressed it to the hospital.'

CHAPTER TWELVE

See Naples and Die

'. . . our road led us suddenly into the most delightful country you can imagine.'

Ibid.

VESUVIUS, with its pillar of cloud by day and its lurid glow by night, dominated the sky to the south of the city and gave a Satanic welcome to travellers, reminding them of Pompeii, Herculaneum and the state of their own souls.

In the end, it was Carey who had accompanied Dame Beatrice to Rome and southwards, for Miss McKay had decided (reluctantly, she admitted), that it would be unseemly and frivolous for her to leave Calladale in the middle of term in order to disport herself in Italy.

Before leaving the college, Dame Beatrice had had a long talk with her and had ascertained that the absent Mr Basil was in hospital in Scotland; that he had broken his leg by falling down in the Cairngorms; that Miss McKay thought it most unlikely that he would have attempted to take a girl student as his sole companion on holiday, but that she was prepared to believe anything of anybody in these days; that he would have been in no jeopardy of losing his post at the college as long as the student had gone with him voluntarily; that the college was a nursery for plants but not for silly girls, and that, if the students of agriculture and dairy farming did not know enough to come in out of the wet, she felt inclined to wash her hands of them and their affairs and write the college off as a failure.

'But would your staff know that those are your views?'

Dame Beatrice had enquired. Miss McKay had shrugged the question aside, with an intimation that it was scarcely the sort of thing about which she could be expected to make a public announcement.

'Of course, if parents or guardians complained, I should have to take a line,' she had concluded, and had added, as an afterthought, that it was all a great nuisance.

'I expect your absence from the college in the middle of the term is also a great nuisance,' Dame Beatrice remarked to her nephew, as, in a taxi driven by an extremely fat Neapolitan, they took the road southwards on the morning after their arrival in Naples from Rome. They were driving to the hotel at which Biancini's relative was known to have worked.

'I say, though,' Carey had volunteered, at one point, before they left England, 'is our journey *really* necessary? This holiday the Biancinis took doesn't cover the time of the murder. That came after their return.'

'Yes,' Dame Beatrice had replied, 'that is the case, certainly.' But, in spite of her ready acceptance of the fact, she still seemed to think that the visit to Naples *was* necessary. Carey, pleased with the chance of a short break in routine, had said no more. He had gone sightseeing by himself in Rome while, for three days, Dame Beatrice visited her learned friends, and now he was prepared to escort her to what he thought would turn out to be a hostelry of only modest if not actually of dubious type.

In this he was mistaken. After the squalor of some of the city streets, the lines of washing hung high from tenement to tenement, the careless heaps of fish and fruit in the markets, the *Hotel Vittorio* came as a pleasant surprise. Its façade was gloomily magnificent. Its interior gave the impression of a monastery, and this was not at all strange, as that is what it had been up to the beginning of the twentieth

131

century. It was cool and pleasantly shadowed. The clerk at the desk greeted them in English.

'Good-day. You have reservations?'

They had reservations. Dame Beatrice was shown to a stone-flagged chamber, immensely vast, which contained, besides the bed, a washstand of nineteenth-century veneered mahogany and a dressing-table in bog-oak. There was also a wardrobe of indeterminate wood, capable (she thought) of housing ghosts, coffins, corpses or the whole of the hotel's store of linen.

She unpacked, bathed and changed, and was downstairs before Carey was ready to join her. The hotel possessed a long balcony overlooking the Bay of Naples. An elderly waiter came up.

'The signora would care for some wine? Lachryma Christi, perhaps? Orvieto? Santa Catarina? Chianti?'

Dame Beatrice, with memories of a honeymoon of long ago spent at Amalfi, plumped for Santa Catarina, and sat for half an hour watching the Neapolitan sea.

'Tell me,' she said to the hovering, elderly waiter when he had reappeared to tell her the time of the next meal, 'have you had here a Signor Biancini and his wife?'

'And daughter, signora. Yes, yes. The wife and daughter are English, a second marriage, as I understand from Giovanni Biancini, who works here but is off duty today. The daughter is of her mother's first marriage, and was born, one would suppose, when the woman was very young.'

'What makes you think so?'

'She was of thirty years, this daughter. Giovanni Biancini told me so, and one could well believe it.'

'Indeed? It is this daughter in whom I am interested.'

'The signora is thinking of engaging her as a companion? But that needs one who is virtuous and of a quiet and docile disposition. This young woman was not quiet or docile. I have heard her revile her mother. Besides, unwisely she liked her stepfather, I think. The signora will understand. It is not nice to explain.'

This remark terminated the conversation and Dame Beatrice went to the dining-room.

'You seem very quiet tonight,' said Carey, as they sat, after dinner, on the terrace with their coffee. 'Scarcely a cheep out of you during the whole of the evening. Are you tired?'

'By no means. I have found out what I came to find out, but how much use it will be to me and to the police is problematical.'

'You haven't been long about it. Does that mean we go home tomorrow?'

'No, no. Why should we not enjoy ourselves here while we can? The news I have gained will not stale for the keeping. We will visit Pompeii. We will study Herculaneum. We will climb to the crater of Vesuvius and go to see the bubbles of volcanic mud at Solfatura. We will demand spaghetti cooked as they do it in Sicily, with bacon, mushrooms, onions, garlic, black olives and anchovies, with the Parmesan cheese on a separate dish. We will eat *pollo in padella con peperoni* and pigeons prepared after the Roman fashion. If we can get it (but the time of year may not be right) we will have a hare washed in vinegar and *sauté* in butter with sliced onions, ham, sugar and vinegar, grated chocolate for colouring, almonds shredded fine and some raisins.'

'I can hardly wait. What about going to Amalfi, Sorrento and Capri? I know everybody does, but I like tripperism. Anyway, I'm glad we don't have to leave at once. I *must* give my young ladies time to miss me from the piggeries. I should think my predecessor's leg must be on the mend by now, though. I don't much want to be at the college after Christmas.'

Characteristically, he did not ask his aunt what it was

133

that she had managed to find out since they had been at the hotel. It was not that he took no interest, but he felt sure that she would tell him when she was ready to do so. She told him as they came out of the church of Santa Chiara in Naples, on their return journey to Rome, which they made in a hired car.

'I note,' she said, 'that with your usual delicacy and the *amour propre* we have come to expect of you, you have forborne to ask me what it was that I came to Italy to find out.'

'I knew you'd tell me when you were ready, if it was possible to tell me at all,' said Carey, with his slight smile. 'That doesn't mean I haven't been curious, of course. I always thought there was some particular method in this madness that you hadn't mentioned.'

'It was the discrepancy which puzzled me first.'

'The alleged age of the corpse?'

'Yes. It couldn't have been the body of a twenty-two-year-old that we saw, and yet the mother identified it as that of Mrs Coles, chiefly because of the college blazer, it seems.'

'So . . . ?'

'I guessed at once that there must have been another daughter, an older one, but sufficiently like Mrs Coles for the mother, in her natural grief and agitation, to have confused them—and certainly to have confused *us*.'

'English is a wonderful language. Well, your guess turned out right, as your guesses are apt to do, being not so much guesses as a species of second sight, but you didn't come to Italy to prove there had been two Miss Pallisers. You knew that before you came.'

'Quite so. I did want to establish that it was the elder daughter who was here on holiday, though, and, in doing so, I was given a very broad hint from the waiter that she made herself a nuisance to Mr Biancini.'

'Probably she was led on. These amorous Italians!'

'Quite. But you see what follows?'

'If the waiter noticed what was going on, so did Mrs Biancini. Oh, ho! Quite so! Mrs Biancini had it in for elder daughter, did her in, and deliberately confused the issue by identifying the corpse as that of the *younger* daughter, with whom it could be proved she had no quarrel at all.'

'The daughter who fled from home, in fact, rather than live in the same house as Biancini.'

'Well, well, well! Of course, the snags are pretty obvious.'

'The biggest snags are the college blazer—Norah Coles surely would not possess more than one of those at a time—and the extraordinary choice of a hiding-place for the body. It seems highly unlikely that Mrs Biancini would have known of the existence of that coach.'

'Norah Coles might, at some time, have mentioned the Highpepper rag in which it figured. I've had students at Calladale tell me about it, you know.'

'Yes, certainly it seems to have been regarded as a classic. All the same, even if she knew of it, I *cannot* see her choosing the coach as a hiding-place.'

'What shall you tell the police about Carrie Palliser now?'

'I shall not mention Biancini yet, if at all. I don't want to set them on what might well turn out to be a false trail. All I shall tell them at present is that Carrie saw Naples and died.'

As soon as she was back in England at the Stone House, Dame Beatrice sent a reply-paid telegram to Mrs Biancini:

Which daughter was with you in Italy query Bradley.

The reply she received was equally succinct.

Carrie why query Biancini.

She thought the message oddly cool, but concluded that it had come from Biancini himself and not from the dead woman's mother. In any case, another conversation with one or both of the Biancinis appeared to be necessary before she went again to the police.

Accordingly, she called on them next day. Biancini was out, but his wife welcomed her with what seemed to be an air of relief.

'We couldn't make head or tail of your telegram, Dame Beatrice,' she said. 'Of course it was Carrie we had with us. It couldn't have been poor Norah, as I thought you knew, her being with her aunt at the time.'

'Sit down, please, Mrs Biancini,' said Dame Beatrice, who had been given a chair whilst her hostess remained standing on the hearthrug in the fireless, over-furnished little parlour. 'What I have to say may give you a shock.'

'Nothing to do with Carrie would give me a shock. She's been a bad girl, bad through and through. It was only me paying back the money as quick as I did that saved her from prison, you know. I did it for poor Norah's sake, not to ruin her career by having a sister behind bars. If it hadn't been for that, and me wanting to marry Mr Biancini, I don't know but what it wouldn't have taught her a lesson to have let her go to gaol.'

'She has received the last lesson she will ever be taught in this world, Mrs Biancini. Tell me, when you were called upon to identify your daughter's body, did it not seem to you that you were looking upon Carrie and not Norah?'

Mrs Biancini did not answer for a full minute. Then she said, in tones husky from shock:

'But—but she was wearing the college blazer. I never thought—I hardly glanced—it was all too much for me. They were ever so alike to look at. I never could understand why their natures should be so different. But—I mean, are you telling me it's *Carrie* who's dead?'

'I do not think there is any doubt of it.'

'Then where is my Norah?'

'That is a question for the police,' said Dame Beatrice sadly. 'I do think, Mrs Biancini, that you would be well advised to tell me all you know.'

There was a struggle going on in Mrs Biancini's mind. It showed in her face. At last she said :

'Perhaps I'd better tell you. My Carrie was a real bad lot. Biancini—Tony, you know—always thought we could reform her, but I felt I knew her better. But what you've just told me has knocked me all of a heap. So where *is* Norah? And is she dead or alive?'

'It is impossible to say, Mrs Biancini. We must hope that she is alive, but it would not do to build on it. There is one ray of hope. You identified the body wrongly; you say the girls were much alike. It is possible—mind, I have nothing to go on in saying this—but it is possible that somebody else made the same mistake and that Carrie was killed instead of Norah.'

'But nobody on earth would want to hurt Norah!'

'What about Carrie?'

'That might be a different kettle of fish.'

'But you know nothing definite? You cannot think of anyone who might have had a motive for compassing Carrie's death?'

'I couldn't say. We'd been out of touch until Tony suggested having her with us for this holiday in Italy. His idea, I think, from what he said, was to get her a job as hotel receptionist or perhaps in a tourist office. She'd learnt Italian, you see, when she knew I was set on marrying him, and she'd taken French at school, my first husband being alive until she was nearly nineteen.'

'Mr Biancini took sufficient interest in her, then, to think about her future? What sort of work had she been doing before this holiday in Italy?'

'School-teaching. Oh, not at a proper school, you know. She was at one of these little private boarding schools where they employ the staff term by term.'

'Term by term?'

'Yes. You get the sack at the end of every term so they

137

don't have to pay you for the holidays. Then you apply again at the beginning of the next term and they take you on again, automatic, as it were.'

'But,' said Dame Beatrice, who had heard of this hand-to-mouth system before, 'isn't it true that the summer holiday at such schools can last as long as ten weeks?'

'Oh, yes, with a month at Easter and three weeks at Christmas. Either Carrie used to get a holiday job or else go on the Unemployment. She managed somehow, or else got into trouble with debts and stealing, which I had to see to, as I told you.'

'Did she ever spend her holidays, or part of them, with you?'

'No. It wouldn't have done, once I'd married my Tony.'

'But you were sure that it would work when you agreed to having her join you in Italy?'

'It seemed safe enough at the time. She told us she was engaged.'

'To whom?'

'She never said, and we didn't press it. We didn't think it could be to anybody very much, or else she'd have been the first one to crow about it. Putting two and two together, we reckoned it might be to a garage hand or a barman, or something of that—that is, if it was true, and not just a tale she'd made up.'

'Did anything transpire during the holiday which caused you to think that she might be in any trouble, difficulty or danger?'

'Not without it might have been the man who kept following us around. And, of course, she was a nuisance with Tony. But this man——'

'Indeed?'

'Yes. We noticed him first when we went to visit Pompeii. I don't understand these old ruins and things, but Tony was very proud of them and insisted on me seeing them all. I suppose it was because I wasn't interested that I noticed this man and pointed him out to Tony. But Tony seemed to think he was only creeping in on our party to hear what the guide had to say. Personally, I thought the man was up to no good, but, as he behaved himself and even gave the guide a tip at the end, I couldn't do anything, and tried to persuade myself it was just my fancy.'

'Quite so. Did your daughter seem to notice the man particularly?'

'No, I can't say she did, but you couldn't ever tell, with Carrie, from quite a little girl, what she noticed and what she didn't. She never gave herself away.'

'Except over Mr Biancini, I think you hinted.'

'Even then, I'll admit, *I* never noticed anything. I suppose it wouldn't have occurred to me. It was Tony himself tipped me off and told me she was getting embarrassing, so, of course, I made a bit of a scene and turned her out.'

'That, surely, was drastic treatment?'

'You didn't know Carrie. Half-measures didn't mean a thing to her. I told her to get back to her boarding school and be quick about it. She got short shrift from me, I can tell you.'

'Was it your first visit to Italy—this holiday?'

'Yes. Tony and me had often talked about it, and then, quite suddenly, he said his relations had invited us over, and he'd like to go, and what about me. Well, I wasn't all that keen, but I could see he was dead set on it. Of course, Italians are great family people, even if they *do* get excited and quarrel with each other, and I could tell I'd better say yes. But, oh, dear! When we got there! Well, really, Dame Beatrice, I couldn't tell you! To begin with, there were *dozens* of them, all living (if you can call it that!) in one of those dreadful tenement houses in the back streets of Naples.'

Dame Beatrice made sympathetic noises and suggested

that it depended upon what one was accustomed to in the way of living accommodation.

'I packed it up at the end of the third day,' Mrs Biancini continued. 'I told Tony he'd got to find us a hotel. I will say for him that he did see it my way, and so we went to the Vittorio, and, my, what a nice change that was!'

'He chose the Vittorio, I believe, because one of his relatives worked there.'

'That's quite right. It was out of the season, I suppose, and his brother Giovanni got us special terms, but, I must say, that didn't seem to make any difference to the way we were treated. Always respect shown, and doors opened for you and a light for your cigarette, just as it might be the Ritz or anywhere else. I really enjoyed myself.'

'And your daughter Carrie was with you all the time?'

'Well, until I gave her her return tickets and sent her back to Naples until the boat sailed. Mind you, the noise and smells and dirt didn't seem to get on her the way they did on me, but then, as she said, being used to crowds of kids, and the stink of everlasting cabbage, and not being able to get housemaids, it wasn't so very different from the boarding school. She gave me plenty of cheek before she went.'

'She preferred the Vittorio, I take it?'

'I suppose so. Anyway, she paid her own bill. I insisted on that. "You can't expect Tony to treat you. He isn't made of money," I said. She said Tony had invited her and that if we'd stayed with the relations, as was the first arrangement, it wouldn't have cost her anything, because he'd paid her fare. First I'd known of *that*, I must say, although I ought to have known when he handed me three sets of tickets. Anyway, I thought I had to put a stop to her nonsense. "You can take it from me, my girl," I said, "that, what with treating them to cigars and drinks, and taking them for outings and giving them parting presents, you spend quite as much staying with relations as you pay at a posh hotel. What's more," I said, "at the hotel you don't have to help wash up and make the beds." She saw it my way, in the end, I suppose, although I can't see *her* doing much for her keep *or* giving presents, either!'

'Yes, I see. So you all three travelled home together? She joined you on the boat at Naples?'

'Yes, but we said good-bye at Victoria.'

'Oh, yes? And did you see Carrie after that?'

'No. I wasn't having her in my house again! There was quite a bit of her school holiday still to run, and she'd got a job as temporary shop-girl, or so she said.'

'Do you know where?'

'Well, you couldn't rely on her word, exactly, but she *said* it was the B. and T. shop in Canby New Town.'

'The B. and T. shop?'

'Babies and Toddlers. I don't know it myself. She said it was a new shop in a nice district, and they were going to pay commission over and above her wages, and that the shop had been opened in response to a big demand for babies' and toddlers' clothes and toys and that.'

'I see.'

'They—they won't dig Carrie up, will they? To know whether it *is* Carrie, I mean.'

'Not at present. As things stand, your identification of the body as that of your younger daughter will not be challenged.'

'Then . . .'

'It is obvious, isn't it, that if we find Norah, it will prove that Carrie is dead,' said Dame Beatrice gently. 'What can you tell me about that? Have you no idea at all where Norah might be?'

'You'd better ask that young Coles. Do you think he *really* married her? He never seemed the marrying sort to me.'

'It should not prove impossible to obtain a copy of the

marriage certificate, if such a document exists. Just one more question, Mrs Biancini, if you won't resent it. Do I understand that Carrie was left out of her father's will?'

'You do, and serve her right. "If she can lift the money off somebody else, she can do without mine," he said. "It's for you and little Norah," he said. "You've been a good wife to me," he said, "and if you can find a man to suit your fancy, that's quite all right with me," he said, "and it won't make any difference to the way I leave my money." Well, I waited seven years, Dame Beatrice, before I took up with Tony, so nobody can't say I didn't respect a good man's memory.'

CHAPTER THIRTEEN

Nobody Asked for Bloodhounds

' "My dear," said I, "I see so many things wanting to be done, that I know not to which to give the preference." '

Ibid.

'So I take Hamish with me to this B. and T. shop and set him up with a garment or so and a toy or two and generally snoop around collecting data on Carrie Palliser, do I?' said Laura, who had listened with deep interest to the story of the Italian holiday.

Dame Beatrice cackled.

'It could do no harm, I suppose,' she conceded, 'but I doubt very much whether it would do good. You cannot furnish a convincing description of Miss Palliser and, of course, she may not have been employed there under that name.'

Laura was not prepared to be influenced by such arguments. Short of an absolute veto, she was determined to assume responsibility for finding out the truth about Carrie Palliser's employment at the shop in the hope that this might furnish a clue to the mystery of her death. She borrowed Dame Beatrice's car and chauffeur and drove in state with her infant son to Canby New Town, a dormitory suburb to the south-west of London.

The shop was in the High Street. George pulled up, opened the door and handed Laura out. She scooped up her lively baby and together they went into the shop. Laura made several small purchases and then asked to see the manageress.

This request was received with a curious mixture of hauteur and alarm by the assistant to whom she proffered it.

'Well, I don't know, madam, I'm sure. It wouldn't be a complaint?'

'Kindly arrange for me to see her,' said Laura haughtily. This attitude was scarcely backed up by Hamish who, toddling tipsily towards a small push-chair, thrust it into a mountain of babies' toilet requisites and knocked over the lot.

'Bang, bang!' said Hamish, delighted.

'Oh, dear!' said Laura. 'Now you'll *have* to get the manageress, won't you?' she added in a fierce aside to the woman who had served her. This assistant, helped by another, both with pursed lips, cleared up the mess. Nothing was broken. Hamish helped them by presenting them with a small enamel bowl. He then clasped a large sponge in the shape of a frog to his chest. From this sponge he declined to be parted, so Laura paid for it and the triumphant child dropped it into her basket. He then added a rattle and a pair of bibs. These Laura turned out again.

The two assistants went off and conferred together, then the one who had served Laura retired behind the scenes and emerged with a sharp-faced woman who wore a gold chain and a disdainful expression, both apparently symptomatic of her office. Laura addressed her without preamble.

'I should like to speak to your temporary assistant, a woman named Palliser, if you please.'

'Palliser?'

'Certainly. She wrote to me for a position as children's nurse and gave this as her temporary place of employment.'

'I'm sorry, madam. No assistant of that name has ever been employed here. We had a Miss Chalmers.'

'No, no. Palliser was the name. A woman of about thirty. Had been on holiday in Italy.'

'I'm sorry, madam.' It was final and brooked of no argument. Laura left the shop, her basket in her left hand and her enterprising son, who had had to be dispossessed of three pairs of woolly mits and a Teddy bear, under her right arm.

'Home, George, and don't spare the horse-power,' she said dejectedly, tossing Hamish on to the back seat of the car, and climbing in beside him.

'*Pot!*' said Hamish insistently. 'Pot, pot, pot!'

'Oh, well!' said Laura. 'Sorry, George.' She extracted herself and the infant and went back into the shop.

'Well, there's only our *own*,' said the assistant who had served her. 'The little staircase marked *Staff Only* on the second floor, madam.'

When they returned to the ground floor, a young assistant, who had been standing by while Laura made her first purchases, went with her, ostensibly to open the shop door. Something about Laura must have appealed to the girl, for she said:

'We don't mention Miss Palliser here, madam. She was sacked for pinching money out of the till.'

'Oh, thank you,' said Laura. 'That certainly settles that. You don't know where she went, I suppose?'

'No, I'm sorry, madam.'

Laura returned to the Stone House to report lack of progress. Dame Beatrice was sympathetic, but added that she had expected nothing to result from the visit.

'They wouldn't have known her address, even, I'm sure,' she said. 'Never mind. It was an outing.'

'Especially for Hamish,' said Laura. 'Well, the next thing is to find this school she taught at. Did the mother give any clue?'

'No.'

'Then that would appear to be my next assignment,' said Laura. 'I think, perhaps, if you don't mind, I won't take Hamish this time. He tends to complicate matters.'

145

'Well, I don't know,' said Dame Beatrice, regarding the child with leering affection, 'we ought to be fair. The only thing you found out—that Miss Palliser had retained her light-fingered habits—you owe to your son.'

'Hm!' said Laura, looking critically at her offspring. 'Something in that, I suppose. I still think I'll manage better without him. Have you Mrs Biancini's address? And can I have George again? I feel he lends an air of respectability to my excursions.'

George, impassive as ever, drove her to Mrs Biancini's house. Biancini was at home and opened the door to her. His wife, he regretted to say, was out at a local whist-drive.

'Momma,' said Mr Biancini, with an expansive, gold-toothed smile, 'is apt to win prizes at whist-drives. Now it will be an umbrella, now a silver-rimmed flower-vase, at another time a tea-trolley. All very nice for the home, and will you wish to come in and wait, or can I, perhaps, take a message?' He leered invitingly at her. Laura flexed her muscles.

'Neither,' said she. 'All I want is a piece of information which I dare say you can give me. Mrs Biancini's elder daughter, Miss Carrie Palliser, taught for a time at a small boarding-school. Would you mind giving me the name and address?'

'Of the school?' He looked both troubled and perplexed.

'Yes, please.'

'So?' He brooded. 'Carrie is in trouble again, eh?'

'I've been to the shop where she took a holiday job,' said Laura obliquely. 'It appears that there *was* some trouble there. The till, you know.'

'Naturally. You better come in. The neighbours, you know.' He led the way to the nearest door, opened it, and stood aside so that Laura could go in. She found herself in a stuffy little parlour and immediately recognised the portrait of her host, once purloined by Dame Beatrice and now

146

restored to its place. 'May I ask why you have come here? Carrie is not in prison, is she?'

'I have no reason to think so. I want a nursery governess for my small boy, and was given Miss Palliser's name.'

'Why?'

'I've really no idea. It was just that one of my friends thought . . .'

'You have come here,' said Mr Biancini fiercely, 'to snoop. Nobody recommends Carrie. What do you want to find out? No one knows anything about her.'

'That's nonsense,' said Laura sharply. 'All I want you to do is to give me the name of the school at which your step-daughter taught.'

'Teaches.'

'All right—teaches.'

'You are not on the level. Are you from the police?'

'No, of course not. Do you refuse, then, to give me the address I ask for?'

'No, no. I think you are phony, but it is none of my business. Carrie is not a nice woman, so I expect her to have some not nice friends. The school is called How Red the Rose House. It is in the village of Seethe, in Suffolk. Now tell me why you want to know.'

'Thank you very much.' It was a triumphant Laura who returned to the car and ordered George to drive home. 'So I go to this How Red the Rose place tomorrow,' she said, when she got back to the Stone House.

'Do you really think it is a good idea?' Dame Beatrice enquired. 'All this rushing about must be extremely fatiguing for you.'

The Amazonian Laura laughed.

'It's fun,' she said. 'And, even if I'm not doing much good, at least I'm doing no harm. Besides, I've definitely established one thing.'

'Yes?'

'This Biancini certainly has no idea that it may be Carrie and not Norah who is dead.'

'You mean he *had* no idea,' said Dame Beatrice. Laura stared at her.

'Could *be*,' she said. 'Oh, Lord! Talk about "the hounds of spring upon winter's traces!"'

'Talk, rather, of "fills the shadows and windy places with lisp of leaves and rustle of rain." That is what you may have contrived to do.'

'It can't be as bad as that!'

'Why not?'

'This Biancini isn't capable of it, you know.'

'Your meaning, obscure though it may seem, is not without interest.'

'Well, honestly, now I've seen him I'm inclined to think it's a case of Pass, Biancini, and all's well.'

'We are agreed.'

'Really?'

'I think so, child. I never *did* suspect poor Biancini of being anything but what he is.'

'The child of God,' said Laura, inconsequently, 'and an inheritor of the kingdom of heaven. I suppose,' she added, 'that the address of that school is the right one?'

'You can but go and find out.'

Laura studied her employer.

'I thought you thought I shouldn't interfere any more.'

'Heaven forbid that I should stand between you and your desires.'

'Hunches, not desires.'

'Have you ever heard of Don Quixote?'

'*Ad nauseam.* He tilted at windmills.'

'That is what I mean. You will do no good by enquiring for Miss Palliser at that dreadful little school, but any harm you may do has probably been done already. What you propose cannot help us, but it will satisfy your curiosity without further prejudice to the enquiry.'

'I don't like you in this mood,' said Laura. Next day she went to London and stayed the night in Dame Beatrice's Kensington house. On the following morning she caught the fast train to Ipswich, had lunch and then hired a car and set out for the school. As she had expected, it was indeed a small one, but it was housed in a beautiful Georgian mansion with a fine, simply-designed doorway and the broad windows of the period. Laura studied the house appreciatively and then rang the bell. A girl in a dark-blue overall answered it.

'Miss Palliser?' she said. 'I don't think there's anybody here of that name. Would you care to step inside?'

Laura stepped into a squarish hall from which rooms opened on either side. She was not kept waiting long. A tall, thin woman swam towards her.

'You have a child?' she asked.

'Actually, yes,' Laura replied. 'But he is of masculine gender and tender years.'

'But of course! We have special teachers for the nursery age.'

'It was about a former member of staff that I came to enquire—a Miss Palliser.'

'Palliser?'

'Carrie—I'm sorry that I don't know the full name—Carrie Palliser.'

'Really?'

'I'm afraid it's rather important,' said Laura. 'The police . . .'

'I am not in the least surprised. However, you can hardly expect me to jeopardise the good name of my school. I fear that I must decline to assist you, Mrs . . .'

'Gavin. I may add that my husband is a Detective Chief-

Inspector at Scotland Yard and that what we are investigating is a case of murder.'

'I cannot help you.'

'But Miss Palliser *did* teach here?'

'Certainly, but that is hardly the point now.'

'Why not?' asked Laura. 'The point is that somebody has done away with Miss Palliser. Surely you are interested in that fact?'

'Why should I be? Miss Palliser was thoroughly unsatisfactory in every way. Her teaching was slovenly and incompetent and her character was undesirable. Do you wish me to say more?'

'Lots more,' said Laura crisply. 'You seem just the person to be able to tell me why she should have got herself murdered.'

'Murdered? But . . .'

'Oh, yes, I know it looked like the younger sister, and that the mother identified the body as such, but there seems no doubt now that it was Miss Palliser and not Mrs Coles who was killed.'

'But—we had better go in here, Mrs Gavin. This news comes as a great shock. You see——' She opened a door on her right and led the way into a large, high-ceilinged room panelled in white. 'You see, Miss Palliser left here under a cloud.'

'Stealing?'

'Please sit down. Embezzlement, I suppose one would term it. Money collected for a school journey, you know. I had to make it good, and there isn't much margin when one runs a school of this type. I had to dismiss her. I could not keep her on.'

'But you didn't go to the police?'

'For the sake of the school. I cared nothing about Miss Palliser. In fact, she had caused me so much worry and expense that I own I felt vengeful. But it would not have done to take her to court on such a charge—the parents, you know. There would be a lack of confidence in me if they thought my staff capable of stealing money paid in by the children. Of course, I could not give her a testimonial which would have helped her to secure another teaching post and she left here threatening suicide. It was quite dreadful. And now you say that she is dead.'

'Murdered.'

'But who would have wanted to do such a terrible thing?'

'That is what we hope to find out.'

'We?'

'Yes,' said Laura, resolved not to be more enlightening.

'I did not know that the police took their wives into partnership.'

'Oh, it happens.'

'Dear me! I had no idea! But, then, of course, I know very little about police procedure. In any case, I don't see why you have come to see me.'

'We are leaving no stone unturned. We are trying to reconstruct Miss Palliser's past life to see whether something will come to light which will give us a clue to her murderer.'

'I see. Well, there is no way in which I can help you. It won't be necessary, I hope, for you to make it public that a—that a murdered woman was once on my staff?'

'That shouldn't be at all necessary. I understand . . .' Laura hesitated a little in order to choose a tactful wording for her next remark, '. . . that is, I believe you have a system here by which the staff do not receive an annual salary, but are employed from term to term, so to speak.'

'That is so. It is often done in schools of this type. It is necessary. We have no government grant of any kind.'

'No, I appreciate that. Then . . . for how many terms did you employ Miss Palliser?'

'Five.'

'Have you any idea what she did during school holidays? Where she worked? With whom she stayed?'

'None at all. She was well aware of the terms of her employment. She had agreed to them. What she did when she was not teaching here was none of my business.'

'I suppose,' said Laura, 'you would have no objection to my speaking to any member of the staff who was here with Miss Palliser?'

'There is none.'

'None?'

'Staff changes are very frequent, Mrs Gavin. There is nobody, except myself, who was here in Miss Palliser's time.'

'Oh, I see. Well, thank you very much for giving up your own time like this. So far as you are concerned then, the dead woman is still Mrs Coles, not Miss Palliser.'

The thin woman smiled in frozen fashion and rose. A minute later Laura was standing outside the front door with it closed behind her. Suddenly it opened again.

'Mrs Gavin!' The blue-overalled girl was standing on the step.

'Yes?' said Laura, filled with a sudden, wild hope.

'Miss Cummings wants to speak to you again. Will you come in?'

Laura followed her and was shown into the white-panelled room. The proprietress of the school was standing at the window. She turned as Laura came in.

'You did say *murdered*?' she asked.

'No doubt about it.'

'It couldn't possibly have *been* suicide? She did threaten it when she left here.'

'The police don't think it was anything but murder.'

'But a mistake was made in identifying the body?'

'Yes, indeed.'

'That must be very unusual. Who . . .?'

'The mother.'

'The *mother*? Oh, but surely, of *all* people, a *mother* would know!'

'There were good reasons, in this case, for making a mistake, but I'm afraid I can't disclose them.'

'Of course not, of course not! I just wanted to be quite sure it wasn't suicide. Not that I should feel the moral responsibility of it. I mean, people must expect to be dismissed if they show they can't be trusted. But—well——'

'I quite understand. Well, it doesn't seem that you can help us. Still, thank you, all the same.'

'You could have a word at the village post office if you wanted to know any more about Miss Palliser. Mrs Pock is renowned for being indiscreet and loquacious.'

'Thank you very much.' This time Laura was not called back at the front door. She strode down the gravel drive to the waiting car and told the man to drive into the village and stop outside the post office.

The post-mistress turned out to be a brisk, grey-haired, bright-eyed little woman with a Suffolk accent so pronounced that Laura, waiting while she conversed with a woman who was buying bacon at another counter, wondered whether she would be able to make head or tail of any information about Carrie Palliser which might be forthcoming. She discovered, however, that Mrs Pock's conversation was not, after all, very difficult to follow. Laura opened the floodgates by buying a book of postage stamps and asking to be directed to the school. She was coming away from it; must have passed it, she was told; not that that was any wonder, for the board saying it was a school was almost hidden by that laurel hedge, and, anyway, it looked like a gentleman's house, which is what it had been throughout Mrs Pock's girlhood and almost up to the time that Pock was taken. Of course, it brought trade to the village. There were the children, just twenty of them, poor little things, with their pocket-money to spend, and then there were the parents coming down to see them, and take them out, which was why the Devil's Advocate had been able to build on a dining-room and call itself an hotel, and then there were the sales of paint-brushes and crayons, exercise books and pencils . . .

Laura wanted to keep the school in the foreground as a subject of conversation, but could perceive no opportunity of stemming the tide of Mrs Pock's reminiscences long enough to put the questions she wanted to ask. Her opportunity came with the entrance of another customer. Mrs Pock broke off in mid-sentence to wish the newcomer good afternoon. It was not long before Laura gathered that this customer was the vicar's wife. She wanted a packet of macaroni, and appeared to be able to cut short Mrs Pock's remarks by addressing her sternly as Lizzie and adding that she was in a hurry.

'And who're you?' she demanded, turning on Laura. 'Don't seem to know your face.'

'It would be extraordinary if you did,' retorted Laura, whose worst instincts (she told Dame Beatrice later) were aroused by the vicar's wife. 'This is the first time I have ever been in Seethe.'

'What are you doing here?'

'Looking for a murderer.'

'What!'

(So the Colonel's lady and Judy O'Grady *were* sisters under their skins, thought Laura, as both her hearers made the same exclamation.)

'I am helping to investigate the murder of a certain Mrs Coles, sister to a Miss Carrie Palliser, who, I am credibly informed, once taught at the How Red the Rose School in this village.' (It was better to stick to the newspaper reports in talking to these two, Laura thought.)

'A chair, Mrs Pock,' said the vicar's wife, 'and another for the woman police-constable.'

Mrs Pock, apparently hypnotised by the incumbent's spouse, disappeared into the room behind the shop and came back with two dining-room chairs. These she brought round and placed one at each end of the counter.

'*Now!*' she said, beaming at Laura. 'This *is* something like!'

It seemed a good plan to Laura to accept this as an invitation to speak, so she plunged in before Mrs Pock could continue.

'There has been nothing in the newspapers about Miss Palliser,' she said, 'but you may have seen that the body was identified by a Mrs Palliser. She is the mother of the Miss Palliser who taught for five terms in the private school here. I have been commissioned—perhaps I should say that I have had occasion to commission myself—to investigate Miss Palliser's past life in order to find a clue which will lead to the identification of her sister's murderer.'

'But this is incredible!' exclaimed the vicar's wife. 'Somebody's sister murdered . . . from *our* village!'

'Well, that's only partly true,' Laura pointed out. 'Miss Palliser wasn't exactly a native of Seethe, was she?'

'All who live and work in Seethe are our flock,' said the vicar's wife. 'How did she come to be murdered?'

'But that's what we want to find out,' said Laura. 'We particularly want to trace Miss Palliser, who seems to have disappeared. We want to know where she went and what she did during school holidays, for which, I am assured, she was not paid.'

'I never *did* see why teachers were paid for school holidays,' said the vicar's wife. 'At least three months in every year are unproductive of education.'

'The teachers would be nervous wrecks, otherwise,' retorted Laura, who had been trained for teaching but who had never embraced that profession. 'Doesn't *that* ever occur to their critics?'

'Beside the point. What about this Miss Palliser? You want to find out where she spent the holidays?'

'And what did she do besides serve in a shop which I have already visited. Yes, please.'

'She stood-in during one holiday at a college for gentlemen-farmers, a place called Walborough,' said Mrs Pock. 'I do know that. The secretary left, and the term wasn't finished.'

'Walborough? You mean Highpepper,' said Laura excitedly. 'Think! Think, Mrs Pock!'

But Mrs Pock shook her head.

'I read all the telegrams, hers and theirs,' she said definitely. 'Walborough Agricultural College it was called. She sat-in to take phone calls and the pay was nineteen and sixpence a day.'

'Where *was* this place? In which county, I mean.'

'It was somewhere in Berkshire.'

'Berkshire?'

'Yes. They paid her fare there and back. It was all in the telegrams I handled.'

There was nothing more to be gained from Mrs Pock, and Laura fled very soon from the vicar's wife who literally talked her out of the shop. She returned to the waiting car and said, 'Ipswich.' In the train, going back to London, she suddenly threw off the feeling of depression which Mrs Pock had engendered, and said aloud, to the consternation of two women who were sharing her compartment, 'Blimey! I see it all now! It's the one thing Mrs Croc. doesn't know! I bet she's guessed, but she can't *know*! After all, the course at one agricultural college must be much the same as at another.'

CHAPTER FOURTEEN

The Counterfeit Patient

' "The pig, with his large fat belly, will have no trouble in supporting himself . . . I own that I would willingly sacrifice the pig to save the others." '

Ibid.

'THE connection seems to me a bit thin,' said Detective Chief-Inspector Robert Gavin, when he was informed of his wife's adventures. 'What makes you think—apart from the coincidence of Carrie Palliser having some connection with this place in Berkshire—this agricultural college, I mean— that what you've found out can be of any help over the Calladale affair?'

'Piggy Basil,' said Laura. 'I always connect Berkshire with pigs.'

'Piggy Basil? Oh, the chap who had Carey's present job and smashed himself up climbing during the vacation!'

'*If* he smashed himself up!'

'Eh? Oh, don't be a chump!'

'I repeat—*if* he smashed himself up,' said Laura firmly. 'When Mrs Croc. begins talking about sending grapes to a hospital, there's more in it than meets the eye.'

'Pips.'

'No, really! I'm perfectly serious. I can read Mrs Croc. like a book and I assure you that she's suspected Piggy Basil from the word Go. And if you want to know what *I* think— well, I think his *bona fides* could bear closer inspection. I feel positively certain in my own mind that it was Piggy who accompanied Norah Coles to that holiday camp.'

Gavin looked thoughtful. Although, equally with Dame Beatrice, he distrusted Laura in the rôle of sleuth, he felt that, this time, her theory might bear close testing. As it was not, officially, his case, he handed Laura's idea to the police who were investigating the murder.

'I wish,' said Laura to Dame Beatrice, 'you would depute me to interview this Basil. I'd turn him inside out in ten minutes. Do we know the name of the hospital?'

'Certainly, but I go there unaccompanied,' said Dame Beatrice with finality.

'All right, then. But I know Scotland a lot better than you do.'

'But you will not obtain more useful information from your fellow-countrymen than I shall. Believe me, this is not a task to be undertaken by a young woman.'

'You mean by a bone-head, I suppose,' said Laura, with resignation. 'When shall I expect you back?'

'Oh, you are welcome to come with me to Scotland. Carey's Jenny will take care of Hamish while we are gone. All I meant was that I do not wish you to accompany me to the hospital. There I shall function very much better without you.'

They set out on the following morning, proposing to spend the first night in the city of York.

'I could get you to Newcastle easily, if you wished, madam,' said George. 'Then you could hop into the Highlands from there.'

'No, no. York for the night, then Edinburgh, then on to our destination,' said Dame Beatrice.

'The police will beat us to it,' Laura pointed out. 'You know Gavin has passed on my great thought about Piggy and the holiday camp.'

'I particularly wish the police to reach Mr Basil before we do, child.'

'Oh, you think their visit will put wind up him, and soften

him up, do you? Something in that, perhaps. Anyway, it will make a much more enjoyable trip if we don't rush it.'

'And, of course, we may have to allow for bad weather at this time of year, madam, I suppose,' said George respectfully. As it happened, the only bad weather they encountered was a certain amount of rain. They reached the village of Tynmally at three in the afternoon, had tea at an hotel which seemed too big for the place and then, while Laura took a short, brisk walk before it grew too dark to admire the prospect from the bridge over a salmon river, Dame Beatrice drove to the hospital.

It was considerably smaller than the hotel and was perched at the top of a sharp incline which rose just out of the village on the north-east side. The matron had had notice of her coming and her welcome was cordial but dignified, after the manner of the Highlands. She was pressed to take tea, declined it and was conducted to the patient.

He could walk, but was still in hospital, he explained. They were keeping him under observation because of an obscure complication which had caused severe dermatitis on the injured limb. From the matron Dame Beatrice had already learn that (a) he had been a model patient, (b) he had been in hospital since the last week in August, (c) they would be extremely sorry to part with him, (d) he was terribly shy and could scarcely bear her young nurses to look at him, (e) that the leg had shown a compound fracture and that, owing to a night's exposure in wet weather on the mountainside, he had been in very poor shape when he had been brought in, and that that was the reason why he had not been discharged.

Dame Beatrice felt considerable interest in the picture thus presented. Compared with the description she had already received of Mr Basil, the picture of the patient seemed strangely out of focus. She analysed the evidence she had just received of the characteristics of the man in hospital and cross-checked it with the stories she had heard, either vicariously or at first-hand, of Piggy Basil. Her interest mounted. A model patient might or might not be a fair description of Piggy in hospital. It was her experience that people who behaved with the utmost selfishness in their own homes and to their wives or mothers, often did become model patients in hospitals. There was nothing extraordinary in that.

The time-sequence fitted. There were no comments to be made, either, upon the matron's second heading. August— yes. That would be right.

Even the reflection that they would be sorry to part with him could go by the board. Nurses—even Sisters—said such things. Matrons, a law unto themselves (on the whole) could concur, and, knowing no better, frequently did. But that Piggy Basil was *shy* was a shot so wide of the mark that the truth was obvious, she thought. This man was not Basil.

Dame Beatrice had then announced that she would be very pleased to visit the patient. He was a thin, attractive young man but he greeted her, as she had expected, with a certain amount of reserve. After the news of his injury :

'Awfully nice of you to come and see me. Let's see—you must be——'

' "Thy evil spirit, Brutus !" '

'Oh, no, surely not ! I mean to say . . .'

'So do I,' said Dame Beatrice, seating herself beside the bed. 'I mean to say that you are an impostor, Mr . . .'

'Simnel.'

'Extremely apposite.'

'Basil,' explained Mr Simnel, 'needed an alibi. I supplied it, that's all.'

'Have you read the papers since you have been in hospital?'

'More or less. I've read the football reports and the racing news. Why?'

'The sister of a girl at the agricultural college where Mr Basil was employed has been murdered. I think you had better tell me where he is.'

'You don't mean he had anything to do with it!'

'We do not know whether he had or not, but you yourself have just used the word "alibi." Why did he need an alibi? Can you tell me that?'

'Well, yes, I *could,* but I don't think he'd want me to.'

Dame Beatrice rose.

'In that case, I have no option but to leave you with my curiosity unsatisfied.'

'Old Basil wouldn't hurt a fly, you know. Tell me about this girl. Why should it be supposed that he even knew her? You don't *know* that he knew her, do you?'

'No, but the circumstances are so serious that I consider you would do better to assist the police.'

'You're not the police?'

'No, but I was brought into the affair before they were, and I have no intention of keeping from them any information which may assist them in their attempts to find the murderer of this unfortunate young woman.'

'So you'll tell them it's not Basil in hospital with a broken leg, but his friend and holiday companion, George Simnel.'

'Yes.' She sat down again.

'How did you tumble to it that I'm not the person I ought to be?'

'I was told you were shy.'

'Oh, I see. Yes, that wouldn't be a word you would use to describe Basil, I admit. Was that all?'

'Apart from a feeling I had.'

'Of something fishy? How extraordinary!'

'Not so very extraordinary. You see, the dead girl's sister is missing from the college. We were led to suppose, at first, that it was the student who had been killed. I will not—in fact, I need not—give you all the details, but the police will have to find the girl. Is she with Basil?'

'Honestly, that I *don't* know. Look here, Basil's in Ulster—somewhere near Londonderry, I believe. But you can take it from me that he hasn't done any killing. He runs after women all right, but he doesn't murder his little friends; he simply discards them.'

Dame Beatrice nodded.

'What would he have done, I wonder, if you had not broken your leg?' she said. Simnel laughed.

'I suppose he'd have been a good boy and gone back to his job at the right time,' he replied. 'Anyway, I can see he'd better get himself straightened out with the police. When was the job supposed to have been done?'

'That cannot be answered exactly, but, from the medical evidence given at the inquest, the girl probably died towards the end of September.'

'Then, if it can be proved that Basil was in Ireland at the time. . .?'

'Yes, it would clear him.'

'You see, I busted my leg on the thirtieth of August, and after he'd seen me into hospital and let my people know and all that, he told me he'd need this alibi and asked whether I was prepared to play ball. Well, we were pals, anyway, and then, you see, my cracking up like that had spoilt his holiday, and then, again, he'd been very decent in getting me fixed up, so, as I took it for granted that he wanted to go off with some woman, I agreed to take his name and let him use mine.'

'But was all this arranged before you came to hospital?'

'Oh, no. Nothing was fixed up before I had the fall. The hospital part of it helped him to get away with things. He just registered me in the name of Basil and wrote the letter explaining about the broken leg to the principal of the

162

college, and there he was—all set and everything in the garden lovely.'

'I am surprised that the hospital has kept you here so long.'

'Oh, I'm a mess, you know. They keep grafting bits on to me and taking bits out—the surgeon has had the time of his life. I don't believe he'll ever let me go.'

'I'm sorry.'

'Oh, I don't know. The grub's good up here.'

'There is one more thing, Mr Simnel. You said just now that Mr Basil informed your relatives of your accident. Surely they apprised the matron here of your real name?'

'No. They live in Australia, and would take for granted what they were told.'

'I see. Will you give me Mr Basil's address in Ireland?'

'You'll find it in that small diary in my locker. Help yourself.'

'By the way,' said Dame Beatrice, when she had found the entry and had copied it into her own diary, 'you have already had the police here, I suppose?'

Simnel looked genuinely surprised.

'News to me,' he said. 'I suppose they interviewed the matron.'

This supposition proved to be correct, as Dame Beatrice discovered after she had taken leave of the patient. The police had asked whether she had a patient named Basil, and, when she had answered in the affirmative, they had asked some questions about his injuries and were particularly interested to hear that he had been admitted to hospital on the date she gave them.

'They were satisfied,' she told Dame Beatrice, 'that he was not the man they were looking for, and begged me not to worry him by telling him of their visit. They might have spared themselves the trouble. Police or no police, no patient in *my* hospital is going to be worried by anybody, let alone by me.'

163

'So now we know,' said Laura, when, at dinner that evening, Dame Beatrice gave her a report of the interview. 'It looks like this Piggy Basil, doesn't it?'

'We shall find out when he crossed over to Ireland and whether he can prove that he was there when the murder was committed. We had better put through a long-distance call to the police, and give them Mr Basil's Ulster address.'

'How many flies do you think there are on this Piggy?' demanded Laura. 'He seems to me a very smooth type. This alibi now. How do you really think of it?'

'As the work of an unscrupulous man.'

'Unscrupulous enough to commit murder?'

'Murder is often not only the result of unscrupulousness but is also a matter of expediency.'

'I can see why he should kill Norah Coles if he took her away and, as they say, "done her wrong," but I can't see how the sister Carrie comes into it. Still, they must be pretty well alike for their own mother to have mixed them up when she identified the body.'

'As we have already realised, that attempt at identification was a horrid and difficult matter. Perhaps, after all, we had better go over to Northern Ireland and see Mr Basil for ourselves. Armed with the college photographs, we should be able to ascertain whether his companion is Mrs Coles.'

'We don't know that he's got a companion. He may simply be hiding from the English police.'

'Then Northern Ireland is not the most sensible place to choose. Kindly obtain reservations for our journey and rooms at an hotel in Londonderry, and we will be off at the earliest possible moment.'

Nothing could have suited Laura better. By the end of the week they were established in the Hotel Fingal, just outside Londonderry, the hotel in which, according to Simnel's diary, their quarry was also staying. At that time of year the hotel was by no means crowded and it was not long before they felt certain that they had identified Basil. He was a hearty, uninhibited creature of about forty, fattish and going slightly bald. The hotel employed waitresses only, and his manner with the girl who looked after his table was what Laura had been led to expect. He was loud-laughing and brash, and appeared to embarrass the girl a good deal.

'This,' said Laura to Dame Beatrice, 'is where I scrape acquaintance with Piggy. His looks give point to his name. I am observing him closely, and, as soon as the time is ripe, I suggest that I spring myself upon him with a moot question about holiday camps. What do you think about that?'

'It might be as good a way as any other of giving him either a shock, a warning or a chance of telling you that he has never been to such a place in his life.'

'You don't think he would simply come clean and give me the low-down about himself and his girl-friend? Wonder where she is? Nobody seems to be sharing his table.'

'I hardly think he will be prepared to confide in you. Still, do your best and bravest. The repercussions should be of interest.'

Laura's opportunity soon came. In fact, Basil himself provided it. She arranged so that they reached the door of the lounge together. Piggy opened it with a flourish and an unnecessary obeisance, Laura thanked him, sailed through and seated herself on a settee. From the reputation he had been given, she felt certain that he would join her, and so he did. Dame Beatrice, who, by arrangement, had left the dining-room earlier, watched the little comedy from an armchair near the fire.

Laura took out a cigarette and Basil's lighter was immediately brought into play. Laura thanked him again and asked how he liked the hotel.

'Oh, I'm leaving tomorrow,' he said. 'At least'—with a gallant smirk—'I *was*. Not so sure now, Mrs . . . ?'

'Gavin.' (He had been quick to spot the wedding-ring, thought Laura. A mistake, perhaps, not to have removed it.) 'You *do* like it here, then? Do you know the country well?'

'So-so. You can't do much without a car, and I didn't bring mine over.'

'Do you fish or sail or anything?'

'I've sailed a bit. As a matter of fact, I'm over here on a job.'

'How interesting!'

'Pigs. Wanted to study the bacon industry over here. Been all over the place—up here, in Eire—everywhere.'

'I adore pigs.'

'Really? That's surely very unusual in one of the fair sex. Tell me more about yourself.'

'I'm afraid I'm not an interesting sort of person. I'd much rather hear about *you*. Has it taken you long to—er—study the bacon industry?'

'I've been over here since the end of August.'

'Indeed? I'm afraid I'm gregarious. I couldn't do even an interesting job unless plenty of other people were doing it, too. My husband always says that I'd be the last person on earth to be a Robinson Crusoe.'

'Oh, I had my Man Friday—or, rather, girl Friday—all right, but only for a week or two. She had to go back, then, to complete her education.'

'Oh, your daughter, you mean?'

Basil found this suggestion immoderately amusing.

'Now, I *ask* you, Mrs Gavin!' he protested. 'Do I look the sort of bloke to cart adolescent daughters about with me? No, my dear lady, I want a chance to enjoy myself when I'm off the leading-strings.'

'Oh, I see. A college student, then?'

'Yes, and a very charming and quite sophisticated one.'

'I should have thought a Youth Hostel would have suited a student better than a hotel like this, or, possibly, one of those holiday camps.'

'Yes, but, you see, my dear Mrs Gavin, they wouldn't have suited *me*. And as (if you'll forgive a rather crude statement) I was paying the piper . . . !'

'Yes, I see. Students aren't usually very well off, although they certainly seem to have more money to play with than *I* was given when I went to college. I suppose they get paid jobs in the holidays.'

She gave Dame Beatrice the sign they had agreed on, and Dame Beatrice got up from her chair and walked slowly towards the door. Laura said :

'Ah, my boss is ready to go, so I'll say good night.' When she and Dame Beatrice were alone, she said disgustedly, 'Not a word of sense did I get out of him. He was stalling the whole time.' She repeated the conversation *verbatim*, and then added, 'Wouldn't it make you gnash your teeth?'

'No,' Dame Beatrice replied, after a moment's pause. 'I can see how to go on from there. I think you've done well. He has admitted coming here with a student and his denial of having stayed at a holiday camp is really immaterial because the police will soon prove whether it is the truth or not, and if it *is* the truth, that has cleared a red-herring out of our way, and if it is a lie there is some reason for his telling it, and that reason may be important.'

'I'd better pass him on to you, then. There's one thing, though. I don't care a bit for his type. He's definitely a bounder. But I can't see him as a murderer. He might hit another man over the head with a bottle or a pewter pot if he had a row in a pub, but I don't see him harming a woman beyond, perhaps, slapping down on her. I'm certain he wouldn't use poison.'

'We seem to have lost sight of the fact that poison, and a

167

particular poison, was the vehicle. When we get back I think we might spend a little time in research. My knowledge of the properties of coniine could be more profound, I feel.'

'You've changed the subject,' Laura pointed out, 'and rather unfairly. Shouldn't you be agreeing or disagreeing with me on the question of Piggy Basil's tendencies to commit murder?'

'I understood from you that he has no such tendencies.'

'Well, that's what I meant. What *do* you think about that?'

'I am no judge. Probably everybody has the tendency.'

'All right. Stall, if you want to. As for the hemlocks, spotted or other, I don't see that they matter any more. The cause of death is known and the poor girl is buried, so what more can we do, apart from finding the murderer, or helping the police to find him?'

'Well, child, as I pointed out just now, you believe that Mr Basil would not use poison, even if he were capable of committing murder by other means. It will be interesting to find out who *would* use poison, and, in particular, *this* poison. Opportunity is important; so is knowledge.'

'Yes, I see. He could, so he did. That sort of thing isn't evidence. It's only a pointer. And why do you say so confidently that it *will* be interesting to find out who used the coniine? Are you hot upon the trail? If so, I think you ought to bring me abreast of the march of events.'

'To say that I am hot on the trail is too optimistic a statement, I fear. All the same, I do feel that we have made some progress. We know now that Mr Basil never was a patient with a broken leg, and, apart from that, do you not realise that we have learnt one fact of primary importance since we have been here in this hotel?'

'There's only one thing I've learnt,' said Laura, 'and that is that, wherever Norah Coles may chance to be, she certainly isn't with Piggy.'

168

'And you do not consider that a fact of primary importance?'

'Well, it means that he isn't as black as some people would like to paint him, but that only bears out my argument that he wouldn't commit murder.'

'At any rate, the girl will have to be found. Finding her may or may not help to solve the mystery of her sister's death, but as her complete disappearance, so far as we are concerned, is a mystery in itself, I feel a certain amount of interest in it.'

'Yes, I see what you mean. If she isn't here with Piggy, where is she? It's quite a point, isn't it? Shall you tackle him along those lines?'

'Possibly. You remember that she disappeared well before the night on which Miss Good says she saw the large and ghostly horseman?'

'Yes. Do you think they *will* exhume the sister if Norah Coles isn't found soon?'

'I have no idea. Of course, it is only a question of time before she *is* found.'

'Yes, once the police hit the trail they don't easily give up and they're usually successful. She can't remain hidden for ever.'

'She might remain hidden longer dead than alive, child.'

'*Dead?*' cried Laura. 'Good Lord!'

'Let us keep open minds upon that subject,' said Dame Beatrice. 'I should have been happier, I confess, if we had found her here with Mr Basil. But there is one thing I am very glad to know.'

'Yes?'

'I am very glad to know that the dead girl worked for a time in that agricultural college in Berkshire. It clears up the only point which has been troubling me. A little knowledge can sometimes be a useful thing, you know.'

'Are you speaking of yourself and this "little knowledge" I got from Mrs Pock at the post office?'

'No, not exactly. Think it out for yourself. Like most young mothers, you are neglecting your intellectual gifts, child.'

CHAPTER FIFTEEN

Piggy Comes Cleanish

'. . . for if there are hours when it is good to reflect and be prudent, there are others when we ought to know how to take a sudden resolution, and execute it with energy.'

Ibid.

'My secretary informs me that you are interested in pigs,' said Dame Beatrice, seating herself opposite Basil at a small table in the lounge. It was a quarter to ten. Laura had breakfasted early and had gone for a walk. This was partly personal choice and partly to leave Dame Beatrice a clear field. 'I am so glad to hear it. More people—many, many more—ought to take to pig-breeding. My nephew now—you may have heard of him—Carey Lestrange of Oxfordshire—has bred pigs almost from boyhood, and look what a fine man he is!'

Basil, who had lowered his newspaper as soon as she had begun to speak, crushed out his half-finished cigarette and looked ready to take flight, but Dame Beatrice, emulating the Ancient Mariner, held him grounded as though by some magic spell.

'I'm afraid I've never heard of him,' he said. 'I only go in for pigs in a small way . . .'

'But that's just what I'm urging. People *should* go in for pigs in a small way. Just think.' She gave him no opportunity to do this, but treated him to a lecture on small-scale pig-breeding until the unfortunate man was too much deflated to follow his first instinct and escape. It seemed easier, he decided, to humour the pestiferous old creature.

'Yes,' he said cautiously, 'I agree with you almost entirely.

But don't you think that your scheme would bring down the price of pork until the game was hardly worth the candle?'

'That may be so. I do not contest it. But think, Mr . . .'

'Basil—er—Simnel.'

'Mr Basil, of the effect on the human soul if everybody talked, bred and ate pig!'

'Yes, of course,' said Basil in a soothing tone. (She must be humoured, he supposed.)

'Right,' said Dame Beatrice, with sudden and startling briskness. 'Now, Mr Basil, to the matter in hand. Exactly how did we persuade Mrs Coles to accompany us on our holiday? I refer particularly to the time spent at the camp at Bracklesea.'

'Oh, that!' He did not appear to be put out of countenance. 'Well, yes, we did go there, of course.'

'That is not what you caused my secretary to believe.'

'Well, of course not. After all, how was I to know what she was up to? She might have . . . Oh, we'll skip that!'

'So there *was* something shady about the visit to Bracklesea?'

'Shady? I don't know what you mean by that. Your ideas and mine probably wouldn't tally. However, for what it's worth, I'll tell you the truth. I'm an instructor at an agricultural college for women. I suggested to Miss Palliser—that is, Mrs Coles—that she might care to come with me to Bracklesea—strictly on the q.t., of course—for the fun of it. She agreed, and we went. At the end of a week we separated, she to go home, presumably, I to go to Scotland. It seemed providential, old Simnel breaking his leg. It gave me the chance I wanted of coming over here for a few weeks instead of going back to work. So there it is.'

Dame Beatrice shook her head and pursed her beaky little mouth.

'I fear not,' she said gently. 'For one thing, Miss Palliser had been Mrs Coles for some months before you took her to the camp. For another, although she returned to college at the beginning of term, she left it under circumstances which remain unknown. She has completely disappeared. It is possible that she was abducted.'

'I read—there was a report of an inquest——' said Basil. 'I understood that the poor girl was dead. You can't call that a disappearance, exactly.'

'Neither *do* I call it a disappearance, exactly or otherwise. As you may find yourself in a very awkward situation shortly, perhaps I had better remind you—for I am certain you know —that the dead girl was identified as Mrs Coles by her mother. However, the body was not readily recognisable, and it seems certain now that it was not the body of Mrs Coles but that of an older, unmarried sister. The police have been unable to trace Mrs Coles, and one is forced to wonder whether she, also, may be dead.'

'If she was abducted from college, I can't possibly be suspected of having anything to do with it. I was over here long before the beginning of term.'

'Yes. That would clear you, of course. You know, in your place, I would go to the police and tell them about that week you spent at the camp with Mrs Coles. If you have this complete alibi, it could do you no harm to contact them.'

'No. But what good would it do if it had no bearing on what happened? And how do you come to be mixed up in it, anyway?'

'To answer that first, I come to be mixed up in it because my nephew has taken over your work at the college, *pro tem.*, and when Mrs Coles disappeared I was asked to look into the matter.'

'I'm a bit dense, so may I ask why? I mean, it doesn't seem to me that being a pigman's aunt is necessarily a qualification for tracing missing girls.'

'I have traced people before, most of them candidates for

173

life imprisonment or, in less enlightened times, the noose.'

'You're not—yes, of course, you must be! Oh, Lord!'

Dame Beatrice studied him. A porcine individual in a ferment was not that individual seen at his best. Piggy was perspiring. Leaving him to his thoughts and his too-obvious fears, she went to her room, put on a fur coat and a witch-like hat of black, white and scarlet, and went downstairs to get the hall-porter to summon a hired car to take her for a drive until lunch-time. She lunched alone, as Laura had not returned.

Basil came to her table as she was about to leave it, and asked whether she could spare him a few moments in the hotel writing-room when she had had her coffee. It would be private in the writing-room, he added, and what he had to say was for her ears alone.

He proved to be correct about the writing-room being private, for they had it entirely to themselves. He switched on the electric fire, drew forward an armchair for Dame Beatrice and another for himself and took out cigarettes. Dame Beatrice declined his offer of one, and prepared herself to receive confidences.

'It's like this,' he said, taking the cigarette out of his mouth and gazing not at Dame Beatrice but at the toes of his shoes, 'I'm in a bit of a spot. You see, I haven't been over here quite all the time I said I had.'

'No?'

'You couldn't be definite, I suppose, about the date Mrs Coles disappeared?'

'Why do you not say at once that you were the ghostly horseman who abducted her?'

'What ghostly horseman? What on earth do you mean?'

'A student named Good was out on a late leave pass that night, and saw you.'

'But—not to know me?' He did meet Dame Beatrice's eye this time.

'She certainly did not recognise you or Mrs Coles. But what was the idea of the abduction?'

'It was nothing of the sort. I was a bit bored with pigs and what not, and, as we'd had a pretty good time together at the camp place, I thought she might be willing to team up with me again.'

'But what did you suppose the college would do when they discovered that she was missing?'

'Oh, but she wasn't going to be missing. That wasn't on the agenda at all. I've got a cottage where I spend weekends sometimes. It's quite near the college. I thought of going there with her and bringing her back in plenty of time for college breakfast.'

'Then how was it she did not return to college at all?'

'How should *I* know? I'd given her plenty of notice that I was going to see her again. The horse and the sheets were *her* idea. It was essential, of course, that neither of us should be recognised. She broke out of her hostel, as we had planned, we togged up in the kitchen garden, which isn't overlooked in any way, and got to my cottage by about a quarter to twelve. We had a couple of drinks and a cigarette and went to bed, and when I went to rouse her in the morning she was gone. Naturally I concluded that she had woken up early and decided to get back to college while it was still dark. Equally naturally, I couldn't follow her there. The arrangement had been for her to show up at the same time on the following night, but she didn't come, and I thought she'd got cold feet at the thought of the risk she was running by breaking out at night, and that was that.'

'Are you a sound sleeper, Mr Basil?'

'No. I wake very easily. You do when you're accustomed to looking after animals.'

'So Mrs Coles must have stolen very gently from your side, not to wake you.'

'Good heavens!' exclaimed Piggy, opening his eyes very

175

wide. 'You don't think I *slept* with the girl? One of my own students! Really, the suggestion is most indelicate!'

'This is astounding,' said Dame Beatrice. 'Are you serious?'

'Of course I'm serious. The thing is, what am I to do? If I go to the police and tell them what I've told you, I'm going to find myself in a very, very awkward situation. They couldn't help but think that I know more than I do. They might even arrest me. I shall have to think things over, unless you can help me. Where can the girl have gone, and why did she go?'

Dame Beatrice shook her head.

'I think you had better tell the police the truth,' she said. 'The *whole* truth,' she added gently.

'Then you don't believe my story?'

'It rings strangely in my ears. I also must think things over.'

'If you go to the police, and tell them what I've told you, I shall probably deny it, you know. It would be your word against mine.'

'The police are accustomed to accepting my word. I do not know how much experience you have had of confiding in them.'

She got up, but, before she reached the door, it was opened and two men walked in. Although they were in plain clothes there was no doubt about their being police officers. Basil rose and looked at them.

'The decision appears to have been taken out of my hands,' he said quietly. 'I suppose I am under arrest.'

'Not at all, sir,' said the foremost man, 'but I shall be obliged if you will answer a few questions.'

'The whole truth, mind,' said Dame Beatrice, grinning at the younger policeman as he opened the door for her.

'Well?' said Laura, who had come in to a late lunch after her walk and was just finishing her coffee in the lounge. 'Any luck? Did he spill any interesting beans?'

176

'He told me—or, rather, I believe I told him—that he and Mrs Coles were the ghostly horseman seen by Miss Good.'

'But I thought he was over here at the time!'

'It seems that he thirsted for Mrs Coles' society, but not connubially.'

'What! Why, the man's known to be a satyr.'

'I am telling you what he told me.'

'You don't believe him, do you?'

'I neither believe nor disbelieve. I suspend judgment until I know more. What he did not tell me is his real reason for getting Mr Simnel to impersonate him in Scotland while he came here to Ireland.'

'Perhaps he really *does* want to study the Irish pig-market.'

'He could have asked for leave of absence from the college, could he not? Why all this elaborate trickery?'

'Probably because a Piggy with a broken leg gets paid his salary while he remains incapacitated, whereas a leave-of-absence Piggy has to forfeit the cash payments until he gets back on the job.'

'Oh, I see. I confess I had not thought about the financial side of it. All the same, I cannot bring myself to believe that Mr Basil came here solely to study pig-marketing. There was some other reason, and, matters standing as they do, we need to find out what it was.'

'Any basic ideas?'

'Yes, but until I find out more than I can prove already, I am not prepared to disclose them.'

'A pity. Hullo, here come the detectives. Shall we confer with them?'

'No. If they have anything to tell us, they will do it without any prompting.'

The policemen came up.

'Do you mind if we ask a few questions, Dame Beatrice?'

'I shall be happy for you to do so.'

'Do you want me to go?' asked Laura. The older officer smiled.

'Certainly not, Mrs Gavin. You may have some information for us, too. We understand, Dame Beatrice, that you found out that Basil wasn't in Scotland when he was supposed to be in hospital with a broken leg, but was here. What was his object in deceiving people about where he was?'

'He told us he wished to study the Irish pig-marketing schemes.'

'Yes, that's what he told *me*. Is that all you know?'

'Yes, although it is not all that I can guess.'

'He confesses to abducting Mrs Coles, the missing girl, from the college, but swears that before it was daylight she sneaked out of his cottage and he hasn't seen her since.'

'It may be true, of course.'

'Yes?'

'You see, from the girl's point of view, it was surely a very risky thing to do, this breaking out of college to spend the night in a man's cottage. I cannot help feeling that Mrs Coles had some stronger motive for taking such a risk, if, indeed, she did take it. She would most certainly have been sent down from college if she had been found out.'

'You couldn't suggest a reason, I suppose, madam? All we can think of, in view of the fact that she has disappeared, is that she wanted to meet somebody in secret, and that the person she wanted to meet could not be interviewed by daylight and in the normal course of events. If so, I suppose you couldn't put a name to this person?'

'Either her sister or her stepfather, I should think, if you are right.'

'The sister who was murdered?'

'And who was murdered at about that time, or some days before.'

The policeman stared at her.

178

'You're not suggesting that this young woman murdered her sister?'

Dame Beatrice shrugged.

'I am neither suggesting it nor the reverse. I am putting it forward as a possibility. Young women have murdered their sisters before now. You see, the difficulty facing us in the case of that particular death has been twofold. Miss Palliser may have been the intended victim, or, as I thought at first (and I have not discarded the thought), she may have been killed in mistake for Mrs Coles. In neither case is there any apparent motive for the murder, and, of course, we cannot rule out the possibility that this was accidental poisoning and that somebody panicked and got rid of the body. If we could only discover the cellar where it lay before it was put into that coach we should be a very long step forward.'

'You mentioned the stepfather, madam. What made you think of Biancini? It seems hardly likely that she'd need to meet *him* secretly.'

'There is the same objection in the case of the sister, is there not?'

'Well, yes, except that they don't seem to have had much to do with one another and may have had some reason for not wanting people to know that they had met. It's all very unsatisfactory, from our point of view. Usually, in murder cases, there's *something* to get your teeth into so that you can make a start, but in this case there doesn't seem to be a thing. We don't want to call in the Yard, but we may not be able to help ourselves. I'm going to have another talk with Mr Basil. The reason he gives for coming here, instead of going back to his job, is a lot too thin to hold water. He's mixed up in this business somehow. I'm certain of that.'

Dame Beatrice nodded several times, but in thought as well as in agreement. The police officers returned to the writing-room and, as they opened the door, they almost knocked into Basil, who was in the passage and in the act of closing the writing-room door behind him.

'Just half a moment, if you please, sir,' she heard the first policeman say. His voice was sharp. It was obvious that he had requested Basil to remain where he had left him and that Basil had not seen fit to obey.

'Looks bad, don't you think?' murmured Laura.

'It does not appear to have inspired confidence in Mr Basil, so far as the police are concerned,' Dame Beatrice admitted. 'Was he proposing to make his escape, I wonder? Extreme measures of that kind would be most inadvisable at this stage. The proceedings must take their course.'

'If "proceedings" means what I think it means,' said Laura, 'I don't think there are any. The police more or less admitted they were baffled. Though I say it myself, they could do with the help of the Yard. I wish they'd call them in, and be quick about it, unless you've got something up your sleeve.'

'Nobody would need to employ the conjuring feat you mention if the police could find Norah Coles,' said Dame Beatrice. 'We ourselves have not the resources for such a search, and although I have given thought to the matter, no idea of where she may be has come into my mind, except that she must have gone back to England.'

'Has the Biancini house a cellar?'

'No, it has not. I visited it, as you know, and it has none. Neither can I think of any other cellar where the body of Miss Palliser might have been hidden, except, of course——'

'The college has cellars. The main building, you know,' said Laura. Dame Beatrice gazed so fixedly at her that she added, '*Didn't* you know?' Without waiting for an answer, she added, 'Then it's "boot, saddle, to horse and away," I suppose, leaving no avenue unexplored.'

'Will you tell George that we shall need the car in half an hour from now?'

'I will do that one little thing. Good gracious me! And here have we been eating, sleeping and continually thinking in terms of cellars, with one, so to speak, right under our noses.'

'It is always the obvious which is overlooked, child, as Edgar Allan Poe pointed out.'

But Laura knew better than to suppose that Dame Beatrice had overlooked the fact that the Georgian house, with its butler's pantry, possessed, for example, at least a wine-cellar.

CHAPTER SIXTEEN

A Confusion of Students

'These were our recreations; other labours abridged the
hours, which sometimes seemed very long.'

Ibid.

DAME BEATRICE gave considerable thought to the problem
of balancing the gain to the enquiry against the possible harm
to the college of her next step, and decided that the step
must be taken.

She paid another visit to the college to put her proposals
before Miss McKay. The Principal, deeply shocked and
horrified by Dame Beatrice's revelations and inferences,
nevertheless agreed without reluctance to all the suggestions
made to her and promised to make the necessary arrangements.

These involved a visit to the college cellars, an interview
with the men in charge of the boiler-room and a visit to the
hostel in which Mrs Coles had been resident. The chief
caretaker, a man of melancholy aspect, accompanied her
to the cellars. These were deep and vast and were reached
by a door next to what had once been the butler's pantry
when the house had been privately owned. The cellars
followed the plan of the ground-floor rooms, but only one,
that at the foot of the steps they descended, was in use and
was electrically lighted. The floor had been concreted and
the room was shut off from the rest of the subterranean
chambers by a steel door.

'It's the rats,' said the caretaker, who had no inkling of
the purpose of the visit. 'Miss McKay puts her trunk down

here, as you can see, and so do some of the lecturers what lives in the college itself. 'Ostels makes their own arrangements for the dishposal of students' 'eavy baggage.'

'I see. Is that steel door kept locked?'

'Why, no. Rats can't push open a door what's closed.'

'Don't the rats become ravenously hungry? There's nothing to eat, is there, in the cellars beyond this one?'

The caretaker wagged his head.

'My perdecer,' he said, ''e 'ad the idea to keep all the artificial fancy manures down 'ere. My oath! Them rats must of 'ad a good time! Hop manure, now! If they eat one sack, they must of eat 'undreds! It got 'em in, you see, and now we can't get 'em out. So we 'as this steel door put in, what they can't gnaw their way through, and we puts down concrete and reinforces the walls, and leaves 'em in outer darkness. Bless you, they uses the cellars now as an 'ome and gets their provender from the veg. the young ladies grows 'ere. Rats! Don't talk to *me* about rats! If you wants my opinion, the Pied Piper of 'Am'lin didn't 'ave nothink on us when it comes to rats.'

'I take it you do not come from these parts, Mr Potts?'

'I comes from 'Appy 'Ampstead on the 'Eath, and that's where I'm goin' to be buried.'

'Do we risk the rats and see what is on the other side of that door?'

'Pre*fer*ably not. I don't want rats in 'ere. Although, that's a funny thing. I comes down one time and finds rat-dirts all over the place. Couldn't account for it nowhow. Carn't see 'ow they could get through the steel door.'

'It must have been opened.'

'But who'd open it? I thought of that meself. But who'd bother to come down 'ere? Not the young ladies, I promise you.'

'All the same, you say that the door is not locked. We shall now return to the ground floor. It would tax your

183

memory too heavily, I imagine, if I asked you to tell me *when* you saw the rat-dirts in here?'

'That it wouldn't. It was midway through third week of this term.'

Dame Beatrice knew better than to question the memories of the semi-literate. She accepted their evidence at its face value. She and the caretaker returned to the ground floor and when they were half-way back to Miss McKay's sitting-room she asked where the boiler-room was. The caretaker looked somewhat disgusted, and told her that they would need to go into the new wing to find *that*. She replied immediately that she was not interested if that was the case, and returned to Miss McKay, who had promised to accompany her to Miss Paterson's hostel.

The head of the hostel, as it happened, was neither lecturing nor demonstrating, and they were shown into her sitting-room where she sat correcting a pile of written work and, at the same time, nursing a large pet rabbit.

'Dame Beatrice wants to talk to you, Miss Paterson,' said Miss McKay, 'about the Palliser girl. Some extremely disturbing circumstances have come to light. After you have heard what she has to disclose, she may need to question some of your students.'

Miss Paterson rang the bell, handed the rabbit to the maid, drew up two armchairs for her guests, and put more coal on the fire.

'I'm not staying,' said Miss McKay. 'Ring me if you need to.' Upon this, she departed.

'The murderer has been located, then?' asked Miss Paterson, taking the armchair she had drawn up for the Principal. 'Jolly good thing, too.'

'He or she has not been located, so far as my information goes. What we seem to have located is the cellar in which the body was hidden before it was conveyed to the old coach at the inn near Highpepper Hall,' replied Dame Beatrice.

'Really? Not—Oh, good gracious me! Not the *college* cellar?'

'It seems more than likely. At any rate, as soon as I have finished here, I am going to telephone the police to that effect. They can brave the rats in the inner cellar to find clues. Now, you had a better opportunity of studying Mrs Coles than any other lecturer or tutor here. In your opinion, what kind of person was she?'

'Extremely reserved and not very sociable. She appeared to have no very close friends, but then, of course, if she had secretly married and wanted to keep it dark, she was wiser *not* to make close friendships here.'

'She *had* confided in one of the students, though—a girl with whom she'd been at school, I believe.'

'Oh, yes, Miss Bellman. They came up together and asked to be housed in the same hostel.'

'I shall have to talk to Miss Bellman again. Then there is Miss Good.'

'She's not one of mine.'

'No. I must seek her in Miss Considine's house. What is the rule about visitors here?'

'Students' visitors?'

'Yes. Is it ever possible, for example, for the college to put them up?'

'Oh, yes, if there is any special reason.'

'What sort of circumstances would furnish a special reason?'

'At half-term, when most of the students take a long weekend, it is possible for a girl staying up to have a sister or friend to spend the weekend here to keep her company or to use the college as a base from which to go sightseeing.'

'I was not thinking of holiday times.'

'Oh, I see. Well, during term we can accommodate very few visitors. In fact, we don't encourage them at all, except for tea on Saturdays and Sundays, and then they are expected not to arrive before three and to leave before eight.'

'How many visitors could you accommodate here at any one time, apart from during half-term?'

'Two only, unless any students have taken a weekend pass. I have two rooms with twin beds. College rules allow each student a room to herself because she has to use it for study as well as for sleep, so, you see, it would be possible for those two extra beds to go to visitors.'

'Have you so allotted them at any time during this term?'

'No, I have not been asked to do so.'

'Suppose that a student in another hostel, or living in the students' wing of the main college building, wanted to have a visitor for the weekend who could not be accommodated there, would it be possible for an exchange of rooms to be made?'

'I should strongly oppose such an arrangement. In fact, unless Miss McKay made a personal approach to me over such an exchange, I certainly shouldn't sanction it. The students get quite enough distraction here without dodging about from hostel to hostel, swapping beds.' She grinned disarmingly.

'I certainly sympathise with your point of view,' said Dame Beatrice, returning the grin with an alligator leer which appeared to startle her companion.

'Of course,' Miss Paterson added, 'what the students can contrive by means of private arrangements among themselves is another matter entirely.'

'Ah!' said Dame Beatrice, with a wealth of satisfaction in her tone. 'May I have a word with Miss Bellman?'

'Certainly, so far as I'm concerned. The trouble may be to find out where she is and what she's doing, and it may be something that she can't stop doing until she's through with it. You know what this place is like! I'll ring through to the secretary's office and find out which group she's in, and then the big time-table outside the Principal's room will show where she's most likely to be, or, at least, who's supposed to be in charge of her.'

It turned out that Miss Bellman was in Private Study, which was (or should have been), by interpretation, in the library. She was not to be found there. This did not appear to cause Miss Paterson the least degree of surprise.

'The little cormorants spend all their private study periods at the buffet counter,' she explained. 'I should have been surprised if we *had* found her in here. Still, one was bound to try. Come along. I could do with a coffee and dough-nut myself. It's astonishing how hungry one gets. It's the very good air about these parts, I suppose. And the students do a great deal of really tough physical work, of course.'

The buffet counter was at one end of the college dining-room and was thronged with students, some of whom looked guilty, some smug (those who had a Free, Miss Paterson ex-plained), some slightly defiant. They made way for the lecturer and her visitor, and Miss Paterson ordered coffee and doughnuts and then arrested the flight of Miss Bellman with a peremptory announcement that Dame Beatrice would like to speak to her and that she was to bring 'that revolting repast' to one of the dining tables so that they could obtain a little privacy away from the other students.

Miss Bellman, bearing two Cornish pasties and two cakes lavishly decorated with synthetic cream, followed her hostel head to a table and returned for a jug of cocoa and a large china mug.

'For heaven's sake, don't stop eating,' said Miss Paterson, herself dunking a doughnut, 'and do try to answer Dame Beatrice intelligently. Now, Dame Beatrice.'

'I think,' said Dame Beatrice, 'that Miss Bellman might prefer that my questions be put and replied to in private. Let us all refresh ourselves, and then, perhaps . . . ?'

'Oh, I see. Yes. All right, Bellman. Rejoin the herd and then, by the time you get back here, I shall be gone.'

Miss Bellman, with a grateful glance at Dame Beatrice, made her two journeys back to the buffet counter with her provender, and Dame Beatrice, refusing sustenance in the form of the doughnuts, sipped coffee and listened to Miss Paterson's comments on the mentality of students past and present whilst the lecturer disposed of two doughnuts and left the others 'for Bellman, who'll be sure to be able to gobble them up, however much food she's had already.'

She had scarcely vanished through the swing doors when Miss Bellman, who, Dame Beatrice decided, must have been watching for this exit, came up to the table. Dame Beatrice presented her with the doughnuts.

'You know P. G. Wodehouse,' said Miss Bellman, seating herself and seizing one of the gifts. 'Well, when he talks about starving pythons, it's really nothing to what we get like in this place. Myself, I think we're overworked and it's nature's way of ensuring that we don't drop down dead. I never eat like this at home. Did you want to talk about Norah?'

'Yes, of course. Miss Bellman, what *sort* of person was she? I know you've been asked this before, but is there anything you can add, I wonder?'

'I'd call her the lone wolf type.'

'Both lone *and* wolf?'

'Eh? Oh, I see what you mean. Yes, I think she *was* a bit predatory. This boy Coles, you know. I bet, if you could find out the truth, that *she* married *him*, if you see what I mean. Otherwise, why an art student with no money? He can't be much of a catch.'

'How well did you know her?'

'Well, we were at school together, and when we both planned to come here she suggested we tried to get into the same hostel. I wanted to be in the main building, but she wouldn't hear of that. She said we'd be so much more independent in a hostel, and that she'd heard there was more chance of getting weekend passes and late leaves if you weren't directly under the Prin.'s eye. So I gave way. You could have blown me over when she told me she was married. She never, in the ordinary way, told anybody anything. Of course, she swore me to secrecy and, as I couldn't see any reason why I shouldn't promise, I did. If I'd blabbed, it would have been all over the college grape-vine in no time, and the lecturers would have been bound to get wind of it. I don't suppose the Prin. would have minded, in a way, but, of course, she'd have been bound to keep an eye on Coles to make sure her work wasn't suffering, and that sort of thing's such a bind! So I kept it to myself until, well, it sort of had to come out after we knew about the murder.'

'Did her sister ever visit her in college?'

Miss Bellman, who had a mouthful of doughnut, choked.

'No. I had heard at school that she'd *got* an older sister, but it seemed there'd been trouble at home and she never mentioned her after we got here,' she said, as soon as she could utter.

'Come, Miss Bellman! You know better than that! Please be frank.'

'I can guess what you're going to ask me, and there's nothing I can tell you,' said the student, very red in the face.

'I see. Very well, Miss Bellman. I respect your loyalty, although I deplore your reticence—at least, on this occasion. Thank you for the help you have so far given me.'

'I'm sorry,' said Miss Bellman, following Dame Beatrice's lead and rising from table. 'I'd tell you if I felt it would be right, but I *don't* feel it would.'

'I quite understand. You must have had a terribly worrying time.'

They parted at the door, Miss Bellman to attend a lecture which she stigmatised as 'poppycock about tap-roots' and

Dame Beatrice to return to Miss McKay. She found the Principal engaged on the telephone. Miss McKay waved her to a seat and soon put down the receiver.

'So sorry,' she said. 'How did you get on?'

'So well,' Dame Beatrice replied, 'that I want an interview with those students who live in college.'

'We have twenty of them. Do you wish to speak to them all?'

'Yes, please. As you know, there is evidence that, after hostel supper, the missing girl was not seen again. I have reason to suppose that she came over here, to college.'

'Really? For what reason?'

'If I wished to be melodramatic, sensational and realistic, I should say that she came over to college that night to murder her sister, but——'

Miss McKay remained calm. She nodded.

'But that is not the right answer. Please tell me all that you know,' she said.

'It is not a question of knowledge—yet. It is a question of applied logic, I think. Are there any rooms in the students' quarters here, which contain two beds?'

'None.'

'Good. May I speak to the men in charge of the boiler-room before I speak to the students?'

The men in charge of the boiler-room proved to be two in number. They wore dark-brown overalls and were brothers. Their ages might have been forty-five and fifty. What they had to report, in answer to Dame Beatrice's questions, was interesting, to the point and, to her, confidently expected. In other words, so far as they knew, nothing except for the fuel that they themselves had shovelled on, had been put to burn in the boiler furnaces since the summer holiday.

'That had to be cleared up,' said Dame Beatrice. 'Well, let us hope that the rats in the inner cellar won't have eaten every scrap of the overcoat by the time the police get here.'

As Miss McKay was not completely in her confidence, she made no reply to this but agreed that Dame Beatrice should address the in-college students immediately before supper that evening.

She made her appeal to them in the full confidence that if they had anything to tell her she would hear it. Her experience of young people informed her that, reserved and slightly suspicious as they were in the face of authoritative pronouncements, they were ready and willing to co-operate for the general good.

'It is essential,' she concluded, 'that the murderer be found if another life is to be spared. I cannot promise indemnity to the student or students who are prepared to help me, but I can promise that the case or cases will be considered sympathetically. Anyone to whom my words may apply should report to me as soon as possible after the evening study period. I shall be in the secretary's office and I shall be alone there.'

'They'll talk their heads off, you know, during supper and even during Study,' protested Miss McKay, when she and Dame Beatrice had left the hall. Dame Beatrice nodded.

'Exactly what I want,' she declared. 'These difficult decisions are not always best left to the individual conscience.'

She parted from the Principal and went over to Miss Considine's house to interview the pulchritudinous Miss Good.

Miss Good was in high feather. Miss Considine's house had finished supper by the time Dame Beatrice arrived, and Miss Good had received by post that morning an intimation from Mr Cleeves that his father was prepared to 'come across with a decent little farm' so that the marriage could be arranged and would take place immediately their college careers were over.

'I want to know rather more about your ghostly horse-

191

man, Miss Good,' said Dame Beatrice, introduced into the hostel common-room at an hour when the rest of Miss Considine's students were busy, or not, at their books. 'Please do not embroider your answers. If you cannot remember, pray say so in plain terms. This is important.'

'I'm not likely to forget *that* awful night,' said Miss Good, seated upon an upholstered stool opposite her interlocutor, who was occupying an armchair. 'What with leaving my ring at the hotel and then being abandoned at the gates and having to trail back in shoes which hurt me, and then meeting the ghost—well, I've never felt quite the same since. What did you want me to tell you?'

'A little more about the ghostly horseman, as I said. What *shape* was he?'

'Tall and broad and, somehow, bulgy. Like the bear, you know.'

Dame Beatrice did know. She added that she was strongly tempted to ask a leading question.

'You can,' said Miss Good. 'You might not think it, but' I'm not easily influenced.'

Dame Beatrice hesitated no longer.

'I know you were taken by surprise when you saw the apparition,' she said, 'but could it have been possible that this rather shapeless horseman was *carrying* something?'

'Gracious!' exclaimed Miss Good. 'Now you *are* putting ideas into my head! No, honestly, I couldn't say. You see, I was so petrified.' She hesitated, and then gave her lustrous hair a childish toss. 'No,' she said, 'I can't say. It's no good. It *is* a leading question and I could so easily agree. You mean a *body*, don't you? I'd better leave it unsaid. I just don't know.'

Dame Beatrice commended her for her good sense and left her. Miss Good had not retarded the enquiry, and Dame Beatrice was grateful to her. Her next step was to telephone the police to tell them that the college cellars might bear some investigation and then she went into the secretary's office, left vacant at her request, to await any developments which might follow her address to the in-college students.

She had been seated at the secretary's desk for ten minutes or so when there came a gentle tap at the door, and a dark, pale-faced, rather good-looking girl came in. Dame Beatrice invited her to close the door and sit down.

'I suppose I know what you want,' said the girl. 'You want to know that I swapped rooms with Miss Palliser the night before she actually disappeared.'

'That *is* what I want to know. Why did she ask you to make the exchange?'

'She said she'd got some photographs to develop and she wanted to use the college cellar as a dark-room.'

'Was that an unusual reason to give?'

'No, not at all. Heaps of people did it. You see, we've got a photography club in college. The staff encourage it. The animals and plants, you know, and students doing the jobs— it makes a nice exhibition when we have Open Day. Only you're supposed to get permission to use the cellar, because staff baggage and stuff is kept down there, and Palliser (she was in my group, so I knew her, in a way, the way you do know people in your group) hadn't got permission and wasn't going to ask for it.'

'Did she say why?'

'Yes, of course she did. She'd got some negatives of herself and her boy, taken on holiday. Nothing to do with college at all. She was rather a cagey, secretive sort of person, so I wasn't surprised she wanted to develop them in secret. I mean, with the best will in the world, no doubt, the lecturers do take such a *kindly* interest in us and our men. Even those ghastly boys at Highpepper seem to give them a heart-throb if they think we're interested. So I swopped with Palliser for the night, she to occupy my S.B. and me to occupy hers. It's easy enough, as long as you sport your oak and nobody

193

sees you. It's often been done for one reason and another. Why, last year a girl named Désirée Something or other smuggled a boy in, and they occupied one of the double-bedded rooms in Paterson's on a swap basis, and Paterson hadn't a clue.'

Dame Beatrice, who had visualised something of this situation and who, privately, congratulated the young on their enterprise, thanked the student warmly. The case was taking shape at last. She returned to Miss McKay to take her leave and indicated that the police would require to have access to the cellars, probably on the following day.

CHAPTER SEVENTEEN

The Gentlemen Raise Their Voices

'Fritz, who was never taken by surprise by events of this kind, had time to fire before the birds were out of reach.'

Ibid.

THERE was one last port of call and Dame Beatrice, having telephoned the local police, made it before she returned to the village of Wandles Parva. She went to Highpepper Hall.

'I want,' she said to Mr Sellaclough, whom she found sipping his mid-morning glass of Madeira, 'if I may, to interview those of your students who were responsible for introducing dead rats and rhubarb into the Calladale soil. Let me hasten to add that this is no punitive expedition. It is from the highest motives that I desire to possess this information.'

'Take a glass of Madeira with me, and tell me more, Dame Beatrice. I have no doubt that the students responsible will give you every assistance in their power if the matter is one of importance.'

Dame Beatrice accepted the glass of Madeira and recounted as much of the story as was necessary for the object she had in view.

'So, you see,' she concluded, 'it would help a good deal if I could establish, once and for all, that the Calladale horseman was not one of your students dressed up to alarm the young women. If it was not, then there is only one thing for me to think, and I have thought it already.' She told the Principal what she thought had happened.

'Good heavens!' said Mr Sellaclough. 'But what a bizarre notion! Why not a car?'

'I have no doubt that a car was waiting, if what I suspect is true. The reasons for choosing to leave Calladale on horseback may have been to avoid making the noise a car would be bound to make and also because the ghostly hood and voluminous attire made an effective disguise. It would be too much to expect that you know of a heavy grey horse in the neighbourhood of Calladale? It had not occurred to me until very recently that the horse must be traced, but my latest researches have revealed that it is essential to find it.'

'I'll put it to the college at lunch about the rats and rhubarb, unless you'd care to address the gathering yourself. It might be quite a good idea if you did. I don't suppose young men in the mass hold any terrors for you, do they?'

So the midday meal at Highpepper was enlivened by the presence at the staff table of a small, black-haired, very sharp-eyed old lady who was introduced by Mr Sellaclough as 'that very distinguished psychiatrist and investigator of crime, Dame Beatrice Lestrange Bradley,' and who rose to the sound of slightly ironical cheering.

'I will not detain you for more than a moment, gentlemen,' she said. 'I am here to invite two of those who interred the rats and the rhubarb to dine with me in the private room of the hotel which I am led to believe you are accustomed to patronise in Garchester. Perhaps I might be permitted to have a word with my guests at the conclusion of the meal.'

'In my study,' said Mr Sellaclough. 'And I am asked by Dame Beatrice to say that nothing in the nature of disciplinary action is contemplated. The matter under review is an exceptionally serious one, but has nothing to do (so far as we know) with the college.'

He took his guest straight to his sanctum and in a few minutes there came a tap at the door. Mr Sellaclough pressed his buzzer and Soames and Preddle came in.

'I'll leave you,' he said. 'Sit down, Mr Soames and Mr Preddle. Gentlemen, you may smoke.'

'I know that your time is very fully occupied,' said Dame Beatrice to the students, as soon as the door had closed behind their Principal, 'so I will come straight to the point. Where did the rats come from?'

The two young men looked at one another. Then Soames replied that they had come from 'an old rat-catcher chap named Benson.' He added that he hoped the girls at Calladale had not been annoyed.

'Where can I get hold of Benson?'

Preddle told her that, far from his time being fully occupied, he had little or nothing to do that afternoon and would escort her to Benson's cottage if she would give him time to change. Beautifully dressed and carrying an impeccable hat, he returned in short order. Dame Beatrice found Mr Sellaclough, with Preddle's help, thanked him for his co-operation and his hospitality and was introduced to Soames' new car, a dashing sports affair in silver and bright blue.

Old Benson's cottage proved to be about a mile from the front gates of Highpepper and to be picturesquely situated in front of a small wood. The old man was chopping some kindling, but looked up when the car braked opposite his garden gate.

'Good-day, sir,' he said to Preddle. 'Job for the college again?'

'No, not this time, Benson. Dame Beatrice wants a word with you.'

'It's the drains,' said Benson. 'If there wasn't drains, there wouldn't be varmint. You wants your drains clearin' out.'

'She doesn't want you to go ratting for her, you old chump! I said she wants a word with you.'

'Not about rats?'

'Yes, about rats, but not my own personal rats,' Dame Beatrice explained. 'What I want to know, Mr Benson, is where the rats came from that you sold to Mr Soames and Mr Preddle at the beginning of this term.'

'It was a bit before the beginning of term, actually,' said Preddle. 'You remember, Benson? You got us a splendid collection. We told you we were experimenting with them as manure.'

Benson received this reminder with wheezy mirth.

'Tell you anything, the young gentlemen will,' he confided to Dame Beatrice. 'Course, I never believed it. Up to one of their larks, I reckoned. Why, I could tell you . . .'

'Yes, another time, you old liar,' said Preddle. 'Dame Beatrice hasn't got all the afternoon to waste listening to your tall stories. Fire away, Dame Beatrice, or he'll talk you into a coma.'

Dame Beatrice accepted this advice.

'All I want to know,' she said, 'is where those rats came from.'

'Where they come from? Why, all over the place. The farms round 'ere is fair drippin' wi' rats. Drop from the thatch, they do.'

'Do you know Calladale, the agricultural college for women, twenty-five miles from here?'

'Ah, that I do. Why, I remember, one time, they 'ad to fetch me in to put down their varmint. Somebody 'adn't 'ad no more sense than to store 'op-manure in the cellars. They was knee-deep—ah, waist-deep—in rats. My word! I never seed so many o' the varmint in my life, and when Mr Soames and Mr Preddle came along orderin' me to find 'em an 'underd rats, I says to 'em, I says, "Why don't you gennelmen go to Calladale College?" I says. You'll mind me makin' the remark, Mr Preddle, sir? "Why don't you go over to Calladale College?" I says. "That's where they grows rats on their gooseberry bushes." Them was my words, wasn't they, Mr Preddle, sir?'

'Just about.'

Old Benson chuckled and threw a bit of stick at a cat which was creeping up on a robin.

'And do you know what?' he said, an expression of great cunning spreading itself over his wizened and grimy countenance, 'That's just where the bulk o' they rats o' yourn came from, Mr Preddle, sir. Never knoo that afore, did 'ee?'

'Good Lord!' exclaimed Preddle. 'Talk about carrying coals to Newcastle!'

'But this is fantastic!' said Dame Beatrice. 'Tell me, Mr Benson, did you find any difficulty in getting into the Calladale cellars?'

'Difficulty? Why should I? Me and the boiler-'and there, we've knowed each other since 'e was born. 'E's me nevvy.'

'Indeed! Did Miss McKay know that you went ratting in her cellar?'

'No need for 'er to know. 'E pops me into the 'ouse, Tom do, and down the cellar, and we makes a goodish rattling noise to scare 'em into their 'oles, and then I ins with me apparatus and smokes 'em out and the dog, 'e gets plenty. That's a good dog, that is. Belongs to the landlord at the Bull. Of course, I don't allus work wi' a dog, but the gennelmen needin' the carcasses nice and fresh like, it were the best way to oblige 'em, so I made out. Never git rid of them rats in that cellar, I reckon, not while there's still the smell o' that 'op-manure about, which it smelt like a brewery first time they called me in.'

'Did any rats escape from the inner cellar to the concreted one where the college staff keep their heavy baggage?'

'Nary a one, mum. We see to that, my nevvy and me. Wouldn't 'ave done to 'ave 'em gnorin' the ladies' baggage. No. We scares 'em into their 'oles and then we opens the door and nips in quick, and shuts the door be'ind us, and then I smokes 'em out wi' me apparatus and the dog done the rest. No, you can rest assured, mum, that if there's a complaint about rats gettin' into that baggage-room down there, it wasn't nothing to do with me nor young Tom nor old Towser.'

'There is no complaint,' said Dame Beatrice. 'I am much obliged to you for your information.' She tipped the old man and Preddle drove her back to the college. 'Seven o'clock this evening, then,' she said to him as they parted.

'With a rose in my hair,' said Preddle, 'and old Soames on a lead with a tartan bow on his collar.'

There was no doubt but that the saloon bar of the hotel had become a home from home to Highpepper youth. The door which led into it from the hotel vestibule was open, and Dame Beatrice, glancing in, discovered it to be crowded with young men who bore the unmistakable Highpepper stamp. They were, for the most part, extremely well-dressed, were large and healthy, had loud voices and brown faces. They held pint pots of beer and exchanged ribaldry and repartee with the two giggling barmaids, and when their pots needed replenishing they threw heaps of small change in a lordly manner on the bar counter where it had to be picked up wet with the overflow of that generous topping from the draught-beer which the barmaids inevitably gave.

Dame Beatrice enquired at the reception desk for the location of the private dining-room she had bespoken and a porter was summoned to show her the way to it. Scarcely was she installed when her guests arrived. Dame Beatrice drank sherry and the young men pink gin, and dinner was served at half-past seven. Goose with apple and prune stuffing followed what Dame Beatrice described as an honest, old-fashioned Brown Windsor soup, and the repast continued with apricot pie and ice-cream and concluded with a savoury.

The young men, respectful of good and plentiful food since, like the students at Calladale, they lived from one meal

200

to another and were always hungry in between, entertained her almost affectionately in a relaxed, delightful way and, at the end, when the waitress had cleared the table, they lounged in two of the armchairs with which the room was provided and invited their hostess to come to the point.

'What do you want to know about the rats and the rhubarb?' asked Soames. 'You know where the rats came from, and we can soon tell you about the rhubarb. At our end-of-term dance it formed the sole subject of conversation of a young girl whom some of us felt called upon, as hosts, to squire round the ballroom. So I said "Why not?" The rats, I admit, were an afterthought, and not a particularly good one. Now to tell us what it's all in aid of.'

'The murder of Carrie Palliser, the young woman whose body was found in the coach. It was owing to the fact that the Calladale students were anxious to return the rhubarb, which they felt certain had come from Highpepper, that the body was discovered at the time. There is not much doubt that whoever put it there hoped it would lie hidden much longer.'

'More difficult to identify it,' said Preddle, nodding his head. 'Wasn't it thought at first to be the younger sister, though? I saw something in the local paper, didn't I, indicating that it was the elder one, after all?'

'That is impossible, Mr Preddle! The police have been most careful to keep that particular bit of information out of the news. The dead girl was buried in the name by which she was identified, and she was identified as Norah Coles, *née* Palliser, a student at Calladale College. Officially, the body is still that of Norah Coles.'

'Then where did I get it from?' asked Preddle, frowning. 'Because it really isn't a new idea to me that it was the older sister.'

'I would very much like to know where you got it from.

201

Possibly from Mr Basil? I believe he was once a lecturer at Highpepper.'

'He was, yes, but that was long before my time. No, it wasn't from Basil. Could it have been from one of the Calladale girls?'

'That also seems unlikely. But, if so, which one, Mr Preddle?'

Preddle, perplexed, scratched his head.

'How can I make myself remember? Let's see. I know so many of them in a vague and amateurish way. All the same, I suppose I *ought* to be able . . .' He frowned. 'Oh, yes, I know! It didn't seem possible, you see, as I pointed out to Miss Colin.'

'How, not possible?'

'Well, we heard that Miss Palliser—Mrs Coles, the one at Calladale, of course—was going off on a holiday toot with Basil. You reminded me that he used to be one of the lecturers at our place. Well, from what I can learn, it was quite incredible that one of Basil's piecee-missies should have gone and got herself murdered. Quite out of character, if you understand me.'

'I don't understand you, Mr Preddle. I knew of the holiday adventure, of course. They appear to have spent a week together at the Bracklesea holiday camp. Then we were given to understand that Mr Basil went climbing in the Cairngorms with a friend and broke his leg. This report of his accident turned out to be false.'

'The Basil *I've* heard about wouldn't have gone nearer the Cairngorms than Sauchiehall Street,' said Soames. 'My older brother was up when Basil was at our place. He seems to have been a bit of a legend. I can't think why Ma McKay took him on. Surely his reputation had gone before him?'

'One can hardly think so. Some facts are known to students, I believe, which would be received with incredulity in the Staff Common Room.'

'You're telling *us*, Dame Beatrice!' said Soames, grinning. 'But to Preddle's point. Why "out of character," old man?'

'Once a girl gets into Basil's grip, she stays gripped until he's tired of her. He hadn't got tired of Mrs Coles. They used to meet in road-houses and motoring hotels and so on, near Garchester, and frequently, at that.'

'The week at the holiday camp may have caused an old man's fancy to shy away from thoughts of love,' suggested Soames. 'Oh, I received some instruction in Eng. Lit. at school,' he added, for the benefit of Dame Beatrice.

'It does not appear to be the case that Mr Basil had fallen out of love with Mrs Coles,' said she. 'When he pretended that he was in hospital with a broken leg, Mrs Coles was keeping house for him in Northern Ireland. She was thought to have returned to college at the beginning of term and then disappeared. Several weeks later came the discovery of the body which was identified by her mother. Of course, the sisters were much alike. But I confess that I do not take your point, Mr Preddle, that it could not have been Mrs Coles' body.'

'Well, thank God for my good dinner and if you *must* know, Dame Beatrice, *she's been seen*. I remember everything now.'

Dame Beatrice was not often completely taken aback, but Preddle's statement astonished her beyond measure. She did not ask him whether he was certain that his information was correct. She felt sure it was.

'Tell me more, Mr Preddle,' she said. 'We cannot leave it at that. Chapter, verse and witnesses, if you please.'

'I had it from my tutor, Gastien. The best plan would be for you to meet him. He was with Upminster, only Upminster doesn't know the girl, so he won't be much good to you as a witness. I don't know how Gastien came to recognise her, as a matter of fact. Oh, yes, I do, too! He is—or was—very pally with Basil, so I dare say he saw the girl several times with him. I don't suppose he realised that she was a Calla-dale student, though. His brain's very myopic except where his job and his beer are concerned.'

'But this sounds as though Mrs Coles went about openly with Mr Basil.'

'Of course she did. Basil always has some wench or other in tow. He's notorious for it. I heard he got the sack from our place—only it was given out that he had relinquished the job of his own free will, because that sounded better—because he bestowed his favours on one of the housemaids. Of course, I don't know whether that's true. It may just be a bit of common or garden slander. Personally, I should think it *is* that; otherwise Sellaclough would hardly have let Miss McKay take him on her staff. Still, straws show which way the wind blows, and there's no smoke without fire.'

'You do not know, of course, what Mr Gastien thought when he saw Mrs Coles, but do you know, more or less, when it was?'

'I do know what he thought, as it happens. Upminster was in the showers with me last Wednesday, and as we were drying ourselves he said, "Rather a rum thing happened this morning. I was in the bar with Gastien, sampling the brew, when in walked a female dressed in black, with a scarf pulled round her face as though she'd got toothache or some-thing, and asked for twenty cigarettes and a box of matches. Gastien didn't turn and look at her, but she was reflected in the mirror behind all those bottles and Toby jugs and tankards and things. When she spotted him she simply turned and bolted without the cigarettes and matches. Gastien turned and looked fairly thoughtfully at the door, which was, as usual, propped open, and said, "My boy, you had better take me home. This is the kind of thing which has made men sign the pledge, and, what's more, stick to it. I've seen a ghost. I thought that a young woman Basil used to trot around came in here and asked for cigarettes and matches." '

'Yes?' said Dame Beatrice.

'Well, of course, Upminster told him a female *had* just been in and asked for cigarettes and matches, and described her. He said that Gastien looked at him in an owlish sort of way, and said, "She couldn't be the girl I'm thinking of. The girl I'm thinking of is dead." You have a talk with Gastien, Dame Beatrice, and get it straight from the horse's mouth.'

Dame Beatrice did this at the following midday. Having been apprised of his habits, she met Mr Gastien in the hotel bar at precisely a quarter to twelve, it being his daily custom, it appeared, to leave college at eleven sharp, whatever duties he was engaged upon at Highpepper, and drive into Garchester for his midday refreshment. He usually brought a couple of Highpepper students with him, and it was understood that these bought his chaser of gin when he had had sufficient beer, and drove him back to the college.

By previous arrangement, the two students on this particular and important occasion were Preddle and Soames, who were in a position to introduce him to Dame Beatrice and include her in the party.

'Basil?' said Mr Gastien, when his thirst was somewhat alleviated and the object of the meeting had been introduced. 'Oh, yes, Basil. About time he came back, I should think. He *isn't* back, is he? Can't be, or that young woman of his wouldn't be knocking about on her own. And she *is* knocking about on her own. Met her—well, I won't say *met* her, because she walked in here last Wednesday morning when I was with Lord Robert Upminster and dashed out again as soon as she realised I'd spotted her. Girl isn't dead, as we were given to understand. Something very fishy must have been going on.'

'Murder has been going on, as we knew,' said Dame

Beatrice, 'but a mistake was made by the person who was called upon to identify the body.'

'So *that* was it! Glad I know. Thought I was seeing things. Thank you, Mr Preddle. A double, eh? Very generous. Very generous indeed.'

Preddle received this tribute—a stock phrase with Mr Gastien—with a polite inclination of the head. His tutor swallowed the gin at a gulp, smacked his lips, licked them and looked expectantly at Soames, who rose immediately and went to the bar counter. The little ceremony was repeated, but this time the gin was sniffed at and sipped. Mr Gastien then glanced expectantly at Dame Beatrice. Scarcely thinking that this was a hint to buy him a third gin, as he still had almost all of that provided by Soames, she continued her remarks.

'Yes. Mrs Coles had an older sister who so much resembled her in appearance that the distressed mother, who was called upon to identify the body, mistook her for the younger daughter because she was wearing the Calladale blazer. The face, in any case, was much disfigured.'

'Oh, well, that would seem to let Basil out. Always afraid the girl had tried to blackmail him or something, and he'd got rid of her. Quite a relief.'

'It is not in the public interest, at present, that the wrongful identification should be disclosed.'

'No, no, of course not. I won't breathe a word. You fellows must be discreet, too.' He sipped gin. 'Murderer must be allowed to think he's got away with it. The police will get him easier that way. Well, this is all very interesting, I must say. Let me get you more sherry, Dame Beatrice. Are you staying here to lunch?'

'No. I am lunching in Calladale College, at the invitation of Miss McKay. No more sherry, thank you.'

'What I can't understand,' said Soames, 'is why the girl chose to come in *here* for cigarettes and matches. I mean, it

206

wasn't early closing day or anything of that sort. She could have gone into a shop. Girls of that age don't usually patronise a bar on their own.'

'For that very reason she chose to do so, I take it,' said Dame Beatrice. 'Dressed as she was, and with her face covered up, she was less likely to be recognised at the bar counter than she might have been at a shop in this rather small town. I don't suppose the barmaids had ever troubled to notice her before. It is not likely that she had ever ordered drinks from them. Her escort would have done everything necessary in that way.'

'I doubt whether Basil often brought her in here,' said Mr Gastien, 'but, if he did, it would be as you say. I mean, look at it! It's always like this in here, especially on Saturdays and Sundays, and those, if I know anything of the regulations at Calladale, are the only days on which, in the ordinary way, she would be able to get away from college. Oh, there's the mid-week half-holiday, of course.'

The dense and noisy crowd of young men who, by this time, were thronging the bar, certainly gave point to his words. Persons seated at the tables would be almost completely screened from the barmaids. Dame Beatrice nodded.

'The most interesting aspect of the whole business,' she observed, 'is that, knowing (as she must do by this time) that a mistake in identification has been made, she does not wish to put it right, but hides and skulks in this extraordinary way. There can be two possible explanations. Either she killed her sister or else she herself is in danger. I prefer the latter theory. I think she goes—or believes she goes—in fear of her life, and that is why the police have not found her. In any case, on their own submission, they are looking for a dead girl, not a living one.'

CHAPTER EIGHTEEN

Squeak, Piggy, Squeak

'This conversation hindered us in unloading the sledge.'
Ibid.

DAME BEATRICE'S first action, after she had left the hotel, was to drive to the Garchester police station and inform the inspector in charge of the case that Mrs Coles had been seen in Garchester on the previous Wednesday.

The inspector invoked what Dame Beatrice took to be a local deity and raised his hands in frenzied appeal.

'I'll skin myself and the chaps I've put on the job!' he said. 'Actually *seen* in Garchester? Who by, madam? I mean, do you think it's reliable information? You see, we'd given up thinking that she was alive, and have been searching woods and dragging ponds for her.'

'As it comes from one of the lecturers at Highpepper Agricultural College, I think we must take it at its face value, although it certainly throws my calculations to the winds. I thought she was still in Ireland.'

'Then the next job, apart from continuing to look out for her around here, is to pull in that Mr Basil who's been leading the Calladale Principal up the garden all this time. I suppose he's been sacked from the college?'

'He received his notice as soon as Miss McKay was apprised of the deception that he had been practising.'

'Serve him right, the twister! Well, I'm much obliged, Dame Beatrice. I've no doubt he can tell us where the girl is. Apart from that, he's got a lot of explaining to do on his own behalf, has that clever gentleman. If he wasn't where he said he was, at the time of the murder, he'll have some rather awkward questions put to him. That broken leg business could have been his alibi, and very likely was intended that way, madam. Now, thanks to you, it's fallen to pieces. He's got to tell us just what he wanted it for. You say he told you it was to study Irish methods of selling bacon, but, to my mind, a man who earns his living by teaching about pig-rearing rather than owning his own pigs, can hardly get away with *that* for a story. What's your own opinion, Dame Beatrice?'

'It coincides with yours. I certainly do not believe that Mr Basil went to Northern Ireland to study pig-marketing. What he did go for we have yet to discover, although that aspect of the matter becomes clearer.'

'Exactly, madam. Right. Well, it won't be much trouble to get hold of him, now that we know where he is, and I'll let you know how we get on.'

The extradition (if that sinister phrase may be used to describe the transference of a suspect from one part of Great Britain to another) of Piggy Basil was accomplished, as the inspector had prophesied, without difficulty or loss of time. The next interview with him took place at the Garchester police station, whose hospitality Basil had grudgingly consented to accept.

'It seems pretty irregular to me,' he had grumbled. 'You haven't got me here on a charge. You've nothing on earth against me except that I knew this missing girl.'

'All right, sir,' the inspector had replied. 'You don't have to spend the night here against your wishes, but we understood you to say that you had got through your money, lost your job and had nowhere to go.'

'It's blinking coercion,' said Piggy, next morning, continuing his overnight grouse. 'You fish a chap back from Ireland where he's harmlessly learning a bit more about his job, get him the perishing sack, shove him in the lock-up as though he's a damned drunk and then haul him up for your blistering third-degree stuff before he's hardly finished his breakfast.'

The time was nine o'clock, the breakfast, served at eight in the inspector's own quarters, had consisted of porridge, eggs and bacon, toast, marmalade and coffee. Moreover, the third-degree was not part of the inspector's method. He pointed out this last fact, and suggested that the sooner they got down to brass-tacks the sooner Mr Basil could follow his own devices.

'Now, sir,' he said, 'we have it on reliable information—from an eye-witness, I may say, who knows her well by sight —that Mrs Coles was actually here in Garchester a few days ago and that she bolted as soon as she realised that she had been recognised. What have you to say about that, sir?'

'Nothing. I didn't know she *was* in Garchester. If what you say is true, your flat-footed gangsters couldn't have been doing their job. How come *they* didn't spot her?'

'That's neither here nor there, sir, and no business of yours, if I may say so. And it wouldn't be against your interests to give us a little help. Now, sir, what about it?'

'I don't like it. I know you busies. Well, what do you want to know?'

'What *did* take you to Northern Ireland, sir?'

'Oh, hang it all! Well, if you *must* know, I was on a toot.'

'You went there with Mrs Coles, sir?'

'Confound you, yes!'

'Why did you stay there after she had returned to college?'

'Because we'd fixed it up that she was to rejoin me there as soon as she could.'

'So that accounts for her disappearance from college, does it?'

'It does. I knew what I was doing, all right. I knew it was a mad thing to do; I knew it was wrong, if you like. But I did it, and we've been together in Ireland ever since. Well, not quite ever since, but up to a week or so ago. Then Mrs Coles got cold feet, I think. She said she was going back home.'

'Not "going back to college?" She didn't say that?'

'Can't see what difference it makes, but she said she was going back home.'

'Did you understand her to mean she was going to her mother's home, or did she intend to live with Mr Coles?'

'Why, her mother's home, of course. So far as I've gathered, Coles hasn't a home. He lives in cheap digs in London.'

'Did you and Mrs Coles quarrel, sir, may I ask?'

'Not that I remember.'

'Was Mrs Coles still in Ireland when her sister died?'

'As I've never been told when her sister died, I can't tell you, but if it was . . .'

'Never mind, sir. Guessing won't help us.'

'Date of murder a deep, dark secret, eh? Well, when you've found Mrs Coles, you can ask her herself where she was when her sister died. I couldn't care less, but I think the chances are she was with me.'

'What do you mean? You couldn't care less, sir? I should have thought her whereabouts would concern you?'

'I mean that you're trying to trap me. Well, I'm not going to be trapped. If I say any more, it will be in the presence of my lawyer.'

'Very good, sir. You are quite within your rights there. But I hope you will soon get in contact with him. Keeping back information which might assist the police in the execution of their duty can be a serious matter, you know.'

'What's Piggy up to?' asked Laura, when Dame Beatrice had been given a report of the conversation and had detailed it to her secretary.

'Trying to cover his tracks,' said Carey. 'Fancy the chump trying to get away with that hospital alibi, though! You'd

211

think he'd have had the sense to realise that it was bound to blow up on him sooner or later.'

'Oh, I don't know,' argued Laura. 'Given a staunch chap in the hospital bed and no snoopers, I don't see why he shouldn't have pulled it off. It was just his rotten luck that Dame B. and I should have rumbled.'

'What *did* give you the clue?'

'The description the matron gave of his character,' said Dame Beatrice, to whom the question was addressed. 'Once our suspicions were aroused, the rest was simple.'

'What's the next move?' asked Laura.

'I think we must track down the ghost-horse. It we can identify him and his owner we may be able to find out who hired him.'

'And for what purpose?'

'If my suspicions are leading us to the truth, we shall not be told for what purpose he was hired. We must imagine it for ourselves. Once we have a correct picture, we may know who murdered Carrie Palliser and the reason for her death.'

'Do you really think so?' asked Carey.

'*I* really think so,' said Laura. 'To go further, I would say that some person or persons stood to gain by her death; but whether they stood to gain in money, in kind or in personal safety is something I cannot postulate, although my feeling is for the last-named.'

Her employer cackled harshly, but Carey asked:

'You mean that the dead woman had the goods on them? Knew some secret or other?'

'And *what* secret or other isn't difficult to determine,' said Laura, with a haughty glance at Dame Beatrice. 'After all, Mrs Coles *was* married and she *did* choose to leave her new-wedded lord and go off with Piggy Basil, didn't she? In other words, she was making the best of two worlds and she was being blackmailed for it, and you can't wonder at it.

She was an absolute gift to anybody unscrupulous enough to accept her.'

'Is that your theory?' Carey demanded of his aunt. She pursed her lips into a little beak and shrugged her thin shoulders.

'It was one of my theories, but there is one circumstance in particular which hardly makes it the most likely. Well, we need not find ourselves at a standstill. There are various courses open to us.'

'Such as?'

'Such as probing further into the dead girl's past,' said Laura. 'It certainly seems to have been a bit murky. I suppose that involves another visit to the Biancinis.'

'First, I think, to Mr Coles,' said Dame Beatrice.

'Who's going to talk to him this time?' demanded Laura.

'I have some definite questions to put to him, so I think I will talk to him myself. Ring him up and find out when it will be convenient for me to visit him.'

When she turned up on the appointed day, Coles presented himself in a new suit, new shoes and with his hair cut. He referred obliquely but intelligibly to these splendours by telling Dame Beatrice that he had an evening job teaching pottery in a youth club and had done some interior decorating. She congratulated him and asked whether his course at the art school would last very much longer.

'I'd thought of carrying on until June,' he replied, 'but now this business of Norah has turned up, I'm thinking of emigrating and taking a job in Australia.'

'What kind of job?'

'Anything I can get.'

'Rather a waste of your training.'

'Oh, I don't know. If Norah had lived, and we'd had that smallholding, I don't suppose I'd have had much time for painting except painting our humble shack. Anyway, I'll be glad to get out of the country as soon as those blistering lawyers will let me have my money.'

'I see. What I really wanted from you, Mr Coles, is further information about your wife's past life.'

'She was scarcely old enough to have a past life. Of course, she was a pretty fast worker, I know, but she couldn't have collected any vast number of purple patches. She wouldn't have had the time, especially once she'd gone to college, would she?'

'You did know she had an older sister?'

'An older sister? Yes, I did, but I never met her. I don't think the two of them got on. Anyway, the sister didn't live at home much. I gathered—yes, I remember now—that she was some sort of a bad hat.'

'Yes, she was a thief.'

'Oh, Lord! Norah never mentioned anything definite, I'm certain. Just gave the impression that she was generally unsatisfactory.'

'I see. Now, please think back, Mr Coles, and tell me of anything or anybody in Mrs Coles' life that could account in any way for what has happened.'

Coles shook his head.

'Complete blank,' he said, 'unless this chap Basil got fed up and made away with her. Such things do happen. I mean, it's more than likely he didn't know she was married. If he found out—supposing he was fond of her—don't you think he might have seen red?'

'Ah, of course, you know she deceived you with this Basil. Even so, the means by which her death was accomplished seem to rule him out. He isn't that sort of man—or so I am told.'

'I should have thought, being at an agricultural college, he'd have known all about vegetable poisons.'

'Yes, there's that, I suppose, although I don't know that there is any real connection between spotted hemlock and

214

pigs. Besides, when would he have had an opportunity to administer the poison? It couldn't have been during the holiday they spent together, because she arrived back home safe and well. Never mind. Let us change the subject. If anything useful to the enquiry occurs to you, perhaps you will let me know.'

'It wasn't *like* Norah to let herself be bumped off. She was a downy bird, you know, with a very strong instinct for self-preservation,' said Coles. He hesitated, looked very thoughtful, and added, 'Besides, she hated celery, she wouldn't eat parsnips, and she always said anything with parsley in it or on it made her sick. So that would leave the spotted hemlock merchant rather at a loss, I should have thought.'

'How do you know so much about the various flavours which are attributed to the stem and root of spotted hemlock, Mr Coles? Are you a botanist in disguise?'

'Oh, no. It's what I heard said at the inquest, that's all. I've a pretty good verbal memory. I don't suppose I'd ever heard of spotted hemlock before that.'

'Well, at any rate, what you have just said is certainly very valuable.'

'Only in a negative sense, I'm afraid.'

'By no means. It strengthens very considerably my belief that I know the identity of the murderer.'

'Really? I say, that's good going. Well, thank you again for coming. When I visited you I so much enjoyed your hospitality and the use of your car. We, the impoverished, do appreciate a touch of luxury now and again. *Must* you go? Good-bye, then, for now.'

The car drove off, and Laura, who had waited impatiently at the Stone House to obtain a report of the conversation, said, as she returned to the warmth and comfort of the library and its fire, taking Dame Beatrice with her :

'A bit imaginative, that young man, wouldn't you say?'

'No, I should *not* say so, child. If he had more imagination, he wouldn't be nearly so talkative.'

'Oh, I see what you mean. What are you going to do next?'

'I am going to ask to be allowed to overhear the next police interrogation of Mr Basil. There is a point I wish to establish, and Mr Basil, if he will, can prove it for me.'

'And if he won't?'

'I have a scheme for persuading him.'

'Oh? May I ask what it is?'

'As I might need your co-operation, you may, but I shall try him with a straightforward appeal first. So let us relax until tomorrow, when we return to Garchester. Before we relax, though, perhaps you would be good enough to ring up the police station there and obtain the required permission.'

Laura did this, and returned with the news that the police were not satisfied with Basil, and that Dame Beatrice would be welcome to listen to his evidence.

'If any,' Laura added. 'The inspector thinks he may turn very obstinate. If he does, I suppose he could be charged with being an accessory to the crime.'

'He *is* an accessory to the crime,' said Dame Beatrice. 'I am perfectly certain of that. The only thing is, I am not sure that he knows the identity of the criminal.'

Laura gazed at her in a silence pregnant with suspicion.

'Is this a leg-pull?' she enquired at last. Dame Beatrice cackled.

'Your legs are long enough already,' she replied, inspecting those handsome appendages, which were encased in tapering trousers of the Menzies hunting tartan. 'I should not dream of pulling either of them. How near to the Arthurian ideal of knighthood do you suppose Mr Basil to be?'

'Miles and miles and miles away from it. He's the bounder complete, I should say.'

'I am not so sure.' She did not enlarge upon this, but sent to order the car for nine o'clock on the following morning. They drove to Calladale College, where Dame Beatrice had a conversation with Miss McKay in which she recounted the talk she had had with Coles.

'Of course, he still doesn't know that the dead girl was the sister, and not his wife,' said Miss McKay. 'Didn't you think you ought to tell him? He's got to know, sooner or later, and you would break the news more gently than most people. Is it right to keep from him what will give him almost unbearable relief and pleasure?'

'At the present stage of the enquiry it would not be at all a good idea to enlighten him,' said Dame Beatrice, very decidedly.

'Oh, well, I suppose you know best. The only thing is, where *is* the wretched Coles girl?'

On the following morning Dame Beatrice went to Garchester police station.

'He's staying as my guest,' said the inspector. 'We've nothing on him, you see, and he seems prepared now to co-operate. He'll be here at any moment. What have you got to tell us before he comes?'

'Nothing, but when the interview is over, if we're not completely satisfied, I want you to witness an experiment.'

'Not a reconstruction of the crime, madam? I don't go for that kind of thing very much. Too French, in my opinion, to suit our English ideas.'

'Not a reconstruction of *the* crime—by which, I imagine, you mean the murder of Carrie Palliser—but a reconstruction of *a* crime, yes. That is to say, a reconstruction of what, I suppose, the *law* would consider was a crime. To my mind, however—but we won't anticipate.'

'As Henry V did *not* say when he tried on his father's crown,' suggested Laura. A constable came in at this moment to announce that Mr Basil was at the inspector's disposal.

Piggy was looking the worse for wear. His heavy face was so pale that it gave the impression that he had not shaved, for the dark hair-roots pigmented the skin on his cheeks and chin. He bowed to Dame Beatrice and seated himself on the chair which the inspector indicated. He placed pudgy, large hands on his knees and leaned back.

'What is it this time?' he asked; but his tone indicated weariness, not curiosity and certainly not belligerence.

'Just another word or two, Mr Basil.' The inspector was brisk. 'We'd appreciate a little co-operation on a certain matter.'

'Yes? Oh, well, fire away.'

'Where is Mrs Coles?'

Piggy stared at him with the eyes of a defunct fish. There was a pause.

'Your guess is as good as mine, Inspector. I haven't a clue.'

'She has been seen and recognised here in Garchester, as I have already told you, and that quite recently. Now, Mr Basil, we want Mrs Coles and we want her badly, and we are pretty sure you know where she is.'

'I don't, I tell you. I haven't set eyes on her since we parted in Northern Ireland.'

'Well, sir, if that's your story, and you intend to stick to it, I have to warn you that you are placing yourself in a very dangerous position.'

'That's as may be. I've done nothing against the law.'

'You failed to report a death, Mr Basil,' said Dame Beatrice. Piggy shrugged his fleshy shoulders.

'You can't prove that,' he said. 'In any case, it was not my business to report it.'

'You admit that you knew of a death which nobody reported?'

'I admit nothing. My conscience is quite clear. What is the charge you are bringing? My failure to report whose death?'

'That of Mrs Coles' sister, Miss Carrie Palliser.'

'But why *should* I report her death? It had nothing to do with me.'

'I propose to take you up on that last statement, Mr Basil. I will undertake to prove to you that I *know* it had something to do with you. I will show *what* it had to do with you, and I will tell you why you acted as you did, and how mistaken you were.'

'Mistaken? Are you sure?' Colour came into his face. 'If you can prove *that*—or don't you mean what I think you mean?'

'I shall leave that question unanswered. It will answer itself in time. Thank you, Inspector. I do not need to stay any longer.'

CHAPTER NINETEEN

The Grey Mare's Ghost

'. . . she would rise, lie down, turn, walk, trot or gallop at
the command of her leader.'

Ibid.

'Now,' said Dame Beatrice, when she and Laura were at the
hotel in Garchester where they had taken rooms, 'we must
hire, beg, borrow, steal or even purchase, a grey horse. A
draught animal would be best, as it has to carry two persons.
I wonder whether we can persuade some brewers' drayman
to oblige us?'

'They take the stuff round to the pubs by lorry nowadays,
don't they? Why don't you let me ring up Highpepper?
Somebody there is sure to know of a grey.'

'An excellent idea! By all means do that.'

Laura returned with the news that nobody at Highpepper
possessed or hired a grey horse, but that the Garchester
cricket team used one to pull the heavy roller and that, out
of the season, it was returned to a farmer who lived on the
western outskirts of the town.

'The same horse as Miss Good saw that night, I'll bet,'
added Laura, at the end of her triumphant recital. 'You said
once that if we found that horse we'd find the murderer,
didn't you?'

'I have no recollection of it. If I *did* say so, I was jumping
to conclusions which have proved to be unwarranted. Nevertheless, we may be able to establish a connection between
Mr Basil and the dead girl if it *is* the same horse.'

The farmer was willing to let his grey horse out on hire for a Lady Godiva item in a pageant.

'Of course,' said Laura, who, at her own wish, was doing the lying, 'we're not actually *doing* the pageant until the spring, but we want time to assemble the props. Will you send the horse over to Calladale College tomorrow afternoon?'

'Too far. Her won't go in a horse-box and it's a waste of a lad's time to ride her over, her being slow-moving, do you see? Why don't you bring your good people over here?'

'Well, *they* can't spare the time, either. I suppose you don't know of anybody nearer the college who owns a grey cart-horse?'

The farmer shook his head.

'There's young Jem Townsend owns a dapple,' he said, 'and there's old Tom Garter owns a blue roan, but for Lady Godiva you'd be better off with an old white pony such as Colonel Grant's got for his little grand-niece.'

Laura thanked him, regretted that they could not come to terms and asked where the dapple and the blue roan could be found. The farmer, slightly surprised that even a stranger should not know where young Jem Townsend and old Tom Carter lived, supplied the required information and wished her good day, asking, with twinkling eye as he eyed Laura's splendid proportions, whether she herself was cast for the part of Lady Godiva. Laura told him to wait and see, and drove to Jem Townsend's farm.

Here her luck was in.

'Want my old Flossie for Lady Godiva *again*? Have they found a young woman brave enough to take it on, then? Last time the gentleman said the one they'd picked lost her nerve, so he brought the horse back next day.'

'May I see the mare?' asked Laura. Old Flossie turned out to be a twelve-year-old Clydesdale and as strong as an elephant. 'You say she's been hired out for a pageant before? When would that have been?'

'A matter of a few weeks back, but I understood they'd give up the idea of holding the pageant. Seems a funny time of year to have a Lady Godiva, anyway. Catch her death, more likely than not.'

'Who hired the mare?'

'Some young woman. I didn't know her, and ten to one I wouldn't recognise her.'

'And did she bring the mare back?'

'No. I've never seen her again. The mare was put back in my paddock, with a pound note pushed through my door.'

'In an envelope?'

'Yes. Nothing wrote on it except *To loan of grey mare. Pageant off. Lady Godiva yellow.* So I read between the lines the girl had turned it down.'

'You didn't keep the envelope?'

'Why, what was wrong with it?'

Laura saw that his suspicions were aroused and that it would be best to beat a retreat. She laughed.

'Just *badinage*,' she said. 'Well, let's come to an agreement about the mare. We shall need her for at least a week. Send her over to Calladale College as soon as you can.'

'Fancy a ladies' college doing Lady Godiva! That's a new one, that is!'

'Oh, I don't know. History, and all that, you know.'

'Have you got a Peeping Tom?'

'I hope we'll have hundreds. We shall take up a silver collection.'

The great, docile animal arrived on the following day in charge of a lad and was stabled. Then Dame Beatrice asked to have a word with Miss Good. Young Cleeves' Thisbe listened attentively and agreed that she might be able to tell whether the horse resembled that from which she had fled

222

on the night of Norah Coles' disappearance, but added that, of course, she couldn't be sure.'

A tableau, or, rather a mime was arranged, therefore, and she received permission from Miss McKay to be a spectator. More difficult to arrange was that Basil should also be there.

'Not being able to charge him at present,' the inspector pointed out, 'we haven't what you'd call much control over him, madam. If he comes at all, it'll mean he'll have to come willing. We can't press the point much.'

'I am going to interview him. I'll invite him to tea at my hotel in Garchester, and then it should be a simple matter to arrange. Now that he has heard what I had to say the other day, I think he will prepared to assist us by every means in his power. I have taken a weight off his mind.'

The inspector made no comment on this optimistic supposition. He said, 'Conditions will need to be the same as before. What kind of night was it?'

'Starry, but moonless. Calm, but not cold.'

'It was a lot earlier in the year, madam.'

'We must do the best we can,' said Laura. 'After all, what Miss Good thinks she saw isn't evidence.'

'We do not require evidence from Miss Good,' said Dame Beatrice, 'but merely a contributory statement.'

She contrived her talk with Basil that same afternoon over tea in the hotel lounge. Laura was ordered to absent herself from the meal, and cadged an invitation from Miss Considine to take tea with her in her private sitting-room at the hostel.

'Dame Beatrice,' said Laura, taking a toasted and well-buttered scone, 'thinks she has some sort of stranglehold on Mr Basil. I can't believe he's a murderer, all the same.'

'I know very little about him,' said Miss Considine. 'Have some honey on that. Our own beehives. Do you keep bees?'

Noting the deliberate change of subject and realising that, in Miss Considine's view, it was not in the best of taste for a lecturer in full possession of her job to discuss a former colleague who had been deprived of his, replied that she had an aunt with a passion for heather-honey, and the conversation developed upon bee-keeping lines.

At half-past five Laura left the cosy sitting-room and its bright fire, and George drove her back into Garchester. Dame Beatrice was still in the lounge but there was no sign of Basil. Laura raised her eyebrows and her employer beckoned her to a chair.

'All according to Cocker?' Laura enquired. Dame Beatrice nodded slowly and rhythmically, but did not reply in words. They dined at seven, changed into warmer clothing, put on wraps and thick shoes and gloves, and drove back to the college.

Here there were preparations to be made. The mare was brought round to the kitchen garden, and Laura, who was inclined to regard the proceedings as an entertainment, not realising until afterwards what they portended, suggested that the sight of somebody attired in a sheet would scare the horse into bolting.

Dame Beatrice agreed.

'The animal is wearing blinkers. You will mount him and then clothe yourself in the ghostly vestments.'

'That's another thing,' said Laura. 'What happened to the other ones—the ones the original ghost used?'

'They have yet to reappear. The college laundry list is not short of the two sheets which we have found to be necessary to clothe the ghost, so, obviously, they did not come from here. May I request you to array yourself? The student who is to assist us should be here anon, but the construction of these trappings requires that the major character in the drama should be robed before the party of the second part can be inserted. You had better try it on first, to learn its intricacies, but keep behind the horse.'

Laura climbed into the tent-like and voluminous apparatus. It came to half-way between knee and ankle, and had adequate eye-holes. She gathered in the slack—there were slits for her arms—and announced that she thought she could manage. At the top of the cellar steps two students were waiting for them. Dame Beatrice greeted them, identifying them by the light of a torch, while Laura wriggled out of the trappings.

'You do not object to taking part in our small experiment?' Dame Beatrice enquired.

'Well,' said Miss Good, 'no, I suppose not. What do you want us to do?'

'Vastly different things, dear child. We want *you* to repeat, as exactly as you can, your actions and behaviour on the night you saw this horse and its rider.'

'Oh, dear!'

'Have no misapprehensions. My nephew, Mr Lestrange, will be with you.'

'Darling Piggy! What a heart-throb!'

'I beg your pardon?'

'Oh, I'm sorry. We always call the pig-lecturer Piggy.'

'I had understood the *soubriquet* to be a pet-name for Mr Basil. By the way, should you happen to run into Mr Basil, take no notice at all. Do not speak to him, even to greet him. His equilibrium is not to be upset in any way until, as I hope, the ghost-horse upsets it completely. So now, Miss Good, if you will proceed, as the police might put it, to the college front gate, Mr Lestrange will get out of his car there, and the two of you will dawdle about until you see the ghost-horse coming. As soon as it comes in view, do as you did before—hide from it and let it go by. When it has passed, Mr Lestrange will drive you back here. Please be prepared to tell me of any differences you may have noticed between this apparition and the other.'

'And what about me?' asked the student who was with Miss Good.

225

'You, child? You are wearing breeches, are you?—All right, Miss Good. Off you go.'

'Well, I thought you said I had to ride a horse,' the student continued.

'No; I said that you had to ride *on* a horse. In this particular case the two are not synonymous. You are helpless and a dead weight. Do not assist Mrs Gavin or the policeman who has just put in an appearance. Right, Constable Starling! Up she goes. Now, student, remain inert.'

Laura, who was also wearing breeches, had already mounted the horse, or, rather, had been hoisted on to its bare back by the policeman. Then he and Laura, the one heaving up the student's inert body and the other receiving it and hitching round it the billowing, sheet-like garment in which she herself was clad, contrived (with no little difficulty) to get the double-ghost horsed.

'Right,' said Laura, when she had a firm grip of the student and both were muffled in the sheet. 'Can do all right. Miss Good should have reached the gate by now.'

The grey mare moved at a stately walk down the drive. The night was clear, but very dark, and Laura left the horse to pick the way. The gravel squeaked and spurted under the horse's hoofs. The student, in Laura's arms, grew very heavy. There was a faint shriek, followed by a scrabbling noise as the horse passed out of the gate. It broke into an uncomfortable trot, taking the direction for which Laura had hoped.

Piggy Basil had accompanied the inspector, but without enthusiasm. He was not told whither they were bound, and showed increasing reluctance to continue the journey as it became more and more obvious that they were on the way to Calladale.

'Look here, what's in the wind?' he enquired plaintively,

226

as the car drew up fifty yards or so from the college gates. 'What's behind all this?'

'We get out here, sir,' said the inspector, not attempting to answer these questions. 'All we want you to do, sir, if you will be so good, is to keep your eyes and ears open.'

'If I will be so good! And, if I don't choose to be so good, I shall be in trouble for obstructing the police in the execution of their duty, I suppose! And they call this a free country!'

The inspector, disregarding this rhetoric, stepped out in the direction of the light which was shining down on the college gates, a light which served to emphasise the contiguous blackness. Just as they were about to enter the tiny pool of illumination which was cast around the gates and upon the ground, the inspector stopped. He caught Basil by the arm to bring him to a halt.

'Listen, sir,' he said. 'Do you hear anything?'

'No,' Piggy replied, after a short pause. 'I don't. Yes . . . yes, I can hear a horse, I think. Sounds like a heavy carthorse!'

'That's what I thought, sir. Let's get into the hedge. I don't want us to be spotted,' said the inspector. 'Who the devil would be riding a horse at this time of night?' he added. This was a disingenuous question; he knew the answer perfectly well.

'Damn the old bitch! I'm being framed!' muttered Piggy. He stumbled into the muddy ditch just as the grey mare and her double burden came into the lamp-light that shone down on the college gates.

'Christ!' he muttered. The ghosts passed on into the darkness, an amorphous glimmer in the gloom. 'The old girl knows! She must know everything!'

'Yes,' said Dame Beatrice, 'I knew. There *could* have been

other explanations of the appearance of the ghost-horse at that particular time and on that particular night, but this, as we came to gather and put together the facts of the case, seemed to me the most likely.'

'*I* always thought it was Mr Basil abducting Mrs Coles,' said Laura.

'No. It was Mr Basil assisting Mrs Coles by removing the body of Miss Palliser from the college cellar. Last night's little plot had a double purpose. I had to prove that it could be done that way, and I had to let Mr Basil realise by the most dramatic means in my power—since I wanted to give him a shock—that I knew the truth so far as the removal of the body to the old stage-coach was concerned.'

'I'll bet you gave him a shock, all right,' said Carey. It was the weekend, and the three of them were in his house at Stanton St John. 'I wonder the chap didn't pass out.'

'Oh, you Piggies are made of stern stuff,' said Laura. 'Anyway, he was so overcome he came clean. Then he said he supposed he might as well hold out his wrists for the handcuffs.'

'But he wasn't arrested, you say? I should have thought moving a dead body so as to conceal it was a pretty serious offence.'

'Yes. He was actuated by chivalry, of course.'

'Chivalry?'

'Certainly. He tells us that Mrs Coles found herself in possession of her sister's dead body, hid it in the college cellar —the inner one, where it was almost certain nobody would find it—and then panicked and called upon Mr Basil to help her get it out of the building. He responded nobly.'

'Then you mean he carried it on horseback to that coach near the back gates of Highpepper Hall?'

'No. He carried it on horseback to his car which he had left about two hundred yards from Calladale in a side road.

He did not bring it to the college for fear of attracting attention at that time of night.'

'It was bad luck, that girl Good spotting him,' said Laura. 'But for that, he would never have been involved. But why did he do it?'

'He thought that Mrs Coles had murdered her sister. When I was able to reassure him on that point, he consented to assist us. He did not know, and it would not have fitted in with our plans to have told him, of the form that assistance was to take.'

'So where do we go from here? You know the identity of the murderer. It wasn't Piggy and it wasn't Norah Coles. The girl was murdered in college. Norah panicked and Piggy, that perfect, gentle knight, helped her out. *Palliser was murdered in college!* ... That ought to ring a bell, but it doesn't. The murderer couldn't have been a student, unless it was an accident, in which case it couldn't be called murder.'

'It was, and it was not, an accident.'

'You mean the dope was really intended for Mrs Coles, don't you? I've thought that one out *ad nauseam*, but it doesn't add up. The sheer, hard fact remains that Palliser *couldn't* have been killed in the college, and yet she *was*. How do you work it out?'

'Impersonation, child.'

'Eh? Good Lord!'

'Cast your mind back a little. I believe I told you of a conversation I had with a certain Miss Bellman, a conversation which, for two particular reasons, intrigued me.'

'Oh?'

'Yes. It appeared from this conversation that the fact of Norah Coles' marriage was fairly widely known to the students in her hostel and that they preferred to think of her as Norah Coles and not as Norah Palliser. Coupled closely with this is the fact that the first student to see the body immediately identified it as *Palliser*. Of course, the college authorities still knew her as Palliser, but I noticed that a warning, in the form of a kick on the ankle, was given to one student who might have become too talkative. You see, the students had *had* to be taken into Mrs Coles' confidence over the matter of this daring impersonation.'

Laura stared at her employer. 'You mean that Palliser was actually in college as Coles?'

'I haven't any doubt of it.'

'But—since when?'

'I do not think that Mrs Coles returned to college after the summer vacaton. I think her sister came back in her place then, and the students in her hostel had to be told, in order that they might help in perpetuating the fiction.'

'What about the head of the hostel, though, apart from the lecturers?'

'Cast your mind back to your own student days, and remember that Mrs Coles was not much of a public figure in the college. Her work was adequate, she played no games, she got into no trouble and her sister was sufficiently like her for the mother to make a mistake in identifying the body.'

'What was Norah Coles' idea, then?'

'To be with Mr Basil.'

'So *that* was the reason for the broken leg business! Oh, yes, of course. What's more, I see the point now of the post-mistress' evidence that Palliser had served in an agricultural college. Well, I'm dashed! Then *who* administered the poison?'

'Presumably somebody who did not know of the imposture.'

'Old Biancini!'

Dame Beatrice shook her head.

'Do not forget that, although the prosecution does not need to show motive in a case of murder, it is, from the lay-man's point of view, a matter of enormous importance. A motiveless, or apparently motiveless, murder, unless it is committed by a homicidal maniac, is a murder unrelished by the public, who, after all, are represented by the jury. "But why should you think he did it, if he had no reason to do it?" they are apt to enquire.'

'One can see their point,' said Laura. 'Anyway, in this case, we *do* know that he disliked the girl.'

'Not at all. It was the girl who disliked him. Besides, the strongest motive in the world (according to the available statistics) is the hope of financial gain. Now, Biancini had no such hope. Mrs Coles' inheritance was already in her possession, and, unless she made a will, it would revert to her husband upon her death.'

'Coles? But Coles wouldn't hurt a fly! He's the complete art student, absorbed in his painting and in his future, and all that sort of thing.'

'Mr Coles has no particular reason to love his wife, you know, and he does need money very badly, I'm afraid. Besides, by that time, he must have known that he'd been cuckolded, and that is not a situation to appeal to most husbands. I think that, although his motive was the expectation of money, he salved his conscience by reminding himself of the other things. He had even found out Basil's name.'

'It sounds likely enough, when you put it that way. The only trouble is that I can't connect it with the man himself. He just doesn't seem the type for a cold-blooded killer. And another thing: how did he know about the coniine? I shouldn't think it's generally known that the spotted hemlock can be deadly. Again, how was it administered? He could hardly have gone to the college and poured it down the girl's throat. Besides, if he had, he'd have known that the person he was poisoning wasn't his wife. How do you work all that out?'

'I don't know how he knew about the coniine, but I suspect that Norah Coles had told him, probably just as an

231

item of interest. There is lots of spotted hemlock about the Calladale grounds and she may have—indeed, I think she must have—told him of its properties. It would have seemed to him a sort of poetic justice to poison her with it, I dare say.'

'I wonder how long it took him to distil the stuff?'

'He may have experimented for months.'

'When you said he would have shown more imagination if he hadn't talked so much, were you thinking about the coniine?'

'Chiefly, yes. He felt himself perfectly safe at our last interview and made the mistake all murderer's make—he underestimated the opposition's brains.'

CHAPTER TWENTY

Painter's Colic

‘ "What, do you think it is a fox?" "Yes," replied Ernest,
"I think it is a golden fox." ’

Ibid.

‘ ". . . you must know that, according to naturalists, the
jackal partakes the nature of a wolf, a fox, and a dog." ’

Ibid.

‘WE find ourselves confronted by a tortuous mind,’ said
Dame Beatrice. ‘Nevertheless, I think we have enough to
convince ourselves of the truth. Whether, on the evidence
we can offer, Coles will be arrested and charged, I cannot say,
but I believe the inspector is prepared to take the risk. The
strength of Coles’ position is that he took nobody into his
confidence except, to some extent, the dead woman.’

‘What! How do you know?’

‘By inference, added to a remark made to me by Mrs
Biancini when I visited her at her home. She said that nobody on earth would want to hurt Norah, a statement which
gave me food for thought.’

‘Well, we both ought to have seen that it was in the college
cellar the rats had got at Miss Palliser. An old house like that
was bound to have cellars.’

‘The ghostly rider was such a very suspicious character,
too,’ said Dame Beatrice. ‘And then there did seem to be a
smell of rats everywhere, both literally and metaphorically,
did there not?’

‘I’m not going to rack my brains any longer. Has Piggy
Basil another job yet?’

‘Miss McKay has another lecturer coming next term, so
Carey has promised Mr Basil a position at Stanton St John.

He regards him as a steady character now. Even if he is not, he seems to be a first-class pigman. Later, I imagine he will emigrate. He says he wants no more to do with Norah Coles, but at present he is not quite himself, so we shall see.'

'Well, let's have the order of events, with your interspersed comments, can we? I think I've grasped the general drift, but I prefer my explanations to be made in words of one syllable.'

'Very well. Norah Palliser, as she was at the time, met and was attracted by Coles. He was handsome, poor, boorish and gifted—in all, just the sort of young man to appeal to a girl who had had to endure the approaches of stepfather Biancini, that crude, gross, amorous foreigner.'

'Don't forget that one of the students diagnosed her as a fast worker. She may have encouraged Biancini,' said Laura.

'Very likely she did at first, until she found that she could not control him. She tucked herself away at the agricultural college, having already planned (I deduce) to marry Coles. I think she must have told him that she was in possession of a useful sum, her inheritance under her father's will. Coles did not want to marry Norah, but he did want to inherit her money. He could see no way of obtaining the latter without doing the former, but Fate played into his hands when Norah fell in love (violently, this time) with her instructor, Mr Basil. She confided this infatuation to her sister and begged her to take her place on the college rota so that she could stay with Basil in Northern Ireland. I imagine that she thought and expected that Coles would divorce her when she could let him know what she had done. Her sister, Carrie Palliser, in trouble all round, impecunious and out of work, and, in any case, thoroughly irresponsible (as her criminal record shows) was only too glad to agree, particularly as she probably saw a chance to blackmail her sister afterwards by threatening to disclose the plot to Miss McKay.'

'Let sisterly love continue! But that wouldn't work, would

it? I thought Norah was so besotted by Piggy that she wouldn't give a hoot what anybody thought or did about it. Of course, there was Piggy's job to consider, I suppose.'

'There is no way, at present, of showing that Carrie did think of blackmail. What we do know is that, true to her nature, she stole from the other students. You remember the thefts of money and valuables mentioned by Miss McKay?'

'Carrie seems to have been a charming soul! Perhaps the rest of us are none the worse for her demise. You still haven't covered the actual murder, though.'

'Here we are on more speculative ground. It is a pity that the letter sent by Coles to his wife, but received and read by her deputy at the college, has been destroyed.'

'What letter?'

'A letter which must have been written and received if anything else is to make sense, child. The letter was mentioned, anyway, by Miss Elspeth Bellman when we first knew of Miss Palliser's disappearance from college.'

'Oh, yes, of course. Well?'

'I believe the letter was sent with some photographic negatives. It would have run something after this fashion : *I took these pictures in Paris and cannot let anybody in a chemist's develop and print them. You will realise why not when you see them. Be a good sport and do them for me in your college cellar. Didn't you say you were allowed to use it as a dark room? You'll get lots of laughs. Don't show them to anybody with no sense of humour, though. You know what I mean. To help you pass the time, there's something for you to drink if you care to collect it from the station. Home-made but potent. Don't worry about the taste. Just wait for the effects. In with it is the hypo. Both bottles plainly marked, so don't go mixing them up.*'

'Good heavens!' exclaimed Laura. Dame Beatrice leered triumphantly. 'You've even hit on the right sort of style and everything! But how did the body get put into the other

235

cellar with the rats? Where are the negatives? How did Piggy Basil and Norah know about Carrie's death? Why did they decide to hush it up by moving the body to the coach?'

'Interesting questions. As I say, I can tell you only what I surmise. The body was put into the cellar with the rats because Coles caused it to be put there.'

'How do you know that?'

'I base the theory on the fact that there was nothing whatever in either the outer or inner cellar to show that the poison had been taken there.'

'But need it have been?'

'Anybody feeling as ill as the victim would have done, having swallowed as much of the coniine as she did, would hardly have chosen to make her way into a rat-infested cellar, or have taken off her overcoat in there. The police found the remnants of that coat.'

'So Coles came along and cleared up? I suppose he removed the films and bottles and things. A risky thing to do, wasn't it?'

'So risky that he did not do it himself.'

'But you said . . .'

'I said that he caused it to be done. Do you remember my telling you that I asked the secretary whether any letters had come to college for Mr Basil while he was supposed to be in hospital?'

'Yes. You mean Coles told Basil he'd killed Norah?'

'Oh, no. The letter would have been anonymous. It came to college, was re-addressed by the secretary to the hospital we visited and was received, no doubt, by Mr Simnel. Mr Simnel must have had other letters addressed to Basil, but a store of fairly large envelopes, each bearing Basil's Ulster address (under the name of Simnel), would soon have disposed of that difficulty. So, in a roundabout way, but ultimately, Basil received a curt intimation that the body of Norah Coles lay in the college cellar.'

236

'I don't see why Piggy Basil took any notice.'

'No, but Norah Coles had to take notice. He was compelled to let her know that her sister was dead. Once the body was discovered, there was no knowing what complications might have arisen, so far as she was concerned. Besides, there were the other students to be considered—those who had held the fort for her, so to speak, by agreeing to pass off her sister as herself. Those students *knew* that Palliser was not Coles, and Coles could see no end to the business unless the fact of the death could be hidden. Mr Basil is weak. He is also, in his own way, a gentleman. He agreed to accompany her to the college. *They* put the body in the inside cellar, threw the coat in, and got rid of the bottles, no doubt. Then they retired to Basil's cottage. But Norah Coles was still in a state of terror and begged him to help her move the body away from the college together.'

'So we get our ghost?'

'So we get our ghost, and, satisfied that all was for the best, the lovers returned to Ireland until Norah's nerve gave way and caused her to haunt this neighbourhood for news.'

'Can't quite see why Piggy let himself in for such a business,' said Laura. Dame Beatrice said :

'Yes, you can. Why do you think he consented to help at all?'

'Oh, of course ! Norah was in such a state that he thought she must have sent the poison and the films herself. I suppose he jumped to the conclusion that the sister was blackmailing Norah. But, if he did, how does he account for the anonymous letter?'

'I don't suppose he tried to do so. He is not very intelligent.'

'What do you make of all that damage done in the Calladale grounds soon after Carey took on Piggy's job?'

'I am convinced it was the work of a gang of hooligans, just as was thought at the time. There seems no other rational

237

explanation. It had some small value, however—it began the discovery of the rats and the rhubarb. But for the rhubarb, remember, the body might still rest undiscovered.'

'Yes, I see. So everything falls into place. The two of them, Basil and Norah, came back to the college and hid the body in the inner cellar. Then she got restless about it and made him move it. They must have had a terrible job. It was no joke for me to transport that student on that great carthorse, and I'd never have been able to get on its back in the dark without the help of that policeman. Could there have been a third party present to assist Piggy, do you think?'

'I hardly think so. They would not have dared trust another person. Desperation is a wonderful fillip and, strong as you are, I feel sure Mr Basil is very considerably stronger.'

'But the planning—the sheets and all that!'

'The sheets came from Basil's cottage, presumably, and the ghost-costume would not have taken long to make. Now that we have decided what happened, police enquiries could readily establish whether the two came here by train or by car, and when.'

'I thought you'd taken Piggy under your protection!'

'I did not say the police were to be *asked* to establish these facts.'

'Oh, I see. Well, after all that, where *is* Norah, and what will happen when she's found?'

This question was answered by the discovery of Coles' body in the pottery room at the art school. The autopsy established that death had been caused by lead poisoning, resulting in a cerebral haemorrhage. The possibility of suicide was taken into account, but the coroner's jury found that, as the deceased had been a potter and an amateur interior decorator, it was likely that an unsuspected allergy to lead, a poison associated closely with his work, had, in eighteenth-century parlance, carried him off.

The result of his death, so far as the enquiry into the

murder of Carrie Palliser was concerned, was the dramatic reappearance of Norah Coles. Dame Beatrice, at home again in the Stone House, Wandles Parva, received a telephone call from Calladale College.

'The Coles girl has turned up. Says she dared not come out of hiding while her husband was alive,' stated Miss McKay. 'Can you come and talk to her? She looks half-starved and is in a fine state of nerves, as you'd expect.'

The Coles girl was housed in the sanatorium when Dame Beatrice arrived. She was sallow and looked thoroughly ill, and was inclined to weep every time she tried to speak. She had been in hiding in Garchester since she had left Ireland. But for the fact that they believed she was dead, the police must have found her, although she had done as little shopping as she could, and that, she explained, at shops where she was not known.

As point after point was disclosed, Dame Beatrice's theorising took the shape of fact. At last the girl said :

'What's going to happen to me now?'

'Nothing,' said Miss McKay, 'if we can help it.' She met Dame Beatrice's eye with a challenging stare, to find that no challenge was necessary. 'You'll get to your work and make up the time you've lost. You've the makings of a respectable farmer if you put your mind to it. Respectable farmers are an asset to the community. People in prison for concealing deaths are not. Mr Basil is going abroad. Dame Beatrice has furnished him with funds. Not a bad sort of man, on the whole, but, of course, he can't come back here.'

Dame Beatrice nodded slowly.

'You're much too good,' said the girl; she began a noisy sobbing.

'Of course we are !' said Miss McKay, snappishly. 'What did you suppose we should be?'